A City Called July

Previous books by Howard Engel:

Murder Sees the Light
Murder on Location
The Ransom Game
The Suicide Murders

A City Called July

Howard Engel

St. Martin's Press
New York

Library of Congress Cataloging in Publication Data

Engel, Howard, 1931–
  A city called July.

  I. Title.
PR9199.3.E49C5 1986   813'.54   86-13796
ISBN 0-312-13986-1

First published by Penguin Books Canada Limited.

First U.S. Edition

10 9 8 7 6 5 4 3 2 1

For Janet
again and always

'Twas in the month of Liverpool
In the city called July,
The snow was raining heavily,
The streets were very dry.
The flowers were sweetly singing,
The birds were in full bloom,
As I went down the cellar
To sweep an upstairs room.

—English skipping rhyme

A City Called July

A City Called July

Chapter One

I sat in my office cleaning out the fuzzy rubble that collects at the bottom of the jam jar I keep pens and pencils in. Also in the litter I found an old watch strap, paper-clips, slightly used Stimudents, clip-on sunglasses and a book of paper matches from Hatch's Surf Lounge in Niagara Falls, New York, three-quarters used. The ashtrays on my desk were empty except for the one with my current Player's nodding off in it. I'd cleaned them all the afternoon before to keep me from falling asleep. It was one of those summer mornings when the telephone didn't ring and I was edgy because it kept looking like it was going to. I'd written a couple of cheques and paid the back rent on the office and my room at the City House. I should have had that warm feeling that comes with my monthly attempt at putting my life in order, but I felt that if I didn't have the pens, pencils and other junk to occupy my mind completely, I'd break out in a sweat.

Outside the window, the traffic along St Andrew Street moved inexorably eastward. Working on the second floor overlooking the one-way main street of this town sometimes gives me the feeling that there is a secret evacuation going on and I'll be the last to hear about it. I tried to settle my mind with the fact that both Church and King went one way in the opposite direction. There must be some law of physics we covered in high school that

1

accounted for that, some Newtonian principle making traffic east balance traffic west. I played with that notion for a few minutes while blowing lint and fuzz off otherwise perfectly good paper-clips.

There was a rap at my door, and before I could answer it or even shout "Come in!" two heads poked through the doorway. I recognized both of them.

"Rabbi Meltzer! Mr Tepperman! Come in! Come in!" I tried to turn the surprise I felt into a friendly greeting, but I don't think I succeeded in projecting it across the room to the door. I glanced for a moment to the trio of bald mannequins in the corner, nude except for a wrapper of unbleached factory cotton. I saw knees and shoulders but nothing to scandalize my visitors. I'd managed to get rid of most of the other left-overs from my father's ladies' ready-to-wear business, except for my three bedraggled Graces. The rabbi and Mr Tepperman, the president of B'nai Sholom Congregation, were both blinking in the bright light of the office after the steep climb up the unlighted stairs from the street. They took their hats off and stood with their backs to the girls.

"Good morning, Mr Cooperman. How are you?" said Mr Tepperman. Good, I thought, let's get over the secular things first. At the back of my mind was the plot in the cemetery I was sure they were after me to buy. I had no reason for thinking this, but a visit from the rabbi and the president wasn't a daily occurrence. I felt my immortal soul was in hazard. They weren't selling raffle tickets on a car for the Haddassah Bazaar. Of that much I was sure.

"I'm fine, Mr Tepperman. Come in. Have a chair. Here, Rabbi, why don't you take this chair?"

"Thank you, Mr Cooperman," said Rabbi Meltzer, tucking his lightweight raincoat under him as he settled into the aged foam rubber of a tubular chair that used to stand near the door of my father's store. It gave my place an art deco look. All I needed were marcelled blonde wigs for the mannequins. The rabbi watched Tepperman settle into the other chair. It matched my oak veneer desk. "We, ah, we are not disturbing you?" continued the rabbi, the thought nearly lifting him out of his seat again.

"Not at all. I'm glad to see you." This wasn't exactly true. It had been some time since I'd seen either one of them, but I remembered the occasions the way a headstone remembers the name chiselled into its face. I pictured the artificial turf at Sally Lenowitz's funeral. I remembered the empty space next to Sally's name when they unveiled the double tombstone. Joe, the widower, made a joke about how they'd never cram him into the narrow space. No wonder my visitors made me fidget.

Once they were both seated, the silence and the embarrassment began in earnest. It was a recognized stage in the interviewing of clients. But it was only my inability to face dealing with plots and eternal upkeep that turned my visitors into clients. I was pretty sure they didn't want me to put up my name to succeed Saul Tepperman as president. It could have been a touch. Something legitimate on behalf of the community that was going to set me back fifty dollars. It could have been anything. I watched Mr Tepperman and the rabbi trying to outwait each other, each deferring to the other's better right to speak first. I sat it out.

"Benny," Saul Tepperman began at length, and started to cough. He called me Benny and that relieved the tension by half a notch. He'd always been Mr Tepperman to me, but I wasn't fifteen any more. He looked like he was ready to begin again. "Benny, we have a problem." Having got that much out, he looked to the rabbi for encouragement. Rabbi Meltzer nodded to show he couldn't have expressed it better himself. This was no time to stop. We had a consensus: there was a problem. Saul moistened his lips with the pink tip of his tongue. From under the bush of his nicotine-stained moustache it

moved quickly, covering all surfaces and retreating behind the white and gold of his smile. "The fact is, Benny,
that we have a situation here in town; like I said: a problem. Isn't that right, Rabbi?" The rabbi jumped like the
spinal cord had snapped to attention. Caught off guard,
all he could do was nod vigorously. Rabbi Meltzer was a
small compact bundle that had gathered arms and legs
together so that they almost disappeared as separate
appendages. Next to him, Tepperman leaned forward in
his chair like a large parcel about to come apart.

"You know, Benny, in a community, we live in and
out of one another's lives. I've known you since you
were bar mitzvah. That's the way it is in a small town.
You scratch my back... You follow me?"

"Take your time."

"A community, Benny, is built on cooperation and
trust," he said. "We have to depend on one another. I
buy from Rosen, Rosen buys from Katz and Katz buys
from me. Sure, today, the circle's a little wider. There's a
Murphy in there and a Mackenzie. But that doesn't matter. The idea's the same. In a community, in any community, big or small, trust is the oil at the joints. You
understand what I'm saying?"

"Tell me in your own way. You're doing fine."

"Most people in town know they can rely on the other
fellow. Take your father. A fine, upright man. Everybody respects him. You could give him your heart to
hold in his hand, and he wouldn't drop it. You understand?" He wasn't moving forward very quickly, but I
bobbed my head to encourage him to move from the
forecourt of his presentation into the vestibule and hall
of his argument. "You take Mel Lowy and Rube Farber."

"Salt of the earth," I said, and we all thought about
that for a while.

"You see," began the rabbi, trying another approach,
"what we have is more than simply a religious community. We're talking about a very complicated social

structure here. There's checks and balances. What I do reflects on Tepperman, and what Tepperman does reflects on you. Don't take this personally. But if Rube Farber robbed the Upper Canadian Bank of ten thousand dollars, it would give all of us a black eye."

"What he means is," Tepperman offered, placing his big hands on the edge of my desk, as though he had suddenly been shown the clear road the argument must take, "we're all in the same soup. It couldn't be worse. My God, I never thought I'd live to see a thing like this." The way was getting cloudy, and he sat back in his chair to catch his breath and try to collect the fragments that he'd been so sure of a second before he began to talk.

"Tell me about it," I said. "Remember I'm a professional private investigator as well as a member of the Jewish community. It's like talking to the doctor. Practically the same thing. Just tell the story the way it happened. Just the outlines. We'll put in the colours later. It's just like doctors. Okay?" Mr Tepperman and the rabbi shifted in their chairs and waited for me to look at one of them to continue. I gave the nod to the rabbi. He cleared his throat.

"You know Larry Geller? Everybody knows Larry Geller. Everybody liked him and trusted him." I made a steeple of my fingers to show that I was taking it all in. Geller was a lawyer with an office on Queen Street across from the post office. I didn't know him well; I'd met him several times. I remembered expensive suits and cologne.

"Sure, I know Larry. What about him?"

"He's disappeared," the rabbi said, as though I'd been missing the point for the last ten minutes. "He's gone. Vanished."

"Two weeks ago," put in Tepperman. "Without a word. Poof! He doesn't even say goodbye to his wife and children. Off the face of the earth."

I swallowed a lump of disappointment. I couldn't see anything but police work in this. Larry Geller, the goodtime Charlie. He could be depended upon at bar mitzvahs and weddings to raise more dust with his back-slapping than anyone else. He was a big wheel in the local chapter of B'nai Brith.

I'd seen his picture in the *Beacon* more than once. In fact I remembered seeing it only a day or two ago. I should have read the caption.

"We all trusted him," said Saul Tepperman, shaking his head.

"You've been to the police about this?" I asked. "At least I suppose his wife has."

"Police!" the rabbi said, lengthening out the vowel until it sounded like a siren screaming. "The police shouldn't be brought into this until the right time."

"The rabbi's absolutely right, Benny. If we can settle this thing within the community..."

"Excuse me, Mr Tepperman. With all respect, when a man disappears without a trace, poof! it isn't a community problem any more. It's police business. I mean, look, this is serious. This has to be handled right. You don't know whether the man's alive or dead. You have to take in all the possibilities. And think of his family, Rabbi. Think of what they're going through. What you've got to do is go directly to the cops on this."

"Benny, it's not that way." Once again an exchange of looks passed between them, making me feel as though I was the butt of a joke I was too dense to follow.

"So, if it's not that way, what way is it? He's disappeared but you're not worried? I can see on your faces how worried you are. Tell me."

"Like I said, Benny," said Mr Tepperman, "we all liked and trusted Larry. He was a lawyer, an educated man. Who would you trust if it wasn't Larry Geller? I ask you? Hesh Riskin from the bakery trusted him with his mortgage money. I'm talking about twelve thousand dollars. Hesh gave it to Larry to pay off the mortgage on the store. Nine months later, when he'd just come back

from Florida, he found a letter from the building's owners
waiting for him. They told him that he could lose the
building because he had stopped making mortgage payments. He didn't know what to do. He had a paper saying
the mortgage had been paid off. What was he to believe?
That's when he came to see the rabbi and me. He was
the first."

"One of the first. Don't forget Naomi Spivak. There
are over fifty people in the same position as Hesh Riskin."

"With some," continued Tepperman, "it wasn't mortgages."

"That's right, Saul. With the Sterns it was investments,
with the Greenblatts it was their life savings. I'm talking
about old people, Benny. People who wanted to put up
their savings in a mortgage. Something to retire on. A
little security. Is that wrong to have a little security in
old age?" he asked me with passion in his eyes. I had a
hard time remembering that he was only speaking rhe-
torically. He did it so well, I felt caught up and wanted
to answer.

"Well it's gone now," said Tepperman. "Mortgages,
investments, savings, security: it's all gone. Disappeared
with that son of a bitch Larry Geller. Excuse me, Rabbi."
The rabbi gave him absolution with a wave of his hand.

"Let me get this straight. You mean Geller has de-
frauded fifty people and skipped town? And you don't
want to go to the police about it? That's crazy."

"You have to understand. Think of the damage to the
community. These people worked hard for that money,
Benny," said the rabbi. "Now you want them exposed as
stupid on top of this? There's a limit!"

"Geller's not going to walk in with the money. He's
not going to see a blinding light and pay back all his
one-time friends and neighbours. It may embarrass indi-
viduals in the community, it may embarrass the Jewish
community generally, but if they want Geller's hide, if
they want a running start on getting some of their own

back, they have to go to the cops. They're the only game in town on a thing like this. They are victims of fraud. They've had the till ransacked and you want them to look the other way. Let me think. There's breach of trust, there's fraud over two hundred dollars, theft over two hundred, uttering forged documents, probably false registration of titles. We're talking about half the criminal code here, Rabbi, and you want it hushed up. I don't believe you."

"We thought that you might consider..."

"Are you kidding, Saul?" I said, trying out his first name. "A job like this requires an army of trained personnel. We are looking for a needle in a haystack, and the only thing we know for sure is that the haystack has moved out of town. You want me to hang around the hotels in Miami Beach in case he walks in, Rabbi? It's more than a million to one that you'd ever hear from either of us again. Should I pack a bag and look for him in Europe? Have you any idea what that would cost? Saul, be reasonable. And speaking of large amounts of money, have you any idea how much he got away with? In round figures?"

The rabbi cleared his throat and said something. I didn't catch it. "I beg your pardon?"

"Two..."

"What?"

"Two million dollars."

"Oh, my God! Two million! And you want to keep it buttoned up! What about his wife? What about his partners? Are they going to cooperate and help keep the lid on? You can't just replace the divot and play through. Somebody's going to want to yell good and loud. Rabbi, you can't honestly tell me that that would be letting the community down?"

"The people I've talked to don't want a fuss. They don't want to see their names in the paper. That's not unreasonable."

"Look, both of you, the Law Society has a fund that tries to pick up after crooked lawyers like Geller. Don't flatter yourself that Geller's the first. There are lots of Gellers. There's a Geller in every ethnic community and Gellers wearing Trinity College blazers too. Geller is universal. Where was I...?" I was riding my rhetorical bicycle too fast again. "Oh, yeah. In order to get some of their money back, first of all Geller has to be disbarred. That's a legal process. And it can't happen unless you go to the police."

"We'd just as soon..."

"Mr Tepperman, if a thief broke into your store, wouldn't you phone the cops right away? Well, this is the same thing." Tepperman was moistening his lips again. He shifted inside his grey tweed coat. His face had taken on a high colour where his skin was pulled tightly across his cheekbones. The rabbi next to him looked bird-like and brittle. They both looked at me like I'd been beating them over the heads with two-by-fours. I felt like I was trying to roll the stone away from the gate to the ghetto. I was dealing with intelligent reasonable men. I'd known both of them for years. They both looked at me with frowns on their lined faces. I was being difficult. All they wanted was no fuss. Fuss was the enemy, fuss got into the papers, fuss was at the root of anti-Semitism. They hated fuss more than they hated Geller or more than they hoped to see the two million again. You had to respect them for it, I guess.

"Tell me about his wife. Does he have a family?"

"A boy and a girl. Ruth, his wife, is a sensible girl. She's Morris Kaufman's daughter. Your family knows them. Morris was in the needle trade in Toronto. Your grandfather would have known him on Spadina Avenue. Ruth is very worried, naturally. She hasn't seen or heard from Geller. She doesn't know where he is; she can't even guess. I don't think she knows about the money. I didn't have the heart."

"And the partners?"

"Only former partners. Geller was independent for the last ten years. He used to be with Bernstein, Wayne and Hart. But that is a long time ago. He used to chum around with Eddie Lazarus and Morrie Freeland. They were at Osgoode together." I began making a few notes to go with the doodles I'd been manufacturing on my block of lined yellow foolscap.

"You didn't talk to any of them?" I failed to establish eye contact with either of my visitors. "I know you didn't because they would have told you what I told you. You have to tell the police about this. I mean, you're talking about two million dollars."

"Think of the old people, Benny. I'm talking about widows and people from the old country who don't understand about our laws and the whole shooting match."

"Saul, you're breaking my heart. Look, I told you my professional opinion. If I told you the only way to make suits was to do them one by one you'd tell me I'm crazy. You know that you cut out dozens at a time. Well, I'm telling you the way to find Larry Geller is to tell the boys at Niagara Regional all about it. I mean, Rabbi, you are talking about fraud with a very big *F*. Call Chris Savas. You'll be glad you did."

"Benny, we aren't saying we won't go to the police. My God, as far as I know maybe the police know all about it. I'm just asking you...both as a friend and as a member of the community...to see what you can see. Find out his assets. Maybe he's left a trail. We don't expect miracles, do we, Rabbi?" The rabbi shook his head. The last think he expected me to deliver was a miracle. I was a plodder, a keyhole-gazer, not a worker of miracles. "For a few days," Tepperman said after a pause. Then there was another silence. If there is such a thing as an unshared silence, this was it. "We'll pay whatever it costs. After all you're a professional." Out the window I could hear a transport truck pulling a heavy load through town towards Queenston and Niagara Falls. At the same moment, I felt in my bones, a truck with an equal load was rolling off the Queen Elizabeth Way and on its way via King or Church to the west end of town and the old highway to Hamilton.

"It wouldn't hurt," said the rabbi. Another pause. Both Tepperman and the rabbi looked at me like the barrels of a Gatling gun. I thought about my other possibilities. I supposed I could continue cleaning the jam jar.

"I'll do what I can," I said.

Chapter Two

As soon as I heard the last of the clatter of the tailor and the rabbi on my stairs, I called Staff Sergeant Chris Savas and got instead my old friend and schoolmate Pete Staziak, who also serves the forces of law and order in the Niagara region. To be truthful, Pete wasn't really a friend from school-days. We'd both been there at the same time, I'd been in a play with his sister, but we only took one class together in five years. Much more recently, we'd been mixed up in a few cases, and since we were both stamped with the indelible impression of Grantham Collegiate Institute and Vocational School, we gave support to the fiction that we'd been pals. With some of the teachers, it didn't matter when you had them, you ended up with the same memories. Pete could finish any snatch of poetry I could remember, and I could complete the Three Results of the Persian War if he gave me a start. Being pals made introductions easier and in the end we'd come to believe it.

"How's the private sector, Benny? Busy?"

"Have to beat the business away with sticks, Pete. How about you?"

"Routine stuff, Benny. I think time this week is running slower than usual. I start to doze off around three-thirty in the afternoon."

"Yeah, time behind a desk crawls on all fours."

"It's summer. That's what does it. I'm sweating just talking on the phone."

"Well, you can comfort yourself with the fact that the days are growing shorter already," I said. Pete grumbled and I told him I wanted words in person. He told me to drop over towards lunch-time and we'd grab a sandwich together at the Di.

The Di was Diana Sweets. It was the oldest establishment on St Andrew Street. It must have been started when the street was still an Indian trail curving along the high bank above Captain Dick's Creek. Ella Beames at the library told me once that Captain Dick was a "man of colour" who was reputed to have hidden a crock of gold not far from the water. If anybody ever found it, I never heard about it. I tried to imagine the captain sitting in one of the stained cherry-wood booths of Diana Sweets, with shining, knowing eyes.

Pete and I took a booth for four and surveyed the menus. When I was young, my father and mother brought me in here for a "Newsboy," a single scoop of ice-cream with a dollop of marshmallow on top. It came with a glass of water and the curled paper check for five cents. In those days the Di had one menu totally given up to sundaes, sodas, *frappés*, fizzes, phosphates and other frosty desserts.

Pete ordered a cheeseburger and I tried a tuna on white, toasted, with a glass of milk and a vanilla sundae. The girl claimed she'd never heard of a Newsboy. I didn't push it. I was on the second triangular half of sandwich when Pete brought me back to business.

"You got something on your mind, Benny?"

"Yeah. This morning I had a visit from Rabbi Meltzer and Saul Tepperman. Two worried men, Pete."

"I'd be worried too, if I was in their shoes. Not that they are liable in any way." Pete wiped his mouth on the tiny paper napkin. A bit of paper was lost on a face that big. He leaned his weight into his forearms along the edge of the table and examined the melting cheese running down his cheeseburger.

"So it's no secret, then?" Pete's face split into a smile that showed me more of his mouth than I wanted to see just then.

"Oh, the *Beacon* hasn't tumbled to it yet, but that'll happen tomorrow or the day after. It's no secret at Niagara Regional." He took another messy bite of the cheeseburger. He was looking at me with an indulgent smile drawn over his working jaw. "They get you in to try to keep it quiet? No way, Ben. I know this isn't going to make anybody look too smart, and nobody wants that kind of publicity. But we aren't in the publicity business. We don't get it for you when you want it, and we don't stop it when it comes looking for you."

"I'm glad you heard me out, Pete. You know, a lot of guys would have jumped to the conclusion that I'd been retained to hush something up." I tried to look indignant. Pete took another bite of his cheeseburger. We continued to banter and eat.

"And don't give me that crap about your even-handed righteousness. When was the last time the sitting member got his name in the paper for driving while impaired?" Pete looked at his plate. "Since you ask," I said after swallowing, "I've been retained to look into this business, not put the cork in it."

"For the Jewish community?"

"Right." He smiled like he'd been right all along. "Okay, okay," I admitted, "naturally they don't want publicity. Nobody wants to look stupid or have a trusted member of the community exposed as a crook. They'd rather see their money back, but I guess you know the odds on that better than I do. You taking bets?"

"Not on that. Geller's made the cleanest flit I've seen since the carnies stopped coming to town. As closely as we can figure it he got away with two point six million. Money like that can inspire a lot of careful detail work.

As far as I can see, he's free and clear. Unless he does some quarter-baked trick like leaving a trail of credit card receipts, or signing his real name on hotel registers. But he's not going to do that. Hell, he's smooth as pus."

"I'm talking to the right guy, aren't I?"

"That's no secret. Yeah, I started the file nine days ago. There's a lot of this stuff going around, Benny. Your guy isn't breaking any new ground. There are a couple of cases in Hamilton just like it, and half a dozen in Toronto. The Law Society has hired an ex-Toronto Metro cop to run interference for them. There are so many lawyers with their hands in the till there isn't room for money. Funds held in trust are the first place hit when the economy takes a downward spiral. Where else is a lawyer going to get his hands on fast free money. For most it's only a temporary measure, a stop-gap."

"You sound like they're all doing it."

"I just got carried away. There's always an element. The rotten apple. I mean, look: it's very tempting. A sweet old widow comes up to you with thirty or forty thousand and asks you to pay off her mortgage. You hand her a phony discharge of mortgage and tell the mortgagee that you'll be making monthly payments on behalf of your client."

"So that's how it's done."

"One of the ways. You get to use the money at the cost of the mortgage payments. Now multiply that fifty or sixty times and you quickly come to the point where you're running around so fast covering yourself that you don't have any time for the good life you thought you were buying. Pretty soon you have to make the big flit."

"So off you go to find him in Florida and Nassau?"

"I do my finding here. We've got out a Canada-wide warrant for Geller. We've got Interpol notified. And I'm sitting near the phone. What more can I do? The world's his oyster. He's not going to look up old friends in all the old familiar places. Geller's smart. He could be at the next table or he could be anywhere in the world where a dollar makes you top dog. Oh, Geller's cute as a tick." Pete finished off his cheeseburger, which he had been neglecting, with three massive bites. Coffee had arrived and I spooned in two large helpings of sugar then watched the cream marble the dark surface of my cup.

"Have you seen his family?"

"Wife and a son and daughter. That wasn't much fun."

"On the up and up?"

"She reported him missing."

"All by herself and out of the blue?"

"We were following up a complaint from one of the old-timers about him not making mortgage payments on time. Kaplan, a farmer from out in Louth township. He must be a free-thinker or something, because he didn't go to the rabbi first. He phoned us as soon as he smelled something funny, and that's when we started looking for him. At first Geller's wife just said he wasn't in. Then I put on my best Department manners and she broke down saying she didn't know where he was and would be happy to see him again herself."

"Sounds up and up. You buying it?"

"Nobody could act that befuddled. I mean, she was completely out of it. She needed both kids and her sister-in-law to calm her down. She understands the operations of high finance the way I understand Chinese. I feel sorry for the lot of them. They don't know where they stand. She couldn't even tell me whether the house was in her name or in his. I hope he at least left her that much, because they won't leave a shingle or keyhole if he didn't. Creditors are going to settle on that house like locust on ripe corn."

"Mortgage Hill, I'll bet."

"Give the peeper a chocolate mouse: 222 Burgoyne Boulevard. Between an alderman and the president of Secord University. We don't live right, Benny. You still at the hotel?"

"Sure. They don't bother me. The sheets are clean, and the music quits at midnight sharp."

"You'll settle down one day. There's a cunning skirt with your name on it heading your way. She'll get you same as Shelley got me. Don't fight it. I never had it so good."

"Stop selling. I haven't got time to settle down yet. How can I support a wife on what I make? A well-fixed private investigator is as rare as a wealthy panhandler."

"Maybe you're too honest. Thought of that?"

"Yeah, I'm not sharp enough to be crooked. Take this guy Geller. A scam like his took planning. No smash and grab. Dealing in mortgages, bonds, investments, stuff like that, and not keeping a record in your books. It's easy to step into your own traps."

"You don't give yourself credit, Benny. You're swifter than you think. Savas and I've talked about it." I was feeling a little warm where my tie was pulled too tight. I put my last sip of coffee in my mouth and let it chill all the way down.

"Well, I'm not fast enough to make a successful villain. I'm not in Geller's class."

"I don't know. A little work and..."

"Go to hell!"

I tried to get the conversation bent back to the subject at hand, but Pete was stubborn sometimes. After all, I wasn't even offering to pick up his share of the check. But before we even got to the point where I might have arm wrestled him for it, something on his belt had started beeping and that put an end to our conversation.

I walked back to the office slowly thinking about a noisy glad-hander like Geller taking the Jewish community of Grantham for two point six million dollars. Why should a guy like Geller come into money like that, while I pick up nickels and dimes looking through keyholes and tracing people who've defaulted on their credit-card debts? How does a guy get the guts to pull off a scam like that? Does he keep up his courage with a vision of himself sipping long cool drinks on some southern marina with white-coated waiters fussing about the tilt of the awning over his table? When was I in Florida last? When was my last long cool drink? Was I going to make enough this month to sustain me through the dog days of summer?

St Andrew Street was a griddle, frying tires parked along its shadeless curve. Even the awnings in front of the stores seemed to be rationing the amount of shadow they cast. I looked across the road into the window of Cottonland Ltd. to see if I could see Geller's reflection in the glass laughing at me for getting mixed up in his little gold mine.

Chapter Three

It wasn't a warm invitation I got from Mrs Geller, it was more like come if you must, come while the fit is raging and get it over with. Even when I told her that I was acting on a request from the rabbi and the Jewish community, I felt like I was as welcome as an eviction notice. By the time I'd parked the Olds in the circular drive I'd worried the invitation into a "no trespassing" sign and when I heard the sound of chimes exploding on the other side of the uncompromising front door, I was ready for the old heave-ho at the very least. But within five minutes of being admitted and introduced, I had a rye and ginger ale in my hand and was sinking fast into a chintz-covered chair that felt like it had no bottom. There were two Mrs Gellers in the room, and it took me a couple of minutes to figure out which was the much-abused Mrs Larry Geller.

This distinction belonged to the frail-looking beauty in a knitted casual suit of burgundy wool. I was able to put a price tag on it and found myself impressed. Those Saturdays helping out in my father's store had taught me plenty, even if I hardly ever needed to draw upon the lore. She kept nervously brushing a wispy strand of strawberry hair out of her green eyes, and made passes at her drink with a very pretty mouth from time to time. The ice in the glass had melted, and it looked warm and watery in her long curved hand.

19

"I should explain, Mr Cooperman, that Debbie is both my sister and my sister-in-law, or I should say former sister-in-law. She was divorced from Larry's brother Sid...How long is it, Deb? It's nearly ten years, isn't it?"

"Ten years, on the nail. Is all of this information important, Mr Cooperman? Would you like us both to give you a character sketch, or do you pick up that sort of thing from the neighbours?"

"When I can't get it from the servants," I said, not much liking the sister.

"Servants?" the sister snorted. "He must mean Bessie. She's the cleaning woman, Mr Cooperman, and she comes every Thursday at nine in the morning. Ruth'll give you her address and phone number so you won't cut into time she's being paid for."

"Deb...!" Ruth Geller said with a whisper of warning in her voice. "It doesn't make things easier."

"Sorry, Ruthie. I forgot I was here to lend moral support, not moral outrage. I've got my wires crossed. I'm sorry, Mr Cooperman. This hasn't been easy for any of us."

"I understand that. And I'm sorry that I'm here at all. If it helps to blast away at me, feel free. I'm well paid to take verbal abuse."

Debbie, the sister, was standing with her arms stretched behind her touching an imitation antique table. The light coming through the curtains sent flattering shadows along the topography of her figure. She was taller than her sister, a little fuller, but not so that you missed the sculptured cheekbones or the large dark eyes they set off. "You see, Mr Cooperman, first we heard that Larry was missing, and then we heard what he is supposed to have done. That's two shocks for the price of one."

"Then you know the worst?"

"The worst?" Ruth said with surprise in her voice, and as she said it her hands inexplicably covered her ears.

"I mean, Sergeant Staziak has explained the magnitude of what has happened?"

Debbie abandoned the table and sat in a large wingchair where she could watch both her sister and me. She found a cigarette in a package of Menthols on a coffee-table and flicked it alight with a silver butane lighter. "Please come to the point of your visit, Mr Cooperman," she said. "We'll forgive you a tactful approach. What is it you want to know? I suppose we'd better help if we can, although I don't like it. We want the bastard's hide as much as his creditors do."

"Please, Deb!" It was more than a warning this time. Her voice had hurt in it, and signs that the breaking point wasn't far over the next hill. I held out my package of Player's to Ruth. I wanted to do some genuine human act of sympathy before we got to the questions. Ruth shook her head. "We don't smoke. I mean I don't. I don't have to answer for Larry any more." I put the pack of cigarettes away quickly. I wondered what else I would do that would remind Ruth of her missing husband. "Mr Cooperman," she said at length, "you know I'll be happy to try to help you any way I can."

Ruth relaxed a little after this speech; her sister pulled menthol-tasting smoke through her cigarette, sending it off towards the sheer curtains, where, according to my mother, it would turn them yellow. I tried reaching for a point of departure, a logical opening question. "Can you give me some idea of the time sequence, Mrs Geller? When did you see your husband last?"

"Not counting dreams, he means," said Debbie. "Remember the boy being interrogated in that old story? 'When did you see your father last?' That bit?" Ruth didn't answer her sister's question; she was trying to answer mine.

"He got up and went to work on Wednesday, two weeks ago today. He didn't take anything with him at the time, just his usual briefcase. He must have come back or been taking things over a period of time, because when I started looking, he'd taken several of his suits and most of his shirts and socks. He hadn't said anything about what time he was coming home." Ruth looked up at me trying to find the solution to the mystery written on my face. She continued, "He came and went as he pleased these last few months. Wednesday wasn't unusual."

"Could you go into that, please?"

"Well, Mr Cooperman, in the old days you could set a clock by my husband. He was never late. He never forgot a birthday or an anniversary. A man of regular habits. For years he used to come at night and I'd make dinner or we'd go out to a show, or we'd just stay home and watch television. He read stories to Sarah and Paul. We were a real family."

"But that pattern changed? He didn't come home so often, was less regular in his habits? Could you describe these last few months?"

Ruth was staring at an orange plastic truck under a chair across the room. "I'd get a call in the middle of one of my afternoon soaps: 'He's not coming home for dinner. Give his love to the children.' That would be Rose Craig, his secretary. That'd happen three or four times a week beginning around the end of March. For the last couple of weeks before he disappeared, he didn't even get her to call, and never called himself. Not once. But I just thought it was business, you know? I knew he was busy."

"Do you know of any business problems?"

"No. We never talked about the office."

"Did you ever suspect that he might not be working?"

"A woman, you mean? Sure, I thought about it. I worried a lot about it, but by the middle of June I was so sick and tired of everything that it would have been a relief to know that it was another woman."

"If it's the Jewish community you represent, Mr Cooperman," Debbie said, butting her cigarette in an ashtray, "you are certainly giving them their money's worth. Is there a corner of our lives that you are going to skip over, or will you have to await further instructions?"

I tried to ignore the question and Ruth went on as though there had been no interruption. "I tried to organize our lives so that it would work without Larry. I mean, since I couldn't depend on him, I had to plan without him. I bought a little Honda to run around in. Second hand, but it meant I wasn't trapped in the house waiting for him all the time. I hadn't driven since I was in high school, but I kept up my licence. You never forget."

"Mrs Geller, has he ever acted like this before? Were there similar but shorter incidents in the past? Maybe a couple of days?"

"No. I told you the way it was," she said, glancing towards her sister to see if she had anything to add. Debbie shook her head. Ruth looked up at me again. "He was universally liked and respected in this city, Mr Cooperman. It must be an illness, mustn't it? I mean a man doesn't just abandon his family after all these years."

"I wish I could answer that, Mrs Geller, but I can't."

"Mr Cooperman's not in that line of work, Ruthie. He just wants dates and facts. Isn't that right, Mr Cooperman?"

"When I can get them, yes, facts are very helpful. Most of the time you have to deal with the shadow of a fact or the footprint where a fact used to be." She was trying to get my goat for some reason and I couldn't figure out why. I could tell that they both were nervous. But that wasn't unexpected. I would have been surprised if they hadn't been. I felt like I was walking over the grave of some dark family secret and they were holding their breath waiting for me to look down. The trouble is in this business you walk over so many graves that your feet stop noticing shallow depressions after a while. "And what about these recent allegations about fraud? Was that a total surprise?"

"Well, I..."

"Let me try this one, Ruthie. Mr Cooperman, how would you feel if everything you touched had slime on it? The chair you're sitting in is probably stolen goods. Ruth doesn't know what's going to happen to her. The house, thank God, is in her name, so at least she'll have a roof over her head. But there's no telling where Larry's creditors will stop. And can you blame them? Widows, old people: how can you not feel sorry for them? The trouble is that Ruth has nothing but the house and some insurance in the clear. What's going to happen to her and the kids is not the question uppermost in their minds. Nor should it be." Debbie was reddening around the well-defined cheek bones as she spoke. She folded her arms across her chest as though she suddenly felt scantily clad on a public platform. Ruth was nodding agreement behind her sister. "As for the surprise, Ruthie, tell him about that."

"He'd become very strange in his habits, Mr Cooperman. He was forgetful and preoccupied in private, although he tried to hide that when we went out. Maybe it didn't show to anyone but me. I think Sarah—that's our daughter—sensed something. He just wasn't the man I married."

"Did he own property that you know about? Would you object to my having a look at his office?"

"The police have been all over that. I'm not sure whether I could prevent you looking if I wanted to. Anyway, the police have the keys to the office. What's his name, Deb?"

"Staziak. Staff Sergeant Staziak."

"Yes, I know him. I think that's everything. I want to thank you for being so helpful." I backed out of that plush living-room and found myself lighting a cigarette in my Olds. I'd come to listen, and I'd heard nothing Pete Staziak couldn't have told me. But I had that feeling about walking over shallow graves. I never liked that feeling.

Ten minutes later, the Olds was parked beside my father's rusting Cadillac in front of my parents' town house off Ontario Street. A coolish breeze off the lake was playing with the flowers in the flower-beds around the side of the house. Pa was digging in the garden in back. When he saw me, he took his foot from the spade and left it standing in the earth.

"Where are the tomatoes?"

"I've got them along the south side of the house. They get the heat from the brick wall that way. I'm just turning over the ground here for some late annuals. I'm glad you came, I'm getting short of breath."

"I hope you're not overdoing it." He looked at me with that mocking look that reflected all the terrible things that could be hinted at by shortness of breath. On Judgement Day, whatever else happens, I know he'll be there with his hair combed. We both sat down at the weather-beaten table that had been abandoned to the elements some years ago. I remember when it was carefully stored in the cellar of the old house. Here the cellar was a small room behind the rec room, and to get things to it you had to drag them through the living-room. The table surface was battered by frost and sun and scarred by neglected cigarettes and peeling paint. Pa pulled at the knees of his old tweed trousers as he sat down on the bench. We talked about the weather for a minute and let that hang out to dry. My health and his joined it there on the line after a short, worried cross-examination about breathlessness. Pa's retired and I worry about retired people who have only gin rummy to fall back on.

"Pa, you know Larry Geller?"

"Who doesn't? He's treasurer of the shul, on the executive at B'nai Brith. I don't know him well. He doesn't go to the club any more. I don't play cards with him. Not at his stakes. But I've played golf with him. Your mother knows his wife, Ruth. Her father was a friend of your grandfather. Two sewing-machine jockeys on Spadina Avenue years ago. Morris Kaufman and his two girls. Lives alone in Toronto since his wife, Pearl, died."

"When was that?"

"It must have been after Ruth and Larry's first kid was born, because they didn't name her after Pearl. They named the boy Paul. That was after her." Pa took a cigar from his pocket. It had been smoked down about a quarter of its length. He looked at it, then neatly trimmed the burnt end with rose shears. He surveyed the job, lit the result and tried it. He was wearing a red wool sweater which showed elbows through vents in the arms. On his head he wore an old yachting cap that made him look like a commodore at the very least. After three or four puffs of the cigar, he held it for a moment at arm's length then threw it into the garden with an underhand shot that spoke of disdain and slight regard. He pulled an aluminum tube from another pocket and lit a fresh cigar.

"What do you know about the girls?"

"What's to know? The older one, that's Debbie, married Sid Geller before she'd finished high school and left him in less than no time. She made a good settlement and she still gets along with Sid's family."

"I guess that made things easier, with her sister marrying the other brother?"

"Well, I'm telling you they all got along pretty good. I don't hear any complaints."

"Oh, so this is where you've got to." It was my mother coming out the French windows with a wide-brimmed hat on and a pair of gardening shears in her hand. She looked like a leading actress making her first entrance in a Coward play, only there was no applause. "Benny, what are you doing here?" She looked critically at Pa, then began to collect a bunch of irises for the living-room. "Is something wrong, Benny? I'm not used to seeing you without a warning any more. And as for your father, I thought he'd gone to the club."

"I'm trying to find out about the Gellers. Pa said that Grandpa knew Ruth's father."

"Morris? Oh, yes, they were great friends on Spadina before you were born. He was a pallbearer at your grand-father's funeral."

"And the girls?"

"They stick together. I'll say that for them. Debbie's always looked out for Ruth. And Ruth has always stood up for Debbie even after the divorce. Do you know Sid Geller? He looks like a Mafia hood. I don't know why she married him in the first place. They say that Larry has left Ruth. Is that why you're asking? He never seemed to be the type to settle down."

"Larry's a lawyer. What does Sid do?"

"You know the new bridge over the canal? Well, his company built that. Bolduc Construction, that's Sid Geller. You see their signs everywhere. They're building the new fire hall uptown."

"Where does Bolduc come into it?"

"Oh, he wasn't ever in it, was he, Manny?"

"Bolduc was a French Canadian with a wheelbarrow. Sid taught him to call himself a contractor. Soon Sid had the wheelbarrow and a contract to build seventy-five sewers in the north end. That was the beginning. I think Bolduc still hangs around the yard out Facer Street. Drinks all the time. Useless."

"Are you saying that Sid Geller cheated this guy?"

"He didn't have a nickel, so what was there to cheat? He had a licence, that's all. The only thing he knew was how much sand and water go into a cement mix. Sid didn't even know that much, but he knew the angles and soon he could hire people who knew all about making cement. They left the name, that's all. At least the old man won't ever die thirsty, not while Sid's around. If it weren't for Sid, Bolduc would have finished in the poor-house a long time ago."

"I think I knew his son in school. He played lacrosse and hockey. Alex Bolduc. Sure."

"I hope you've had your lunch, Benny. Your father hasn't been to the store yet. I'm down to two eggs and I've had them since April."

"I ate in town, Ma, but I'm coming to dinner on Friday night."

"That's right. Rain or shine every Friday night," she said. "And here it is Wednesday already. No sooner do the Friday candles burn down but you have to light them again." Pa tried to catch me with a subversive glance; I avoided it.

"Tell me, both of you: do you like the Gellers? Are they likeable people?"

"Well, the old man Geller died such a long time ago, I guess the boys went a little wild. Sid was always a hard man in business. Not that I ever had anything to do with him." Here Pa stopped as though he was thinking over the relevancy of what he had in mind to say next. I tried to encourage him with a look. "One time they were put-ting asphalt on Hillbrow Avenue and I tried to get Sid to have them run the machine up my driveway. He wouldn't do it. I would have paid for it."

"And Larry's so smooth," my mother said, "you have to watch your step around him so you don't slip and fall."

"This town should have asked you a month ago."

"And there's Nathan," added my father.

"Who's Nathan?"

"He's the other brother. He's the youngest, some sort of artist making statues. He has a workshop or studio you call it, someplace near the Bolduc yard on Facer Street."

"He took Doris Feinberg all over it," Ma added, "but she didn't see anything she liked. She tried to give him a tip for just looking. Doris says he's expensive."

"Is that the whole family, then? Sid, Larry and Nathan?"

"What is this, Benny: Twenty Questions?" Ma asked.

"He's on a case," Pa shrugged, like he was in on it from the beginning. "Being tight-lipped," he explained.

"Sid Geller's in with a bad bunch, I hear," said Ma, looking at the irises.

"What bunch is that?"

"I'm just repeating gossip. That's the sum total of what I know. So, I can't help you there. Is it Sid you're investigating, Benny?"

"Wait, wasn't there something in the *Beacon* about Larry?" Pa was the quiet member of the family, but he didn't miss much.

"I'm doing a job for Rabbi Meltzer and Saul Tepperman. It's hush-hush right now, but I'll be able to take you into my confidence by the end of the week."

"Benny," Ma said. "You look so serious when you say that."

"I'm only your father. Do you think you're adopted?"

"Maybe before the end of the week."

"As if we have to wait, Benny. Everybody knows that Larry Geller's a crook. His teeth are so real they look false."

"Ma, I don't know why I try to keep things from you."

"That's right. I always find out, don't I? I'm just a little juvenile delinquent that's what I am." Pa looked at my mother like he was about to move out. I beat a hasty retreat after reminding them I'd see them as usual on Friday night.

Chapter Four

The Bolduc Yard began about a quarter of a mile before a gate made a break in the chain-link fence. Inside I could see heavy, earth-moving equipment, trucks looking massive on great wheels, sheds made of corrugated iron, hangars sheltering mountains of sand, wooden frames, steel scaffolding and a range of cement in bags piled higher than the largest of the yellow earth-disturbers. Everything bore the stencil: BOLDUC. The gate itself was built so that it would admit vehicles twice as high as the fence. It stood open first thing on Thursday morning as I steered the car into a clearing and parked in front of what looked like the main office. The car was dotted with mustard-coloured stains from the puddles I'd splashed through. I walked around two more on my way to a boardwalk leading to the door.

The outside suggested that I might find a dozen barrels of assorted nails on the other side of the door, but I was wrong. It was a modern office inside with coloured plastic IN and OUT trays, banks of cabinets and files, desks with pretty girls behind them. Any roughness implied by the exterior had been smoothed away with wallboard streaked to look like real wood, but unable to fool a four-year-old.

"Mr Geller is expecting me," I said to the first face to look up from her typewriter.

"Mr Cooperman, is it?" she asked, and I wondered whether the whole office knew my name and the reason for my visit.

"That's right." The girl was already opening the gate and holding it so I could follow her to the door at the rear of the office. She knocked and went in for a second, then came out to show me the rest of the way.

Sid Geller was a huge man cramped into a small compass. He should have been six feet five instead of five feet six. It would have given more scope for a body that seemed to be bursting with energy even as it slouched in a high-backed leather swivel chair. He was wearing a three-piece, lemon-coloured business suit which set off a pink shirt and purple tie. The sun came through a window to his left, leaving no detail of the outfit to the imagination. His head was big, dark and I could find no trace of a neck. The face was darkly tanned, the eyebrows nearly meeting above a large squarely centred nose. The wide mouth was smiling as I came into view, and the figure rose from his chair; Sid Geller came towards me with his hand outstretched. When he finished with my right hand I was glad I'd broken off piano lessons at an early age. He motioned me to a chair, and as I pulled it over the bare floor, I saw that Geller's shoes and trouser cuffs were spattered with the same mustard-coloured mud that marked the Olds outside.

"Well, now, Mr Cooperman. Can I call you Ben? I hate all that formal crap. Call me Sid, and let's get right down to it. You said over the phone that it was about Larry's disappearance. What do you know? Are you buying or selling? Ruth told me she'd let you get your foot in her door. That's the only reason I'm talking to you, see? Ruth is going through hell, so I don't mind doing what I can to help out. I can talk to you as the rabbi's representative and be done with it. When some *schmoe* from the community comes asking after Label—

that Larry to you—I can tell him I already gave." He laughed at his own joke and I joined in to try to soften his steamroller methods. If he didn't shut up, I'd never get to ask a question. When I tuned in again, he was taking off with more of the same. "But I'm warning you, Ben, Label's my goddamned brother and I'm not going to do dirty on him. You get me?" I got him and told him so. He lit up a cigarette that looked like he'd rolled it himself, and leaned back until the chair squeaked. Above him was a framed photograph of the Flatiron Building in New York with a skeleton of girders showing through the front. I tried a question.

"What do you know about the trouble your brother's been involved in?"

"Nothing. Next question?"

"Back to the first one. You mean that Larry's taking-off came as a complete surprise to you?"

"Sure, if I knew he was leaving, I would have tried to stop him. For Ruth and the kids' sake. I didn't know he was involved in all this crap with his trust funds. Why should he tell me? When he was a kid he took my bike without asking and when he punctured the back tire he filled it up with a length of garden hose so I wouldn't know. Can you beat that? I knocked him into the middle of the next week when I found out. He knew what to expect from me. I'd be the last man in town Label would trust. Not that I'd turn him in; I'm his brother after all. But I never minced words with him when he was asking for it. Most of the time we were on good terms. But when he did some jackass stunt, he heard about it from me first. You can bet on that."

He placed his dark palms on the desk blotter and leaned on his arms. There was sweat on his forehead.

"When you heard about his confidence scam was he still around?"

"When I heard first, it was from a little guy who owed me. Never mind his name. He came asking for advice.

He explained what had happened and I could see the
game Label was playing. Only usually lawyers don't get
in that deep and don't get caught. It was the economy
that was against him. He should have levelled with me. I
might have helped. I could have put him in the hospital,
that's what I could have done, and he'd thank me for
doing it."

"How long was that before he skipped out of town?"

"Couple of days. I told him I wanted to talk to him. He
knew what it was all about, told me he couldn't talk then,
but promised to come and see me on the Wednesday."

"That was the day he disappeared?"

"Yeah, that was the day. I didn't know he was playing
such a big game. That kid brother of mine got away
with over two million. Crazy bastard. Can you beat it?"

"Yeah, I can think of a lot of people in this town who
can't wait to give him a medal."

"Don't start in with me, Cooperman. I have to live
here too. He gets away with two million and I have to
face those people. Sweet prospect, eh?" He folded his
arms across his chest like he was having a hard time
breathing, then asked, "When do you think we'll be reading about it?"

"Tonight, maybe tomorrow. The lid's half off now.
There's no advantage for the cops to keep it a secret."

"I'd skip out of town myself until this thing blows
over if it wasn't for Ruth and the kids. They're going to
need all the help I can give them. Debbie can't do
everything."

"Are you on good terms with your ex-wife?"

"You're changing the subject, aren't you?" He put out
his cigarette butt in a distributor cap he was using as
an ashtray. "Debbie and I are cordial, that's what we
are." He didn't want to embellish that and appeared to
be looking forward to the next question on a different
subject.

"I hear otherwise. It was a messy divorce."

"Okay, okay. She took me to the cleaners but good. But that was ten years ago. I don't hurt so much any more. I've got a happy situation going in my life, so I can afford to forgive and forget. I don't like fighting in public." He lit another fuzzy-looking cigarette which he took from his jacket pocket. "Neither of us wants anything bad to happen to Ruth and those two kids of hers. I'll back her on that. She has her moments, Debbie. Sometimes she can be as sweet as pie."

"What about your sister-in-law? Is she going to be all right?"

"What are you, Ben, all heart all of a sudden? Ruth's in for one hell of a bad time. There isn't any mud that's not going to be thrown at her. And you're not exactly a disinterested spectator, are you?"

"I'm trying to find her husband. Is that so bad? Are her shoulders broad enough to take some of the heat?"

"Sorry, Ben. I forgot my manners. You know how it is?" I agreed that I knew how it was.

"Do you think that Larry got into this mess because of the economy, being pressed by creditors and so on, or as a matter of policy? Did he plan the whole thing, or did it just happen?"

"That's the big question, isn't it? If I could see the books he kept, I could get some idea, but without them, I'm only a guesser like the rest of you."

"The cops will have his books."

"So, go bother them."

"Did Larry take any part in your business here?"

Sid licked the hair on the knuckles of his right hand as he thought about his answer. Finally he said: "He did some legal stuff for me. Nothing important. He didn't even get paid for it. Never invoiced me, and I guess I never pushed him to."

"Did he owe you money?"

"Christ, they all owe me money! I put him through school so he could learn the law and find out about three-piece suits and which fork to use at parties I wouldn't get invited to. I'm still doing the same for his brother, only I don't get my name in *The New York Times* like Nate does."

"You were the head of the family." That gave him breathing time. He was getting a little excited.

"Yeah, I was the head of the family. I had to look out for the family." His eyes were shining when he looked up for a moment. He didn't look me in the eye. I tried examining the pictures on the wall until he asked if I had any other questions.

"Was there anyone outside the family he trusted and might have talked to?"

"No."

"Is there any place apart from his office and house where he might have left some record of..."

"No. Next question."

"Does he have a favourite watering hole in Florida or Arizona that you know about it?" That's when I got thrown out. He wasn't rude about it. He didn't stop smiling at me through his clenched teeth. It was just that suddenly he wasn't sitting behind his desk any more, he had me tightly by the elbow and we were moving towards the office door at some speed. After I got the ignition started, I could still feel his grip on my arm. I splashed my way out of there fast, nearly skinning the Olds on a silver Audi driving through the gate. There was a woman at the wheel. She didn't stop to get acquainted.

Once again the Bolduc fence followed me for a quarter of a mile along Facer Street. I rolled down the window. Under the sun, the interior had become a sauna without an oak branch. I was warm from my interview with Sid Geller too. Through a windshield pockmarked with yellow mud, a blue sky smiled over the landscape of one-storey houses built during and after World War Two to meet the housing shortage. These bungalows began life as alike as sardines, but now they all had sprouted eccentricities: aluminum awnings, added second floors, porches, extensions, chimneys. While across the road one industrial site gave way to the next. Sandwiched between two such sites, and opposite more depressing grey houses, I came on the two-storey warehouse that a little digging had told me served as Nathan Geller's studio.

I parked the car near a nest of green garbage bags and rang a bell. I couldn't hear it make a sound inside, so I tried the door and found it open.

I was in the biggest room outside a theatre I'd been in for some time. Except for a balcony-like second floor, which beetled over the work area, the room went up to the ceiling. A skylight let in the day and the light pooled in cool circles like theatrical work lights on a stage. In these white spots and bathed in the illumination stood life-sized human figures in plaster. In spite of a rough surface, I recognized the familiarity of these types: a fruit-vendor weighing vegetables, a fat woman on a park bench holding one shoe in her hand, a tourist photographing an unbending Mountie, a bag lady with her supermarket cart loaded with her possessions. That's the sort of thing. These were finished pieces, and arranged to create the effect I'd walked into. Nathan Geller was an accomplished sculptor and it was the first time I'd heard about it.

From under the overhang of the balcony, I could hear hammering. I followed the racket until I found whom I took to be Nathan Geller hammering at a wire armature that was as big as he was. He was dressed in farmer's overalls and wore a railway engineer's cap turned back to front. Welder's glasses covered his eyes, although the torch was turned off near by. When he saw me walking towards him, he paused and pushed the goggles up on his sweaty forehead.

"Mr Rylands? I didn't expect you until tomorrow. Didn't Munby tell you? I left a message yesterday. But as long as you're here..."

"My name is Cooperman," I said, putting on a smile. "The bell doesn't work."

"You're not from Munby?" he said, trying to get a grip on the fact.

"Not so far. I've never heard of either of them. I came to talk to you about your brother." He pulled the goggles off completely now and double checked the valve in the welding torch.

"I heard about you. Debbie phoned and told me to be good. Come on upstairs." He led the way from this work area up a flight of industrial stairs to a small comfortable room with a rug on the floor and books in shelves, a television set on a small refrigerator and a comfortable-looking couch and matching chair. It was a copy of any of thousands of rec rooms built during the sixties in finished basements. Geller had a fine eye for detail.

He also had the family nose and cleft chin with dimples on either side of a frank mouth. He had more hair than his brother but it didn't look like what he had would outlast the decade. Without asking, he went to the refrigerator and removed bottles of imported beer. He settled one with a tall glass near me and began working on his own from the bottle. "This gets to be hot work this time of year," he said. "I always seem to be casting bronze in July and doing outdoor sketches in January. Well, so you know about Larry. Welcome to the club. Club, hell, it's more like a convention."

"Did you have any hint that this was going on?"

"Mr Cooperman, look around you. Does it look like my life gets mixed up with stocks and bonds much? Sid pays the rent on this place and keeps my books straight. I'm a non-starter in the world of high finance. Surprise, surprise. My life is framed by Sid at one end saying 'Go to it, little brother! Have fun,' and at the other by my dealer saying 'Can't you work any faster? I bust my ass getting you a show and what thanks do I get?' Between these extremes I manage to have a pretty good life."

"Where do you show your stuff? Not locally."

"I actually did have a show here about ten years ago. Nobody knew what to make of me. Only sold one piece and that was to an American. When you came in I thought you were from Frank Munby, my dealer. He has connections with the big commercial galleries in Toronto, Vancouver and Montreal. The stuff I do usually ends up there. Ever since he arranged for big shows in London and New York, the Toronto gallery can't get enough of me. Munby phones twice a day to see if he can catch me going to the can or knocking off for a beer. 'You keep your buns moving, boy,' he says, 'and I'll make you as big as Takis or Jones.' Hell, I shouldn't complain. He got me that show in New York and you wouldn't *believe* the press we got. But that's not what you came to talk about, is it?"

Having shut himself off from his favourite topic, it took him a minute to remember the topic at hand. He blinked a bit, like a golfer swatting tall grass, going through the motions of looking for a lost ball.

"Larry," I said. "Your other brother."

"Right! Yes, good old unreliable Larry. He went missing on July 3rd. I saw him the weekend before. As far as I could tell he wasn't taking leave of us. He tried to impress Sid as usual with his inside information and kidded me about all this." Nathan was carefully tearing off the oval beer label as he spoke. The object seemed to be to get it all without ripping it or leaving a white residue on the bottle. "Sid bellowed at both of us the way he usually did. Big brother stuff, very old country. Larry didn't slip me any secret messages. He didn't anticipate his going by giving me my birthday present early. He didn't make any statements full of *double entendres*. No hits, no runs, no misses. Just Larry, with his jaw set tight when he talked about my work. Larry doesn't approve of what I do. It's funny, but Sid, with no education to speak of, understands me better. When I got a Canada Council grant it really fazed Larry; he couldn't understand why anybody'd give a dime to me for these glorified plaster pies. He just doesn't understand what I'm all about."

"Have you any idea where he might have gone? Is there a place he might hole up until this blows over?"

"Come on! What do you take me for? I'm not going to play those cards. He's flesh of my flesh and all that."

"Routine question, that's all. No offence intended. Did he travel much in the last few years?"

"Now you think you're getting clever, eh? Sure he travelled. Winters in Miami Beach. We've got a duplex down there. You can get the address from the cops or from Ruth. He went to Phoenix a couple of times. Do you want to hear about the places he went skiing?" I would have looked sillier with a pencil in my hand taking all this down. As it was, I felt silly enough. Nathan wasn't through with me yet: "...In 1981 he spent some time near Arles in the south of France. He travelled to West Berlin on business that year, and was in London twice in 1982. He stayed at the Dorchester..." I thought of shutting him up, but you never know about these things. Sometimes the first thing you find in a haystack is the needle. "He went to Scotland one time. Can't remember where. Some cranny or is it a corrie north of Edinburgh. Went hunting with some MP he tried to butter up. Did I tell you about his two weeks in China?" He went on with his Cook's tour for a few more minutes then finally stopped.

"What about around town? What were his haunts?"

"He was always going to B'nai Brith meetings as far as I could tell. Tell you one thing: I never once saw him in an art gallery. You can have that for nothing." I put it down in my head with all the other nothing I'd heard. I slipped him a little silence to prime him. He didn't need it. He was still working his joke and didn't look like he was going to run out of places. "His office is on Queen Street across from the post office. He was a member — hell he was treasurer! — of the shul. He had regular habits. And you know what? I think he's a son of a bitch leaving those kids of his to face this alone. That's what I think. He's got the backbone of an amoeba."

"Who drives the silver Audi?" I asked, trying to move on to new territory.

"The silver...? Oh, you mean Pia Morley. She's Sid's girl-friend."

" 'Girl-friend?' That sounds like he's borrowing the family car on Saturday night. Can you be more specific? This isn't for a newspaper. Just background."

"Okay, Pia's his live-in pal. Since they invented palimony, I guess that pal is an okay legal status, right?" He pronounced Pia to rhyme with Hi-yeh. "She's divorced too, has been around, I'm told, and they've been together since a few years after Debbie flew the coop."

"Was she friendly with your brother?"

"Pia and Larry? How should I know? They were friendly enough. Nothing special. But you're asking the wrong guy. I'm not all that fast on the uptake. Relationships are things you have to put down on paper for me to see. My God, I mean I just don't notice."

"If there was something, I couldn't count on you to tell me about it, could I?"

"I suppose not."

"How is Larry's disappearance affecting your family?"

"Shit, Mr Cooperman, you ask dumb questions sometimes. Personally, I'd like to climb into a hole in a Henry Moore and pull it in after me. Ruth's on Valium, with a doctor and Debbie standing by twenty-four hours a day. The kids want to see their Daddy. What would you tell them, smart guy? Daddy's a crook? Daddy's stolen a lot of money and run off with it, but be good and maybe if you say your prayers he'll send you a postcard." Nathan Geller drank off the last of his bottle of beer, gasped and wiped his mouth on his sleeve. I got up to go. Agreeing with him about the questions, I couldn't find any better ones. So I thought I'd save my next visit until I had something to stick to him. I said my goodbyes and started for the stairs. He called after me, "Cooperman? Let me give you some advice: don't mess with Pia. She doesn't fool around, and she has some friends who have a habit of not liking the people she doesn't like. Now if you'll get out of here, I can go back to work."

So I got out and I suppose he went back to work.

Chapter Five

I parked my car in the usual place behind the office and climbed out into the sunshine. It was really doing it today. Even the mossy backs of these ancient St Andrew Street buildings looked like they were giving up the last ounces of a century's accumulated moisture to those perpendicular rays. On my way up the sloping alley, I saw weeds trying to make a go of it against the brick wall of the Standard Bank Building. The weeds would be more successful than the bank. It closed down before I was born.

The glare on the pavement made me squint as I opened the outside door to the office. I tried to imagine the street with a rampart of snow over the curbs and ice on the sidewalk I should complain to the janitor about. It didn't stop the sweat from running down the inside of my shirt. The hall and the stairs to the office were cooler. Old buildings, I thought, as I unlocked my door.

I went through my mail without finding anything of interest, then got busy on the telephone. Pete Staziak couldn't let me have the key to Larry Geller's Queen Street office. It wasn't right for the public cops to go around helping out the private cops even though, as I pointed out to him over the telephone, the private sector had once or twice...

"Don't give me any of that nail polish, Benny. When have you done anything for me when it didn't get you off some hook or other? You're like that goddamned bird that cleans out the teeth of the mud-loving crocks in the bayou down south. Show me once where what you did for me and Savas..."

"I told you about Kogan, didn't I?"

"Big deal, so we pull a drunk out of a doorway so he doesn't freeze to death. Besides it was your doorway he was freezing in, wasn't it?"

"It was next door. Okay, I'll bother Geller's wife for a key, knowing how much you'd love to get me on a B and E."

"Ah, now you're talking. You could loid the lock, set off the alarm and we could waltz around all night together. You know Rose Craig?"

"Never heard of her."

"Geller's secretary. She's got keys. What's more she's still trying to deal with the traffic in there. Which means she has more guts than brains, if you ask me. I don't see any harm in you snooping around there, as long as I don't have to wait until Christmas to find out if you discovered anything."

"You're always the first to know, Pete."

"Only when Shelley's pregnant, Benny. With you, I'm always playing guessing games. I'm at the foot of your Must Be Told list. But I got faith in human nature, that's what I got. So, go to it. Go up there and uncover all the clues we poor working stiffs have overlooked because of our superficial and hidebound ways."

"I'm getting to recognize that line coming, Pete. Get off my back. I'm only trying to make a living. What do you want from me?"

"Damn it, Benny, I just told you, practically told you, to use my name with the secretary. What more do you want, a seeing-eye dog?"

It was a short walk from the office to Queen Street. On it I passed two banks that were in business and one that had become a restaurant. It was one of those places where they serve a vegetable fuzz of shoots on top of everything and you need a PhD to understand the menu. The fish-and-chips truck parked at the corner of St Andrew and Queen was closer to my style. I bought a cone of French fries, doused them with malt vinegar and salt and began spearing them into my mouth. Kogan, the rubby, was asking for handouts near the chips wagon. He was looking elegant in a reclaimed crested blue blazer and grey flannel trousers held up with a few rounds of butcher string.

"How about it? Got any change? I was in the war, mister. Not your war; your dad's war. Help a fella out."

"Hello, Kogan. How's it going?"

"Huh? Oh, hell it's you, Mr Cooperman. Nice day, eh?" I gave him a warm quarter from the change I'd just collected from the purchase of my lunch. "Thanks," he said, and I continued down Queen Street.

Outside the office of the *Beacon*, in one of the handy honour-boxes, I could see the headline through the plastic window: LAWYER DEFRAUDS LOCALS. That tore it. I'd had all the head start I was going to get. Now it was every man for himself. I fed the machine some silver and it clicked open when I pulled the handle. I read the top paragraphs in each of the three stories linked to the headline. The picture of Larry Geller looked at least ten years old. He didn't look a bit ashamed of himself. I folded the paper in half and tucked it under my arm.

Geller's office was in the Hamilton Building, about half-way down the first block on the west side of Queen. The shadow of the post office nearly darkened the entrance, which was formed by four glass doors, all but one locked. The elevator entrance was cut into a wall of solid native limestone, or so it looked. I pushed the button for the fourth floor.

I couldn't miss Geller's office; it was the one with a crowd of seven or eight people in front of the door with uniformly grim expressions on their faces.

"She won't let anybody in," a middle-aged woman, one of a group of three, volunteered. This verdict was confirmed by grunts of agreement from the others. An elderly man, flanked by what I took to be his lawyer, stood first in line at the door. Another old couple, rather formally dressed, hovered near the elevator doors. "She threw everybody out just a minute ago," said the first woman again. "She's cracking under the strain, if you ask me." I wanted to try the door myself, but there didn't appear to be any reason to believe that these people were part of a plot to keep me from visiting Geller's office.

"She'll have to come out for lunch, won't she?" said the elderly man to his lawyer, who didn't jump to give his opinion.

"And what a temper she has!" said a woman with a voice like the ping from a cracked crystal vase.

"Just stay calm, Mr Friedman," the lawyer whispered into the hearing aid on Mr Friedman's chest. "It's not the end of the world."

"Easy for you to talk," Mr Friedman said, moving his arms in exasperation. "You're making money just standing here."

"You should have stood up to her, Doris. I would have backed you up." This from the woman with ghostly facepowder all over the front of her face.

"I wonder," I asked looking at no one in particular, "if she's read the story in the paper."

"Paper? You mean the *Beacon*?" asked one of the ladies.

"Sure. It's got the whole story, with pictures."

All of them squeezed into one elevator car and were out of sight within twenty seconds, and I was alone in front of Larry Geller's office door. "The coast is clear!" I shouted through the door. "They've all gone. I chased them all away. Open up and I'll show you your boss's picture in tonight's paper." For a second or two I heard nothing except the sound of the thought process itself maybe, then a chair squeaked and a voice near the door asked:

"Who are you anyway?"

"I'm not the paperboy, but I've got a copy."

"If this is a trick..."

"Cross my heart. Look, my name's Cooperman. I'm an investigator working with the Jewish community of Grantham. I've talked to Ruth Geller, and she knows I'm here." She didn't know, but I would pass the word along when I saw her again. The spring lock snapped open on the other side of the door. I turned the knob and walked in.

Rose Craig stood before me like she thought I was the leader of a mob come to break the door down. It took her a minute to see that I was alone, then she stopped glaring and took her hands from her hips. I squeezed past her into the office. She grabbed the paper from under my arm and threw it down on the receptionist's desk with the headline staring up at the ceiling.

Geller's secretary was a compact, well-proportioned redhead in a green blouse and tweed skirt. She looked like she'd been tossed in a blanket: she was nervous, twitchy and sloppy. White underwear showed through where too many buttons were unfastened on her blouse, a cigarette dangled from her lips as her head moved up and down the columns, spilling ash over her impressive bosom. Her hands were small and puffy, with short, none-too-clean fingernails. Newsprint was coming off on her red palms. She looked up at me and shot a glance over her shoulder. "They've been driving me crazy," she said. "I couldn't take it any more. You say you've talked to Ruth? That's supposed to make it all right your being here. Let me tell you, Mr Cooperman, not even Ruth is a complete friend. She has her own interests in this too. There are no friends. Not even me. If I don't get paid on Friday, I'll be looking for a new job on Monday."

"Have you found much?" I asked, nodding in general at the inner office.

"What do you mean?" She opened her green eyes with new-born innocence. I liked her for that. If my business ever begins to take off, I'll try to remember Rose Craig. It would be nice to be protected by her "What do you mean?" for a change.

"Come on, Rose, you've been tossing the place, same as I would in your spot." She eyed me thoughtfully, taking the cigarette out of her mouth and babysitting it in an ashtray on the corner of the beige desk. It was her luck that a fleck of tobacco stuck to her lower lip. She didn't take her eyes off me. She stood just far enough away from me so that she could go through all the illustrated steps in a karate manual if I got out of line.

"If that lot got in here, there wouldn't be anything left intact within three minutes."

"What they're looking for won't be found in neatly kept files. You know that better than anybody." She smiled at me in spite of herself, but savaged the cigarette in the crowded ashtray like she was killing a spider with it. "He must have had a wonderful memory, your boss, or maybe a carefully kept code system. He could have done it on slips of paper and made it look like laundry lists. What have you found?"

She eyed me evenly. "That would be telling, wouldn't it?"

"Okay, play coy. I'm not one of those you have to worry about. Geller doesn't owe me six cents. Now that the story's public property you're going to have lots of opportunity to meet new people and develop inter-personal skills. Tell you what, you should get a security company in here to guard the office. You'll need six men in three shifts around the clock. Get them from Niagara Security. They won't cheat you. Probably you'll get a fair rate on the junior men. You must have an office operations budget. Don't tell me he cleaned that out too?"

"No. There's a few hundred in petty cash. Damn it all, Mr Cooperman, I'm so confused. What's going to happen to me?"

"You're going to get your picture in the paper, and you're going to get an unlisted phone number for a year. Do you have a friend or relative who'll put you up for a few days? It's just until you can move from wherever you're living."

"Move? I just moved into that apartment!"

"Well, you're going to have night visitors for a month, and nasty telephone calls for longer than that. You won't be in any actual danger..."

"Danger!"

"Right, you won't be, but people want to get something to ease the frustration. Remember we're dealing with the friends and relatives of the people he cheated. You won't have to worry about the people themselves, I don't think, just the kin, who'll tend to be younger and more hot-headed than is actually necessary. The cops'll help you if you get threatened. Best to disappear for a while; that's what they'll tell you."

"Damn it. I don't need this. You know?"

"Nobody does. All you can do is get through it without skinning your knees. Low profile, that's the ticket. Try not to talk to the paper, try to avoid photographers. Get yourself a lawyer you can depend upon."

"Lawyer?"

"Just in the background. Nobody's going to try to say you did it. Geller got away with a lot of money; a lot of people are cross at him; and they may think you know more than you do. It wouldn't hurt to keep a diary about what's happening to aid your memory if this ever comes to court." It was part of my standard speech to clients. Now I was giving away free legal advice.

"I swear I don't know a thing about any of this. You've got to believe me, Mr Cooperman."

"I believe you. But will they?"

"All I did was the normal legal work. I typed the wills, deeds and mortgages. I billed the clients. I kept the loose-leaf law reports up to date. I passed on messages to Ruth that he left for me. I don't know anything. Honest."

"I still believe you. What about a man named Kaplan? Did you know him?"

"He's a farmer, isn't he? Sure, he came here, but I don't know what they talked about. I never do unless there's some letter or minutes of agreement that Mr Geller wants typed. With a lot of them, he typed his own notes. I heard him do it, but you won't find them in the files. I've looked."

"He must have done his bookkeeping somewhere else. Did he own or rent any other property that you know of?"

"This is the office. This is where he did his work. I mean he usually took an attaché case home with him. Why'd' you think he must have had a second office?"

"He had a second life, didn't he? All he'd need was a room someplace where his records couldn't be traced back to him. He could have rented it under a false name."

"In a town this size, are you kidding?"

"All right, forget it. It was just a notion. How much time did he spend in the office anyway? You know the routines of other legal eagles. How does Geller stack up?"

"He used to get here early. That's one thing I'll say for him. I used to get in by a quarter to nine and he was already dictating into his machine."

"Often?"

"Oh, a couple or three times a week. Then he'd take long lunches. But most of them do that. You can check his desk calendar to see the people he met. Only that's at the police station. A Sergeant Staziak has it."

"Did he work late usually?"

"Sometimes. He'd stay on after I went home and then in the morning there'd be a batch of tapes for me to type up. But there were times when he didn't come back from lunch at all. Or he'd come back and then go right out again saying he wouldn't be back."

"Was he going home, do you know?"

"I just work here, Mr Cooperman," she said. "I'm not clairvoyant."

Rose had been doing some unobtrusive personal tidying while we talked. I noticed without noticing when she'd done it, that she had detected and remedied the unfastened buttons on her blouse. "Would you mind if I had a look at the private office, Miss Craig?" She put down the paper and waved me through.

There was nothing special about Geller's inner sanctum. The desk was uncluttered dark wood with a high-backed swivel chair behind it. On the wall I recognized diplomas, citations and photographs with Geller shaking hands with various dignitaries. The desk was arranged so that the morning light fell on the faces of his clients. A photograph of Ruth and the kids sat in a silver frame next to a brass calendar with the date reading Thursday, July 7th. Rose Craig, who was standing in the doorway, saw that I was eyeing the wall of filing cabinets. "There's nothing doing in there," she said, like a mind-reader. "I told you, I checked."

"What used to be here?" I asked, examining a round patch on the dusty mahogany that showed less dust than the rest.

"That? It was a trophy or something he'd won when he was at law school. He told me a million times what it was, and I'll be damned if I can remember. It had something to do with winning a prize at Osgoode Hall. He was very proud of it."

"So, it's not surprising, then, that it's gone?"

"Oh, he'd take it with him all right."

"Do you know whether he kept up with Eddie Lazarus or Morrie Freeland? They were pals of his from law school."

"Mr Lazarus doesn't live here in town. I think he has a practice in the Falls. I could check. Mr Freeland's office is on the next floor to this. He's with Beamish and White. Mr Geller never called him, but sometimes Mr Freeland would put his head in the door. They went out to eat together last winter sometime."

I was half-way to the door of the outer office when the phone rang. I knew it couldn't be for me, but I didn't hurry away to let Rose answer it without a witness. From the look of her, she didn't want me to hurry away either. It was one of those calls full of exclamations and cries of "You're kidding!" and "What?" that convey absolutely no information to the casual listener. When she hung up, she looked right at me as though in whatever game she was playing I was "it."

"There's a gang over at the Geller house throwing things and tearing up the place!"

"Did she call the cops?"

"I don't know. Shouldn't we do something?"

"Yeah, put in a call to the cops while I collect my car. I'll be back in two minutes. Meet me outside." And I was off.

I don't know why I reacted that way. It was clearly a dab of vindictive violence levelled at Geller's house and family because Geller himself had so successfully fled the scene. So why was I getting involved? I guess I thought it might put me somewhere close to a word or phrase uttered in the heat of the moment that might give me a clue about where this investigation was going next. The Olds, parked in my father's old spot behind my office on St Andrew Street, started up and I backed out of the alley without sending more than half a dozen slow pedestrians to the hospital. Because of the one-way system it took me longer to get from my office back to Geller's office by car than I could have covered the direct route on my hands and knees. Rose Craig was waiting outside the office looking the wrong way for me on Queen Street. I honked. She crossed the street, got in and swung the door closed behind her, smelling of Chanel No. 5.

It took about eight minutes to drive across the canal bridge and find Burgoyne Boulevard. It took longer to make it to 222. I counted at least three police cars and about fifteen other cars blocking the street. A crowd of people were standing on the lawn listening to a cop with a bull-horn telling them to go back to their houses. It was like walking into a scene in the movies. Usually it's staged in front of a jail with one of the mob waving a rope suggestively. But this was no mob. No ordinary mob, I mean. I recognized Mr and Mrs Sokolov, the Wagners, the Epsteins, the Shapiros and even Mort and Cindi Katz. None of them were carrying ropes, but they looked mad and frustrated. I could see blood in many eyes, and for a minute I couldn't be sure whether the cops standing on the Geller porch, in the driveway and about six feet away from the mob were sufficiently intimidating. They all looked serious, and sweat was standing out on the forehead of the cop nearest Rose and me as we pushed our way into the front rank. From here I could recognize other faces. Some were from the Jewish community, but not all. There was Doug Spiers and Michael Rainsbury, neither of whom had ever been inside the shul as far as I knew, and Tobi and Frank McLure along with the Helmsels and Digbys. It was a show for everybody, and as I thought that, I saw a microphone pass under my nose at the end of a familiar arm. It was Wally Skeat, late of the Niagara Falls TV Station. I hadn't even heard he'd moved back to Grantham. But nobody consults me about these things any more. The whole world comes apart and reassembles without a whisper to me about what it has in mind. Wally didn't see me. He kept looking over my shoulder, and when I turned I was looking into the bright lights of a truck with a camera crew on top leaning over the railings at us. To me it seemed

that the timing was unfortunate. The cop with the bull-
horn shouted something at the truck and once again told
the crowd to disperse. Somebody lobbed a cabbage at
the Geller porch, but it was such a lazy, defeated pitch
that I knew that the forces of law and order had tri-
umphed again. The crowd buzzed and turned retreating
towards the tangle of cars. The camera truck followed,
hurrying them up. The news media chased the event out
of sight. The cops breathed a sigh of collective relief,
and the top cop passed the bull-horn to a junior man
who carried it around like a newly won badge of authority.

We joined the huddle to hear what we could of the
post-mortem.

"What set this thing off?" I asked, trying to separate
us from the disassembling hoard, and at the same time
get them talking louder.

"You're Cooperman, right?" asked a uniform with a
red head sticking out the collar. "I've seen you with the
sergeant."

"This is Mr Geller's secretary. She sent in the alarm."

"Her and half a dozen others. Geller had good neighbours. Nobody likes seeing property threatened. On that
they stick together."

"What started the fuss?" I asked again. The policeman
looked at the departing mob.

"I guess it was the paper. It could have been on the
noon news too. I don't know about that." Another cop
confirmed that he had heard the whole story on the radio.
Whether the paper had the scoop or not was something
for the likes of Wally Skeat to argue.

"Who's the officer in charge?"

"That's Chalice." The red-headed cop hoisted his
thumb in Chalice's direction. "He's good, isn't he? I think
he likes it. I wouldn't give three cents to be holding a
bull-horn when a crowd really decides to get ugly. Give
me cruiser duty any day."

Ruth Geller, who must have slipped out of the house without anyone noticing, came into sight and grabbed Chalice by the arm. "We can't go on living like this," she said. "Anything could have happened. What about my kids?" The rest got louder and shriller without making more sense. Chalice was talking to her, his voice low but steady. Ruth nodded to the tune of his words until she caught sight of Rose Craig standing near me. "Rose!" she called, tears overflowing. "Thank God for you, Rose. You are such a friend." They were hugging and crying in that way women have. I didn't hear what they said, they were both talking at the same time.

"Benny drove me over while I called the police." I made out the words but the sense was obscure. Ruth looked over at me and tried on a smile for size. It didn't fit and the colour was wrong. I took advantage of it, though, and ambled over to join the ladies just as the policeman moved off to other duties near one of the cruisers. I was standing on a crushed tomato.

Chapter Six

After picking up three green garbage bags full of dead oranges, cabbages and other missiles, Rose and I were invited into the house for coffee. Nathan Geller was in the living-room putting a square of cardboard over a window that had been broken. Ruth Geller looked like a zombie; she walked around the living-room touching the corners of tables and lamp-shades. I thought she was going to fall on the floor and melt. With a fragile smile at the corners of her mouth, she seemed to be listening in to a stereo station on Mars. Her sister hovered over her like a protective, stronger other self. Although we had been asked in for coffee, no one in fact made a movement in the direction of the kitchen. Nathan was working on his window; the task seemed to occupy him totally. Work was liberating. Debbie made an attempt to make Rose Craig comfortable, although I couldn't hear what they were saying. Ruth kept glancing from the window and Nathan to the stairs, whose broadloomed steps led to the second floor. Nobody noticed when I went into the kitchen to put the kettle on.

A few minutes later, Rose sat with her heavily tweeded knees close together balancing her cup and saucer, watching Nathan now applying masking tape to the spider-lines of a cracked window-pane. He took a professional pride in his work, and kept commenting on each step as though we were a film crew watching and recording the artist at work. "That's good enough for the moment. I'll try to get a man to come around to replace both panes in the morning." Then he took the measurements and made a notation on the inside of a package of cigarettes.

From upstairs I heard the voice of a child calling. Ruth bounded up the stairs without a word. A few minutes later, two kids, a boy and his older sister, appeared with a strange woman and their mother, each carrying a suitcase. Debbie, Ruth and Nathan rallied long enough to try to make the send-off look like an event. They hugged and kissed the children, tried to make a flourish of it, but they weren't up to it and the kids didn't want it.

"I've got to have my bike," the little girl said with a serious expression. "I need it tomorrow, Mommy."

"We'll see, dear."

"I *need* it."

This was my first opportunity to see a fair piece of the family together acting like a family. I watched the aunt and uncle help bundle the kids off in a car with the woman who was later identified as an unmarried cousin of I never did figure out whom.

With the kids out of the house, a source of tension was removed. Debbie lit a cigarette with her butane lighter, and I cadged a light for a Player's off the same flame. Rose rattled her empty cup in her saucer as she got up to return the coffee things to the kitchen. "Leave it," Ruth ordered, but didn't take any notice of Rose continuing her mission anyway. Nobody said anything except in hoarse whispers. If Larry Geller had been laid out on trestles in front of the fireplace with his hands crossed over his chest, the atmosphere couldn't have been more funereal. We smoked in silence. Rose returned to her place on the chintz-covered chair behind the coffee-table. Ruth huddled in a narrow occasional chair. Her painted smile was peeling away. Nathan pulled out a rounded stone from between the pillows of the loveseat in front of the windows. When she saw it, Ruth began to cry.

By now I was feeling like the fifth shoe under a bridal bed. If I'd been looking at this scene through a transom or a keyhole I couldn't have felt more like a voyeur. The room itself seemed to be crawling away from the patched window. In a way it didn't seem like the room I'd been in the day before. Somehow a pile of broken glass glinting on broadloom and masking tape on painted woodwork completed the work the mob tried to do. "Safe as houses," the Welsh say. This house seemed as safe as a circus tent in a hurricane.

"Your wrist, Nathan. Look!" Debbie crossed to where Nathan's bare arms had been dangling between his knees as he sat on the edge of the loveseat. He raised first one arm then the other. A twisted line of darkening blood snaked down his long left arm. He raised it like a surgeon scrubbing up, and then began to lick it.

"Don't!" Ruth cried, suddenly coming to life. "I'll get something." But Debbie was already binding his wrist with a handkerchief.

"It's just a scratch," she said with some colour returning to her face. Nathan looked embarrassed.

"I hate the sight of blood," he said. "Especially my own." His bum joke brought a laugh which cracked the mood down the centre.

"Nathan, you idiot!" Ruth said. "Here we are with the mob at the door and all you can do is make jokes."

"Well, the mob's gone at least. And the house is watertight for tonight. Shouldn't you get out of here for a few days, Ruth?"

"What and have every stick of furniture stolen or smashed? Don't be silly, Nathan. Somebody's got to stick and stay. It's my home. If the cops can't protect the place with people living in it, think of what a mob could do to it empty."

"Good point, I guess," said Nathan. Rose sipped her coffee, which like mine was chilly.

"Will this find a corner in your report, Mr Cooperman?" Debbie asked, returning to that annoying note she kept hitting on the first visit.

"Mrs Geller, I'm not writing a report. I'm not here to judge you people. I'm here now because Rose Craig and I thought you might need help."

"I called the police," Rose added. Debbie shrugged and slumped into the long couch under a large painting of a woman in a hoop skirt playing a cello beside another at a spinet. The women were lush in their velvets and satins. Debbie Geller was wearing a large shapeless white sweater over blue jeans. All in all, she had a good face: a high forehead and clear eyes, focused on the patched window.

"You're a son of a bitch, Mr Cooperman, whatever you say. If this was my house, I'd show you your way out faster than I can think of my own name. Ever get the feeling that you're not liked, not wanted?"

"Sure, it goes with the territory. Look, I'm as sensitive as the next guy, but my business is your business as long as the community is paying the shot. I know that doesn't give me special privileges, and my nose gets slammed in the door often enough for me to wonder if I maybe shouldn't open up a ladies' ready-to-wear like my old man did. But as long as I'm taking people's money as an investigator, I'll have to go on getting my nose slammed. At least it's better than getting shot at in a big city. Here at least you sometimes get asked in for a cup of tea or coffee."

"You're the strangest man."

"I'm just out to make a living."

"But your being here is tantamount to an accusation that my sister was involved in this dirty business with her husband."

"It's happened before."

"Not with Ruthie, it hasn't. I mean, God, just look at her."

"Sure. I'm as susceptible as the next man to appearances. What would you have me do? I can't flash his picture to every airline ticket agent in the country."

"Well, you could try asking the local ones, at least."

"The cops have done all of that, I can't compete with the cops. I'm a one-man band."

"Elastic band and broken. Sorry. I just don't trust people, I guess. I'm not used to strangers."

"Look, in your place, I wouldn't want me around either. What would you do in my position?"

"I know that's not meant as a trick question, Mr Cooperman, but I can't help you. Maybe you should leave it to the police and Interpol."

"Maybe I should. I didn't bid on this case, you know."

"Don't you ever think of the cunning it took to pull off what Larry did? Don't you ever get a sneaking admiration for the criminals you go after?"

"Mrs Geller, I'm just a beat-up divorce peeper. Except for a few odd cases, I've never been on a case where anybody got much of what they were looking for. Most of the time they were so worried about being found out, they didn't have time to enjoy their ill-gotten gains. That's the truth. So, I don't imagine that I'm ever going to become jealous of some poor guy who has to hide under a false name and run around frightened of his own shadow. Now, from what I know about your brother-in-law, he was a smart man. Maybe you imagine him having the horse-laugh on the rest of us. But I doubt it. Every time a phone rings, he shudders. Every time there's a knock on the door, he gets sweaty palms. But, you'll tell me he has all that money. Well, I wonder. How much of it can be flashed in public without getting people suspicious? If it's in securities, the cops will find him; if it's in cash, he has to take a chance every time he crosses a border."

"What about those famous numbered bank accounts in Switzerland?"

"Mrs Geller, your brother-in-law could have spent two million just setting up a deal like that. You're talking big money, political money, exchequer and treasury money. Larry's robbed a bunch of geriatrics in Grantham, Ontario. He's in the Little League. He only hurt a bunch of old-timers. He didn't knock off a bank or run over the premier's dog. A case like this has a lot of local people hot about it, and the cops are going to do their best to find him. I'm going to do my best to find him. But it isn't going to rate a column inch in Vancouver or Montreal. There aren't any votes riding on Larry Geller."

"So what can you do? What can a single private investigator accomplish?"

"Nothing, maybe. Maybe something better than that. Maybe I'll figure some angle that nobody's thought of before."

"Like what?"

"Oh, like, maybe, and I'm just groping for an example you understand, maybe Larry Geller wasn't in this all by himself. Maybe we should be looking for two people. That's at least a different tack from the cops. And it might even pay off."

"I see. Some sort of confederate."

"That was just an example." Ruth interrupted our little talk, drawing Debbie away from me, and I watched the sisters talking across the room.

I could see that Debbie still didn't trust me, and I guess she had good reason not to. I was more dangerous to them in the long run than the mob had been. At the very least I was out to catch up to the father of the two kids I'd just seen shunted off to a safe haven. Any help I could be to my clients wouldn't help the Gellers at all. The best thing for them to do would be to sell up and get out of Grantham as fast as possible. Whenever the law caught

up with Geller there was going to be more publicity and
more newspaper headlines.

"I'm sorry for your trouble," I said without thinking. I
don't know where it came from, it just came. It was probably something I picked up from Frank Bushmill whose
office is across the hall from mine. Frank would have the
tact for a session like this if he were sober, which was
seldom.

Downtown an hour later, I ran into himself at the door
to his consulting room. Frank is a chiropodist on his sign
and a podiatrist in the phone book. Podiatrist is the
metric term, I guess.

"Hello, Benny. You look like you've seen Hamlet's
father. Have a look at your face in the mirror. You'll
swear it's made of Irish linen." He dragged me into the
small toilet at the top of the stairs and made me face my
face in the glass. He was right, I could read the tension
of the last hour in my mouth and eyes, although, with
Frank standing beside me, I couldn't be dead sure the
tension wasn't something he generated. I was never fully
relaxed with Frank around. It was well-known around
town that Frank had an unhealthy appetite for strange
flesh. I always had to be on guard in case it was mine.

"I just came back from a mob scene outside the Geller
place."

"Jayzus! The print's not dry on the paper, and they're
out there like that, eh? Fat lot of hooligans! Hangin's too
good for them. Trying to get them out of the kip, were
they now?" Frank was sounding more Irish than usual.
He must have been reading that Flann O'Brien fellow
again. Frank was always at me to read this or that, and
it seemed that every second book that he waved under
my nose was by this Flann O'Brien. I managed to read
some of the books he lent me, but I couldn't make head
or tail of the O'Brien ones. Frank had taken it into
his head that I needed more education. Maybe for a

chiropodist with a bent appetite I was ignorant, but when I finished at the collegiate I felt I had more education than I could manage. In none of my cases so far had I been able to put $E=mc^2$ to any account. "Come into the office and we'll have a quiet jar together. I've got an hour before my next patient. You can tell me all about it." He led the way to his door then through it into the office smelling of chemicals barely covering the odour of troubled feet. A bottle with his own name on it was produced and in a moment we were both holding and clinking glasses. Frankly, I wanted to talk to somebody about the case. The drink I didn't need. I never do.

"Frank, I feel like I'm in a room without windows or doors. The walls are like polished granite, like on tombstones, and there aren't even inscriptions to get a fingerhold in."

"This Geller business! Families," he muttered. "They close ranks to the world. But I'd like to hear what they're after saying among themselves. I warrant that would bear hearing. I gather they've made themselves into clams whenever you showed up?"

"Sure. And now that the story's public property, it'll be hard to see them on anything but television from now on." I took a sip of drink and Frank poured himself another.

"If you ask me, Benny, that fellow must have had some haunt or other to do his mischief in. The paper said they found nothing in his office. Ergo, he had another office. Some spot where he could leave papers that wouldn't be traced back to him. Maybe he had a girl-friend. He could have left his copybook at her place." Frank began pulling at his necktie to give him better circulation near the thinking parts. "A girl-friend! I like that. She could be the key to the whole business, my lad."

"Geller was a homebody. Regular habits, no playing around."

"There you are. A clever bandit, that's what he is. Never a false step; never a sudden move. Very tricky indeed, is your Mr Larry Geller." There was no stopping him now. He elaborated on his theory for the next five minutes. By the time I'd reached the midway mark of my drink I was getting to like the idea. If Geller could fool all his clients, why not the rest of his kith and kin? It was a point to work on. It was the beginning of a finger-hold in the granite face. If I finished the drink, I'd have figured out the bugger's hiding place, only to find it empty when the sober light of dawn came in my window.

When I left Frank he hardly noticed. He was spinning a fine web of intrigue over the whole case. He remembered a case in Dublin in the 1890s where a doctor was discovered to have been living a bigamous life with two profitable practices. I tried to imagine Geller doing that within the greater Grantham area. Dublin must be a lot bigger, I couldn't see Geller getting away with an act like that for more than forty-five minutes around here. I wondered whether the Dublin doctor took off for the same reasons Geller did. What did I know about Geller anyway? I'd talked to Rabbi Meltzer and Mr Tepperman about him. I'd interviewed his family. But what did I know? Was he the type to have a girl-friend on the side, someone to share the money with down south? I didn't know him that well. I tried to parade the images I could remember of him grinning and shaking hands at a wedding. I could see him slapping Mort Slater's back at his boy's bar mitzvah. I could see him at a head table sitting near the rabbi and the president of the shul waiting for the kiddush to be said and keeping his eyes on the twisted loaf of challah waiting to be sliced. I had to admit it to myself. I was still crawling up slippery sides of smooth granite. The only thing I knew for sure was printed on my driver's licence.

Chapter Seven

Old Man Bolduc, Alex's father, was hoeing in the small backyard on Nelson Street. He was ruddy with short-cropped grey hair. His dark green shirt looked too hot for the day and too big for his frame. The two-inch belt that held up heavy industrial trousers was working on a new hole burned about a foot from the trailing end. The toes of his yellow work-boots peeked out from under his rolled cuffs. The sun shone on the skeleton of a canoe, and through its ribs green shoots were reaching up into the light. Near it, a rusted oil drum was crammed with old lath with chunks of plaster adhering to the wood. The grass in front of the unpainted porch was sparse and defeated, the walk cracked and uneven.

"Mr Bolduc, is Alex home?" The old man didn't look up. I repeated myself and the hoe stopped in mid-air as he turned to give me the once-over. His eyes were a watery blue that looked like they were seeing through wet doughnuts.

"Who wants see Alex?" The hoe was far enough off the ground for me to give him a straight answer. I told him I was an old friend from school. At that he softened, seemed to get even shorter and shrugged in the direction of the pink flamingo on the aluminum screen door. "It's his house. He lets me live here. He's in dere. Go ahead, knock." I did and waited.

I hadn't seen Alex Bolduc since I'd last been to the Grainger Park Lacrosse Box. There he'd been electric. As a hockey fan, I didn't quite approve of this primitive approach to my favourite sport. Screened in, the players ran up and down the box like they were on skates, and the ball whistled through the air and moved from stick to stick with such precision that it must have been guided by remote control from up in the broadcasting booth. But lacrosse doesn't attract the ink that hockey gets. So, it was on ice that Alex became a local hero. The papers watched him for a few seasons and then bounced rumours back and forth about which of the National League teams he was going to. Alex turned whatever he did into something between athletics and ballet.

At school, Alex used to make the announcements for the sports department at the end of the weekly assembly. He spoke in a voice that was down-to-earth, shy and precise all at once. He was one of the people you remembered from school-days. And now I could hear him coming to the door of his bungalow.

He looked sleepy and puffy. His unshaven face looked at me through the screen with suspicion. "Yes? What is it?"

"Alex, I'm Benny Cooperman. I was at the Collegiate with you. I remember you were on the hockey team and played lacrosse for the city." I could feel that my knowing who he was wasn't helping him figure out who I was. He let a suggestion of a smile work away at the left side of his mouth. It gave him pleasure to be reminded about those days.

"Come in," he said, showing me no sign of recognition, but holding the door open so that I could get into the house under his arm. The front room was furnished in a matching wine living-room suite. The rug was a round hooked one and it covered linoleum that imitated the lines of a hardwood floor. The TV set was running. "Make yourself comfortable." I found the couch. The

ancient springs let me slide down through the pillow so
that I was sitting scarcely two inches off the floor. With
my back to the light I could see Alex better. "I remember
you," he said, pulling out a package of cigarettes and
waving them in my direction. I leaned over and took
one, lighted it and his, then settled back into the wine-
dark couch again. "You used to be in plays. Right? You
went on and became a doctor, right?"

"That's Sam, my brother. But I was in plays too. We
both were. Did you see *The Merchant of Venice*?"

"Sure. You were Shylock."

"No, that was Sam. I was Old Gobbo."

"Who? I don't..."

"It's the character part. Some funny lines. An old
clown."

"That's right, you grabbed the hair on the back of
your son's head and said what a beard he's grown."

"I was supposed to be blind. That's right. You remember."

Alex had relaxed completely, and soon we were doing
"Whatever happened to" games, taking turns and finding out that Mary Taaffe had married Bill Inkle and Fred
Cameron was practically running the Canadian Armed
Forces in Ottawa. Finally, I purposely let myself run out
of gas so that I could get on with the business of my
visit. I told him what I'd been doing since I graduated
and that led through my professional snooping to the
present snoop.

"So you want to know about the Gellers from me?"

"Could I come to a better source? Your family has been
tangled up with the Gellers since we were kids, and from
what I hear, your side hasn't won all of the marbles."

"I got to think about that." He got up and looked out
the window for a minute. I tried to imagine his father
out in the back hoeing. "My old man's been through the
meat-grinder, Benny. I just got him back from Wood-
green two weeks ago. Dr Hodgins said that his system

can't take much more abuse. He's always been a terrible drinker ever since I was a kid. It probably killed my mother. When he came to Grantham from Noranda he couldn't speak a word of English, but he could carry a mule on his back without even breathing hard. He was an unskilled construction worker when he met Sid Geller. The two of them started a business that's got millions of dollars worth of contracts today. You can't drive a mile in any direction in this town without running into a sign reading "Bolduc." I'd be lying if I said I wasn't envious of Sid Geller. It may be my old man's name up there, but the money's Geller's. Papa doesn't own one cent on paper. Sure, he gets handouts. He'll never starve. There'll always be a place for him as long as there's a shack in the Bolduc yard. He helps out. He draws a wage when he's working. He knows that yard like I know the Ingram Papermill where I work. I know how he feels because I was dangled on waivers for three years by the Buffalo team. They said it was all settled, but I never even got to dress for Buffalo or any other big league team.

"Papa's a mess today. But I guess he made most of it himself. Geller was the business head of the outfit, and the old man only ran the yard. After he hit the bottle, he didn't even run that for more than a few days at a time. You couldn't depend on him."

"Did Geller get any help from anyone beside your father?"

"Sure. His family had some money. I know that. More than we had anyway. Geller never lived with a Quebec heater in a tar-paper shack."

"Apart from that?"

"He got backing from Glenn Bagot. You know, he was in cement. Used to make concrete pipe down in one of the locks of the old canal. Bagot had a lot of good connections at Queen's Park in Toronto. They used to say that everything he touched turned to gold."

"Glenn Bagot? The name sounds familiar."

"Sure it does. Bagot Street off Welland. The Bagot Block on St Andrew Street. They're old Grantham; go back to the first settlers in the peninsula. United Empire Loyalists. That sort of thing. Glenn got into highway construction, helped put the new highway through to Fort Erie."

"When you say he's well connected at Queen's Park, you mean he has a fix in with the provincial government?"

"There are a few people in this province that the government doesn't burp without consulting. Bagot's one of them. Call him a bagman, call him an influential lobbyist. He has friends in all the right high places."

"And he took an interest in Geller when he was just getting started?"

"And he's stayed interested. Even after Bagot's wife left him and started going around with Sid."

"Is that Pia Morley? Drives an Audi?"

"Morley's her first husband's name. When I knew her she was Pia Antonioni. I always called her Toni."

"But you'd think that trading wives would have soured the business arrangements, wouldn't you?"

"Some people have more respect for business than I have. I do my shift at the mill and I'm glad to get back here. My wife's a nurse over at the General. We mind our business."

"You seem to know a lot about Glenn Bagot and his connections."

"It's the old game of 'There, but for the grace of God...'"

"Tell me more about Pia Morley. Did she come between Geller and his first wife?"

"Hell, no. That was over years ago. No, Sid was a sitting duck when Pia came along. And she brought connections of her own."

"Relatives to be supported?"

"Not on your life. Pia has no relatives as far as I know. She's as close to a self-made woman as I've ever met. No. Her connections are with the leading edges of organized crime. She has friends who try to put their money into legitimate businesses."

"There's a lot of that going round."

"Because it works. Pia counts among her pals Tony Pritchett and his English mob."

"Anthony Horne Pritchett. Our paths have crossed before."

"Then you know he's nobody to fool around with."

"What do you know about Sid's brother, the lawyer?"

"I thought you'd get around to him. I don't know him at all. I admire him, though. Taking those people for a ride like that. Incredible. Over two million. And tax free, Benny, tax free."

We both thought about all of that free money and how it would look on us for a few minutes. I tried to imagine a life away from the City House, with a bedspread without cigarette burns in it and the sound of the rock 'n' roll band downstairs on Friday and Saturday nights. Alex looked at his watch, one of those big things that tells you the time in six different directions. I pulled myself out of the wine velvet couch and found my legs had turned to synthetic rubber. Alex walked me to the door and held it open for me. The old man had worked his way around to the front. Together we watched him pulling off the dry dead blooms from a bed of petunias. Alex shook my hand and I'd started to turn away when a last question slipped into place.

"By the way, Alex, you said that Pia Morley was as close to a self-made woman as you'd ever met. When would that have been?"

"That I met her? Oh, Benny, that's sludge under the trestle. We used to go together when I was playing for the Grantham Ospreys. You could say we used to be room-mates."

Chapter Eight

"What is it Kogan? For crying out loud, don't just stand there hanging in the doorway. Come in and sit down." Kogan didn't move. Kogan didn't look like he enjoyed being up on the second floor, twenty-eight steps from the solid comfort of the street. He was still wearing his grey flannels and blazer with his army discharge pin in the lapel. He looked at my door, trying to read something in my sign that would make it easier. "Come in, Kogan. Nobody's going to bite you."

"Look, Mr Cooperman, I don't want to break into anything. I just thought..." All this from the doorway, like he could smell something unpleasant under my desk, when in fact it was Kogan who smelled like a three-day-old tuna sandwich in August.

"If you're coming in, let's get on with it. If you're not coming in shut the door gently and see you around." Kogan thought a moment, looked at a space about a foot above my head, then closed the door behind him. I got up, rushed around my desk and caught him halfway down the stairs. "Kogan, I'm sorry. I didn't mean to snap at you. I just got carried away by the impulse to share some of the frustration I've been collecting. What's up? You broke?"

"It ain't that, Mr Cooperman. Hell, I'm always broke. Shit, you know that. That's no secret." He wedged his way around so that he faced me. The light behind him

70

coming up from St Andrew Street blanked out his large, leathery face. I leaned against the stair railing, then slid into a hunkering position as we talked.

"I know that. You've had bad luck for a long time now."

"You ain't just whistlin' Dixie. That's a fact. I've been down since we got out of the army. Must be twenty years."

"More like forty. The war was over in forty-five. What can I do for you?" Kogan pulled at the non-existent creases in his trousers and sat down on the steps looking up at me. The light gave his messy hair a halo that needed reblocking. It also picked out highlights on the brass stripping at the top of each step, and the marks on the wall where heavy objects had squeaked by.

"You know Wally? Wally Moore? Me and him's been buddies since we won the war together over in France. I met him first in the lock-up out Niagara Street one winter. You've seen him around. A little guy, with a wide gait and a bamboo cane like Charlie Chaplin?"

"Oh, sure. I've seen him around for years. What's he got up to?"

"Old Wally's been a good friend of mine for a lot of years. We used to do a lot of drinking together."

"I'll bet. What's he got into?"

"Wally—I call him Wally: his right name's Bamfylde. How j'ah like that? Bamfylde! Hot shit. Isn't that sumpin'?"

"What are you worried about, Kogan? You came here to tell me something, didn't you?" The answer to that question had to wait for one of Dr Bushmill's patients to pass us on her way down the stairs. I watched her go, bouncing down each step a little light on her left foot. Corns. Maybe.

"Estelle Kramer," Kogan announced when the air-brake settled the door back in place.

"What?"

"That was Estelle Kramer. You know Otto Kramer's wife? Butcher on James Street?"

"What's she got to do with this?"

"Not a thing. Just practising. In my position you have to know people. Can't depend on looks alone. Otto's given Wally and me a Christmas bird more than once. Stringy, you know, but tasty."

"Kogan. Go to hell! You're never going to come to the point and I'm going back to my office where I can get rid of the cramp in my shin." I got up and went limping back behind my desk. I didn't slam the door, but I felt like it. In a minute he was standing like Samson between the pillars in my doorway again.

"Wally's got a lot more class than you think, Mr Cooperman."

"What makes you think I've thought about it?" I was doodling the names of the people I'd been talking to up at the Gellers' place on a block of yellow legal-sized foolscap. I could still see Kogan holding up the door-frame.

"He could be in a lot of trouble. And you don't even give a damn."

"Sure I give a damn. But his pal won't tell me what it's all about. He's waiting for me to read all about it in my Christmas stocking or something. His old buddy won't give me any hints. He wants me to work it out like Sherlock Holmes from the nicks on your Adam's apple."

"Okay, I understand. I just had to be sure I came to the right place. I gotta be careful like. Wally's the only buddy I ever had. The best pal I could want. Now he's nowhere."

"How do you mean, 'nowhere'?"

"We had a shack behind Maple Street. Wally used to have a popcorn wagon back there, but the kids smashed it all to smithereens. But we had a decent kip: blankets and a sleeping-bag. It beat sleeping in doorways. Even sleeping here in the hall along by the bathroom. You should get that toilet fixed. It runs all night."

"I'll mention it to the landlord. He'll appreciate that."

"Don't mention it. I mean, sure, tell him. By 'don't mention it' I meant 'you're welcome.'"

"Kogan, do you think you can stay on the subject of your pal for a minute without a side-trip? Try it. We are talking about your pal Wally Bamfylde Moore. Get on with it."

"Well, it's just he ain't been around for a couple o' days. He's gone. Like that Geller guy on Queen Street. Only Wally didn't have more than maybe twenty-five dollars tops."

"Maybe he's found another kip? Maybe he's found a nice park bench to sleep on during these warm nights. He'll turn up."

"Cooperman, you're a shit-heel. You know what that is? You're a real poop-and-scoop artist, that's what you are. I told you Wally and me've been together. You know what that means? I know Wally, and I know what he's going to do from Monday to Sunday. He's a shrewd character, but habit-ridden. You know what I mean? He sometimes sleeps near his pitch, but he tells me first."

"I'm sorry, Kogan. I didn't mean to be flip. I apologize." Kogan made a pass at his nose with his fingers, squeezed the bridge of his nose like a bank president, then blinked trying to pick up the thread of the story again. "Kogan, what's your first name? I can't keep calling you Kogan."

"Give me a minute," he said, squinting hard. "Victor."

"The hell it is."

"I seen it in print that way. Anyway, I been Kogan too long to argue. Just don't call me Victor, you hear?"

"Where did you see Wally last?"

"We tucked into some 9-Lives on Tuesday night."

"Did he say anything about going off? Did you have a fight?"

"Certainly not. And I checked the hospitals and the lock-up. Wally didn't get hit by a milk truck, and he didn't get pinched."

"Did he say anything about where he was going or what he intended to do the next day?"

"Well, you finally got down to it. You finally asked. I thought I'd be a fine old bone before you asked that one." Kogan's old wallet of a face creased into a map of smiles. "He told me he was going to see the wife of a Queen Street lawyer."

"He what?"

"I knew that'd get you. He told me he was going to see this woman over on Mortgage Hill. I forgot the name until I saw it in tonight's paper."

"Tell me this again slowly."

"I don't usually chew my cabbage twice. He said he wanted to see this Mrs Geller. Said they had business." Kogan now had all my attention and he knew it. He played the scene like an actor building up the momentum leading to the curtain line. "He said we were havin' our last can of cat food. And that's when he showed me the bottle he'd bought. It wasn't his favourite, Old Sailor, it was Gordon's gin. Where'd he get that kind of money? That's what got me scared, Mr Cooperman. Where's Wally and is he all right?"

I took Wally's pal Kogan with me around the corner to the United for a coffee and a square meal. He had the coffee. I had the square meal. I nearly had to bust his arm to get him to accept coffee. He sat on the edge of the stool like he was afraid of breaking it and pretended not to notice the dirty looks I was getting from the waitress who had "Nicole" stitched on her breast. It wasn't Nicole. Nicole had left the United a year ago. "Nicole" went with the uniform the way a glass of water went with the menu. For the next twenty minutes I pumped Kogan about his friend: where he did his panhandling, what his habits were, and in that time I picked up about two

minutes of valuable information. Wally's favourite
stamping ground was right in front of the Loftus Building at the Queenston Road end of St Andrew Street,
across from the closed-off block where the new fire hall
was being built. To me it didn't look like the best pick-
ings in town, but Kogan put me wise to the stream of
workers coming to and from the building site as well as
the shifts going to and from Etherington's Empire Carpet Works. Together we went around to the liquor store
where it didn't take long to locate the guy who'd sold
Wally his bottle of gin. The fellow remembered him because Wally'd given him a fifty-dollar bill to change,
flicked ashes on his change machine, and asked for a
receipt. And all because he'd been on the Liquor Control
Board list of those whose money was no good for about
twenty years. Then the rules changed.

Kogan had given me the only break I'd had in this
case. His pal had been paid by Ruth Geller for something. What was it and did it have anything to do with
the fact that he was nowhere to be seen? My stomach
told me that there was a strong possibility that his disappearance had directly followed from something that
Wally had seen and reported to Ruth. I'd have to question her about that. In the meantime I was happy to be
helping the little guy. It made me feel like I was a real
taxpayer instead of someone who only had aspirations
to be one. Before we separated, I got Kogan to promise
to keep his eyes open and to be sure to drop in to see me
as soon as he heard from Wally.

When I got back to the office, I found the door standing open. I didn't remember leaving it that way. I was in
the midst of giving myself a sermon on forgetfulness
when I saw that the office had a visitor.

"Mr Cooperman? I suppose you're Mr Cooperman.
It's silly even to ask, isn't it?" The speaker was a woman
in her thirties, about five feet six and not at all hard
to look at with her large eyes and pouting mouth. I

recognized the brunette hair from the time I'd seen it drive into the Bolduc yard in her silver Audi.

"Well, Mrs Morley! This is a surprise. Do you always let yourself in? If I'd known you were coming I would have left the door off the latch."

"Please don't be boring about the door, Mr C. Those old spring locks wouldn't keep the cat out. You didn't actually want me to stand waiting in the hall, did you? With the Water Music from your bathroom? Besides, this old credit card's expired." She held up a mangled plastic card and dropped it with a dramatic gesture into the waste-paper basket. I walked around her, feeling that if I could recapture my desk, I could get the interview on a firm footing according to all the rules on the subject. I already had a feeling that Pia Morley didn't necessarily bend where the rules said "fold." Once I'd claimed my chair, I waved her to one of the others on the client's side of the desk. She took it, composing her skirt under her as she sat. I offered her a cigarette and instead of taking out her own, she took one of mine. She wasn't given to showing her independence in small ways. I leaned across towards her with a lighted match. She steadied my hand and bent to the flame. She was wearing a pink blouse, cut like a man's shirt, that almost failed to contain her. A dim outline of lace appeared through the broadcloth and gave an electric jab to my innards. She wore her hair tied up at the back of her head, but there was enough left over to frame her face provocatively. Her eyes had been made up lightly and her lips parted in a smile that showed straight white teeth. There was no missing the long curve of her neck or the diamond studs in her earlobes.

"To what do I owe the honour?" I asked. She crossed her legs grandly without bothering to check the horizon of her hemline.

"I'm trying to make up my mind whether or not I'm going to like you," she said, missing my ashtray by inches and not worrying about it. "You've been lifting up a lot of stones in the last two days, Mr C."

"Let me remind you now that it was you who spoke of lifting up stones first. Sure I have. I'm working on a case. That's no secret. I'm trying to find Larry Geller and see if I can get him to give back the money he's taken."

"You know the police are doing the same thing?"

"Sure. We're all in this together. Only they have more patience than I have. They can afford to wait until Geller makes his move and then grab him. By 'grab him' they mean get extradition proceedings underway. When I hope to grab somebody, it's a little more physical than that."

"You don't look like a muscle man. You surprise me, Mr C. I can't actually imagine you manhandling people. You don't seem the type."

"Well, between the two of us, I haven't had to man-handle too many lately. I may be out of practice. But I do what I have to do. Mostly talk to people. Sometimes it works."

"You talked to Sid and Nathan."

"No law against that, Mrs Morley. I'm entitled."

"You've been asking questions about me. Me and Sid." I nodded my admission, and she cocked her head to one side and flashed her eyelashes at me. "I don't like to have questions asked behind my back, Mr C. I don't like it. I don't know anything about Larry Geller you can't read on the front page of tonight's *Beacon*. So, I want out, please. I said 'please,' remember. I always start by saying 'please.' "

"And when that doesn't work?"

"But it's going to work, Mr C. Because you're one smart detective, aren't you?"

"Never top of my class."

"But you've learned so much since then."

"And it's built all this." She looked at the hanging fluor-escent fixtures and then at the light coming dustily through the Venetian blinds. She inclined her head as though acknowledging a point. I shrugged it off. A tendril of brown hair fell over her forehead and I wondered how she'd managed that. She leaned over my bleached oak desk trying to look tougher than she could in a pink button-down shirt with lace showing through.

"Mr C. I'm asking you to lay off Sid and me. Sid's already told you everything he knows. Everything he's willing to tell, anyway. He's not going to rat on his brother. You've got sense. Would you spill your guts to me about *your* brother?" I thought of my brother Sam. I could see him in his operating-room greens worrying about a parking ticket.

"You've made your point, Mrs Morley. And you know I'm not lifting stones because I like lifting stones. It's all part of a job I'm being paid to do. With me around it means the stage isn't cluttered up with the aggrieved and the hard done by. I've got the blessing of the whole community. I'm sanctioned." She looked at me evenly while taking a pull at the cigarette. She slowly let the smoke out.

"Supposing, just supposing there's more in it for you to let sleeping stones lie? What then?" I stroked my chin where the beard was beginning to show through at the end of the day. I pushed my swivel chair back from the desk and rocked on the point of equilibrium and thought. She watched me like she had put a bunch of chips down on twenty-two black and the wheel was still going around. And I watched the way the lace came into focus under the broadcloth every time she breathed in.

"Mrs Morley..."

"Don't call me that. Call me Pia. My friends call me Pia."

"Look, you're not making me an offer to look the other way because of the tricks your boy-friend's brother has been playing. You have reasons of your own."

She tried not to let on I'd hit a nerve. That was one way of looking at it. The other way was to admit that I may have been miles from the truth. She extinguished her cigarette butt in the ashtray. Her nails were pink, like her shirt. "You have a wild imagination, Mr C. I can't think where you get your notions from. I want you to be my friend, Mr C. Nobody tells me anything. Whenever I ask Sid, he just grins or chews on his cigar. He never tells me anything. Except that he loves me, I mean. I can get him to tell me that, because I'm so back and forth with him about *us* that it's a joke. He doesn't think it's funny, but what can I do about it? That's the way I am. That's the way I've always been." She reached on the floor for the taupe bag she'd brought in with her and began to make signs of leaving. I got up, and started coming round the desk.

"You must pick my lock again sometime." She ignored that, and pushed herself out of the chair.

"Now, I've stayed too long. I don't want to get a ticket."

"I'll bet you have friends who would take care of a little thing like that."

"Yes, I have friends, Mr C. I hope that you'll be a friend. At a time like this friends are very comforting, don't you think?" She gave me the full force of her pouting smile, held it for a second longer than it took to make its point. She said goodbye and left me standing in the middle of my office wondering where she'd gone. She had that sort of presence that I find confusing. I walked over to the door and shut it, then came slowly back to my desk. Pia Morley had left a lingering fragrance behind her. I hadn't noticed it when she was two feet away from me. Nice, I thought, very nice.

Chapter Nine

I was asleep, having one of those amorphous dreams where it isn't unusual to find Napoleon and Marilyn Monroe on the same football field marking exam papers or folding laundry. At first I thought it was the alarm clock, perched on the usual pile of paperbacks beside the bed, but the dial told me it was only two in the morning. It had to be the phone, and it rang again to prove my point.

"Yes?"

"Cooperman? It's Nathan. Nathan Geller."

"I know which Nathan. What can I do for you at two in the morning?"

"Is it that late? I've been working. I lose track. Anyway, what I'm calling about is this: I've heard from Larry."

"Why are you telling me? I'm practically a perfect stranger."

"Okay, maybe it seems like I'm telling tales out of school, but I don't want Larry to get into more trouble than he's already bought. I don't know what you think of my brother, Cooperman, but he's my brother. My guess is that if he gives back the money he's taken, maybe things won't be so bad for him up here. I mean, a life of hiding is unthinkable."

"Uh-huh. So you decided to tell me about it?"

"I told you everything I know. All I'm saying is I had this call and I thought you should know that he's in Daytona Beach, Florida. Or at least that's where the call came from."

"What did he say?"

"He said he was sorry for what he's putting us through."

"All heart, isn't he?"

"Look, I called you because I thought you'd understand. I don't need any additional insults from the public these days. I've had my fill."

"Okay, okay. What else did he say?"

"He said he won't be coming back to face the music. Not yet anyway."

"What do you want me to do with this information? The phone number of Niagara Regional isn't unlisted." I pulled out a cigarette from the pack on the chair and lit it while waiting for Nathan Geller to find an answer. My mouth felt sticky and my teeth mossy. The room was illuminated by the street light across the street, which flashed an elongated version of my window across the far wall and onto the door.

"I thought you might go down there, try to talk some sense into him."

"I see. Are you going to foot the bill, or do you expect my clients to pay my way?"

"You know I haven't got any money. I'm no millionaire."

"I never knew anybody who ever thought he was. Everybody's just getting by. But you think I should go, eh?"

"It might cut this whole thing short."

"Where do you propose I start looking? I'll bet he didn't give you his address and postal code."

"Well, you're supposed to be a detective, aren't you? It can't be that big a place. You'll find him."

"I guess I can get the phone company down there to tell me about long distance calls to Grantham tonight."

"Can you do that? I didn't know it was so easy. Great!" He made "Great" sound like "What, cabbage again?"

I got off the phone, waited a minute, then called him back. As I guessed, he was on the phone to someone else. I knew the line would be busy. I finished the cigarette in the dark, then pulled the covers over me and tried to get back to sleep. I worked at it for about ten minutes, but it wouldn't take. I turned the bed light on and read the first chapter of a Ruth Rendell mystery I'd been saving.

At a quarter after eleven I was in the United Cigar Store practising my coffee-drinking on a second cup, when Pete Staziak slid onto the pedestal stool next to me.

"Good-morning." I returned the greeting and tried to find evidence of Pete's state of mind in his face. He looked like he hadn't been up all night. He hadn't cut himself shaving, and his breakfast wasn't drying on his tie. I asked him what was on his mind. I always did that when the Holmesian stuff didn't pay off.

"You know who's on my mind: Larry Geller. Not only do we have a fraud situation in this town the like of which hasn't been seen since William Drummond Beal sold City Hall on a domed sports stadium..."

"The less said about that the better."

"...but we are also trying to keep a rising tide of public indignation from slopping over the weir. You saw what happened outside the Geller place yesterday."

"Can't you get them to leave town until things blow over?"

"What we've got over on Burgoyne Boulevard," Pete said, "is either a very gutsy dame or a boneheaded bitch. Frankly I can't tell which."

"They're within their rights to stay."

"That's right, and I'm within my rights when I balk at having three men permanently detailed to that place. That's three men that could be used in better ways."

"Hell, I can rattle my own doorknob," I said. Pete gave me a look. "Just trying to help out." I took a fresh breath. "Pete, for God's sake remember: nothing lasts. That includes public indignation. The hardest expression to sustain is one of prolonged outrage. So take it easy."

"You must have read that somewhere."

"Sure I did. Look, Pete, I got a call last night from Nathan Geller telling me he had a call from his missing brother." Pete's eyes took on a glint which wasn't all reflection from the overhead lights.

"Where was he supposed to be calling from?"

"Daytona Beach."

"Yeah, a lot of them do end up down there. And there's a certain tension between their police forces and ours. Frankly they're a bit galled by the fact that our bandits are starting colonies down among their sheltering palms. You can't blame them."

"But you don't think that Geller's there?"

"Come on, Benny. You don't either. Since when does the family offer tips like that? It's like going to the chief of police to announce you didn't rob a bank. There's something wrong with the way it bounces."

"But you'll check it out." Pete looked at me like I was having trouble seeing red STOP signs.

"Sure I'll check it out. We follow up all leads no matter how seemingly idiotic. There's no guessing the simplicity of some of the bandits I've put away. They think that if nobody saw them pinch the money or forge the paper that they've escaped detection forever. Even some of these computer operators. They're supposed to be brainy types, aren't they? Well, some of them behave like we're still dazzled by anything that lights up, flickers and moves."

"Now you're going to hark back to the good old days when a pinch was a pinch and the noose and the lash kept us all safe as houses."

"You paying for this or me?"

"You get it, since you're asking, and I've been doing the telling."

"Now, Benny, don't start imagining yourself a source. A case like this doesn't need information, it needs time like a boil. It'll come to a head in its own sweet time. If you try to rush it you'll only get into trouble. I know trouble's your dinner and supper, but tell that to your clients, not me." Pete got up. On second thought he hadn't done such a super job with his razor, and he had toast crumbs at the corner of his lips. But I wasn't going to tell him about it. A thing like that needs time, like a boil.

When we hit the pavement he turned east on St Andrew, leaving me free to return to my place of business as he sometimes described the place I keep my full ashtrays in. But he stalled. "You were seen talking to one of the street operators yesterday."

"Is this a warning for me to clean up my act?"

"Just tell your pal Kogan to watch himself. We've got a friend of his at the morgue."

"A friend of Kogan's? Not Wally Moore?"

"He didn't have any ID, but I haven't been in plain clothes long enough to forget the dynamic duo. They used to present themselves at the door of the lock-up as soon as the thermometer dropped below zero, and if we had a drunk that cut up rough after midnight, don't think we didn't hear about it in the morning. They did everything but sing out for croissants and *cappuccino*. Those two, the pair of them, ran on more nerve than..."

"And you've got Kogan's buddy cold?"

"Looks that way. Found around midnight in Montecello Park. From the preliminary report it looks like he was stabbed. So tell his buddy to watch himself."

"Who'd want to hurt Wally Moore, a little helpless slob like that?"

"That's a fair paraphrase of what Priscilla Gesell said when I told her that somebody'd buried a hatchet in her husband's skull."

"Yeah, I know. She put it there. But Wally? His middle name was harmless. I'm not surprised that he's dead. Hell, he could have frozen to death for the last umpteen winters, or he could have given himself an overdose of battery acid or eaten a can of month-old cat food."

"Calm down. I was just telling you he's dead, that's all. Don't get your balls in an uproar." I saw Mr McCartle walking back to his store with his lunch in a brown paper bag. He looked older than I remembered him. "Hey, Benny! You've gone white. What's the matter?" Pete had me hard by one elbow and I was flat against the display window of Dunn's Tailors.

"I'm okay. I was just talking to Kogan about his pal. He wanted me to try to find him. I wish you hadn't told me. Why should I know about all the dead panhandlers of St Andrew Street? Give me a break, Pete."

"You want to sit down or something? Christ, Benny, I didn't think you even knew the guy."

"Well, he's been part of the scenery for so many years. Like old Joe Higgins on his crutches."

"Yeah, and the balloons..." Pete said, smiling as he remembered.

"And the balsa birds. Remember the red-headed hunchback on the bicycle?"

"Yeah. Worked as a delivery boy. I don't know what happened to him."

"And the Mad Scribbler."

"He hasn't been around for a while."

"What are you talking about? He eats in the United at least three times a week."

"Still at his great work?"

"Sure," I said, "he must have covered a ton of paper by this time. And you know how he writes: on the lines, between the lines, across, down the page, diagonally, and always in a great frenzy."

"He once ripped off Grahams. Took a pad of paper. But the old man wouldn't make a fuss about it. I only heard about it because I was buying a briefcase." Pete was looking me up and down, probably wondering if I was going to be all right. "A present to myself when I climbed out of uniform."

"There sure are a lot of them."

"Yeah. Mild crazies like old Joe, the Mad Scribbler and Apple Mary. And where would we be without them? You feeling better?"

"Sure. I guess I felt the dark angel passing by." Pete grinned and then looked down, stooped and handed me a black feather. He walked off without saying another word.

I sat in my office for half an hour after that, waiting for something bad to happen. But nothing did. Not then it didn't. I cleaned the receipts from my wallet. I do that every so often. Having a thick wallet is bad for my character, even when it isn't thick with anything more interesting than lunch and taxi receipts. I played at this for a while, hoping that an idea might drop out along with loose change. I could have used an idea.

I knew I couldn't keep fiddling with this thing. There comes a time with a case when you either have to throw it out the window or start moving on it. I'd been all over town, talked to people until I was bored by the sight of them. Larry Geller was off getting a suntan. I could get excited about that. But I didn't believe for a minute that his own brother would try to put me on his trail. Daytona Beach is a big place, not as easy to lose yourself in as Miami, but the possibilities of finding yourself later on are better. What was Nathan playing at? Did he know that his brother was up in Haliburton running a freshwater marina on Eagle Lake, or that he'd enrolled at Carleton University in Ottawa to get a whole new career for himself. Balls! I wasn't any better off than I was on Wednesday when the rabbi and Mr Tepperman came to see me. Whenever I hear myself say "Leave it with me, let me nose around for a few days to see what I can find," I should have myself committed.

Well, I have nosed around. I've talked to people at every corner in the thing and it didn't lead me home. Time I confessed to the rabbi. I gave it my best shot. Now the time has come to bow out gracefully. In the Toronto paper, there was a story about a guy who'd done exactly what Larry Geller'd done. There was an epidemic. Somewhere down south they must be having a convention and comparing statistics about which of them took the oldest widow to the cleaners for the most money. They might steal a plaque and award it annually.

I lit a cigarette and tried to think why Geller made me so mad. I thought about what Pete Staziak said about computer hotshots who try to fleece the population without figuring that all the cops have to do to identify them is locate the terminal or examine the bank accounts. I looked up the rabbi's number and dialled it. Time to get absolution from this thing. Time to get off the hook. The line was busy. It figured. I found where I'd scribbled Rose Craig's home number. I tried that, hoping to change my luck.

"Hello?" It was a wary voice, but it was hers.

"Cooperman. You didn't go back to the office?"

"I told you that if I didn't get paid, that was the end."

"Yeah, I know you said it, but I didn't believe you. I had you pegged for one of those people who will never desert the ship."

"I know. That's me all right. But I have rent to pay. I hate myself, but Mr Cooperman, I don't think he's going to come back now. Even I believe it."

"Good. It's a start. Tell me, Rose, Larry wasn't in partnership with anybody, was he?"

"Certainly not. He was known all over town as a lone wolf."

"But he used to be in business with other lawyers, in his early days I mean?"

"You're going back farther than I do. He was in partnership with Irving Bernstein. But that must be at least ten years ago. The partnership was dissolved."

"Into what?"

"What?"

"What happened to the pieces?"

"How should I know? Ask me about something that happened a month ago and I only know about part of that. Mr Cooperman, the more I think about Mr Geller and what he did..."

"I know, Rose. You think you know a guy and then..."

"Yeah, that's right. Another thing is you realize that there's a false wall in his life somewhere."

"I like that. Yeah, he had a false wall all right. And what I'm trying to do is tap all the panels until one begins to sound different. Like in the movies. Have you heard anything in your tapping around?"

"Oh, Mr Cooperman, he'd never leave anything in the office that could give him away. That would be like having the false wall behind a bookcase. You know, the first place the movie detective would look."

"Where does this Irving Bernstein hang out these days?"

"He's the senior partner in Bernstein, Carley, Grella and See."

"See? See what?"

"That's her name, Joyce See. Smart girl. She's in charge of their properties, conveyancing and things like that."

"Is she Chinese?"

"That's right."

"Then I've seen her down at the registry office when I've been doing some title-searching for my cousin. I sometimes try to turn an honest dollar. Thanks for your help, Rose. Speaking of my cousin, why don't you call Melvyn Cooperman and tell him all about yourself."

"Do you think that maybe..."

"Just call him. I'm not a crystal-ball gazer. Goodbye."

I left word at Bernstein, Carley, Grella and See that I wanted a word with both Mr Bernstein and Ms See. The rabbi's line was still busy when I tried it, but waiting for the two lawyers to call me back didn't make me feel as idle as I had been feeling. When I hung up I was almost glad. But it didn't last long enough to spoil my day. Irving Bernstein was on the line, his secretary announced. Once she was certain I had no plans to leave town, she put Irving on.

"Melvyn, I hope you aren't going to break our racketball date. With me, Mel, three times and out..." I let him rattle on, mistaking me for my cousin. I didn't interrupt until I thought I had the hook of embarrassment in as far as it would go.

"Oh, *Benny* Cooperman. Of course. Yes, I'm sure I've seen you around. What can I do for you?" I told him that I was looking into the Geller business for the Jewish community and that I had interviewed Larry's family and was now starting on his old friends. "Yes, Larry Geller. That was a damn shame. Not only does it look terrible for the community, it gives every lawyer in town a black eye."

"You used to be partners?"

"That's right, we were, just after we came back to Grantham from Toronto. We did law in Toronto. I'd stayed on and worked as a junior in a big Toronto firm, and he'd just stuck around the law library for most of a year."

"What was he doing?"

"He told me, let me see, what was it? Oh, yes, he was working on a paper about pleading. Very technical, or so I understood. I never read it. I don't even know if he ever finished it."

"Was it part of some course work he was doing?"

"Not after graduation. He was just a bit backward about getting his feet wet, I think. Or, to give him credit, he was very serious in those days. When we set up together, I leaned on Larry a lot. He knew a lot of law."

"So he was bright and serious. Doesn't sound like the Larry I knew: Larry the glad-hander, Larry with the three funny stories?"

"That came along later. I guess practical law got him down. Not enough intellectual challenge. When you've winnowed away the theoretical law that you study from the law as she is practised in a small town, there's not much to write academic papers about."

"Why did the partnership break up?"

"That's no secret. You've talked to Sergeant Pete Staziak, haven't you?"

"Sure, we just had breakfast."

"Well, Larry and I worked well together for a few years. We both made our mistakes and cried about them in each other's offices. We were a young firm in a town full of established WASP firms. It was hard getting a foot in the door in those days, but we did get a start. The good old community threw us some business, couldn't see home-town boys starve. And then we started getting a mixed range of business, not just from our Jewish relations and friends. I think that's where the split came. I tended to play the field, ethnically speaking, and Larry tended to stay with the known and the true. His business got to be at least ninety percent Jewish. Mine was never more than, say, fifty-fifty."

"Is that what did it?"

"Not exactly. We just started thinking differently, wanting different things. He changed a lot too from the pal from law school." He thought about that one for a minute. I could hear the hum of the thought on the silent phone line. "When we split up, Larry wanted to make a lot of money. That's what he wanted more than anything else. Now, don't tell my wife, but I'm not in law primarily for the money, after all the jokes of course, and after I freely confess that I like being comfortable and being able to afford to belong to the club where I regularly beat the bejesus out of your cousin at racket- ball, after all of that shit, I have to tell you that I'm in law because of law. I'm hooked on it. I'm no intellectual the way Larry was when we graduated, but I'm learning. It's getting to be my second skin. I enjoy trying to trans- late it to bewildered people who don't know a writ from a tort. Law can be brutal, especially to people who didn't grow up under English law. It's complicated and it's a lot more than just complicated. Hell, I could do twenty min- utes on the law in a night-club. You should catch my act up at Secord, where we're just starting a law program." Another pause. "What else do you want to know, Mr Cooperman?"

"The partnership was dissolved?"

"That's right. Ashes to ashes, dust to dust."

"What happened to the ashes and dust?"

"We split it up the middle, according to our accounts. It was a fair enough split. I kept the building and the office, so he got a little more cash."

"I see."

"Your cousin should take a few lessons, Mr Cooper- man. He'll never be good, but it will give me a better game. Is there anything else?"

"Not on the order paper, Mr Bernstein. But I'd ap- preciate being able to call you back when and if I get stuck."

"Any time. Any time. The least I can do."

I filed what Bernstein had told me along with all the other stuff and sat there liking Geller a fraction of a scru- ple more. He wasn't a cardboard figure any more. I could begin to see some weight and shading. I thought of call- ing his wife again, but I thought better and didn't. Ruth might be keeping something back. Hell, she was. She'd seen Wally Moore. But I didn't want to strip all the masks away at once. I thought of the murder case that Pete was talking about. Ruth Geller said she'd told me the truth, the whole truth and nothing but the truth and it still didn't amount to anything. I wondered how Priscilla Gesell felt when she discovered she didn't have any little white lies left to tell.

Chapter Ten

J oyce See was shorter than I was, which made me like her right off the bat. She was wearing a short-sleeved summer dress with small flowers on it. Her black hair gleamed and so did something in her bright brown eyes. We were walking under shade trees on King Street from the registry office. She swung her attaché case as she walked, making it seem all the more out of place with that dress which should have been completed by a picnic hamper or a wide-brimmed straw hat with a fat ribbon on it. She'd called and we'd arranged to meet at three-thirty, at the corner of King and Ontario. In the summer, the registry office is the coolest place in town. And it doesn't have air-conditioning. It must have to do with the thickness of those old walls and the rationed windows.

"Did you know Larry Geller?" I asked.

"No. But I've been hearing a lot about him. It's hard to turn on the television for the local news without seeing that picture of him. As you may know I'm the newest partner in B.C.G. and S. This is a town of four-partner firms and they needed me so they could get on with business. I was like the second shoe dropping, the resolving chord on a piano. Why do legal partnerships in Grantham come in fours, just as in English almost everything comes in threes?"

"Like what?"

"Oh, like lock, stock and barrel, like win, lose or draw, like the long, the short and the tall."

"Like *The Good, the Bad and the Ugly?*"

"Same thing. I read it all the time. Maybe it has something to do with trinity. I'll have to look it up."

"What about *The Sound and the Fury* and *The Bad and the Beautiful?*"

"Exceptions that prove the rule. Are you hungry? I usually stop for a cup of tea in a little place by the market."

"Fine," I said, and we crossed King Street's one-way traffic and went into a restaurant with a soda fountain on one side and an out-of-town paper rack on the other. Further back there were booths, one of which was not overloaded with teenagers half-way home from the Collegiate. One head of hair was dyed purple, and another was streaked blonde on black. At least there wasn't a juke-box. They were trading a pair of earphones and gyrating to the unheard beat of a rock band.

"You're doing this for the Jewish community?"

"Who told you?"

"The senior partner. I told him I was going to be seeing you. You feel responsible to the community?"

"In a way, I guess. It's the weak spot in my armour. There's nothing in the book about how to get out of talking to the rabbi and the president of the synagogue when they come to you with their hats in their hands." I thought a second. "And I guess I owe it somehow."

"You're not just involved in mankind, but in certain specific strands of it. Is that right?"

"Isn't everybody? Taking humanity all at once is a little like trying to put your arms around one of those giant Douglas firs they have out in British Columbia." Joyce See ordered tea and I ordered coffee. "And I guess I feel guilty about what Geller did. Because of what he is and because of what I am."

"Yes, that's what it's like being part of a minority."
She nodded as the tea and coffee arrived. A teenager
returned the sugar to our table. "I share an apartment
with an Armenian girl," she added by way of explanation, then went on, "Chinese people are both a minority
and a majority. In my heart I know there are vast millions of us in Asia, but that doesn't seem to mean anything here where the numbers are very small. The closest
I've ever come to feeling like I was really Chinese is walking down Dundas Street in Toronto."

"Your firm handles Geller's legal affairs?"

"Such as they are, we do. It's mostly things going back
to the old partnership."

"Then you know about his property holdings?"

"The file stopped when it got to me. Full of dead ends,
really. Just things Irving and Mr Geller acquired, paid
mortgages on and then sold or traded."

"Traded?"

"There was a property on Woodland Avenue, an office
building. Nothing huge. It was traded for six condominiums. Irving still owns his, but I understand that Mr
Geller sold his three." She sipped her tea slowly, looking
at me over the rim of the cup.

"Who bought the Woodland Avenue place?" I asked.

"It was Tom MacIntyre."

"Who is?"

"Tom MacIntyre? Oh, Tom MacIntyre's a lot of things.
He's been buying up most of unwanted Grantham, he
drives a fast car, has a boat at Port Richmond, keeps an
apartment in New York and is very cosy, in a business
way, with Glenn Bagot."

"Oh, I've heard about *him*. He's connected with Larry
Geller's brother. The one who's in construction. Sid. And
Sid's live-in friend used to be Mrs Bagot."

"You've forgotten to mention the connection with certain powerful names at Queen's Park."

"You mean he's a bagman as well as driving a fast car? I don't believe it."

"Well, he grew up eating local peaches and drinking local wine. What can you expect?"

I got the exact address of the Woodland Avenue property from Joyce and found out where Tom MacIntyre hangs his hat in the daytime. It was still a good hour before closing time, so I walked into the solid marble temple in which he did business. His office was on the sixth floor behind a door marked *McHugh & MacIntyre, Consultants*. The secretary had never heard of a person without an appointment before, and so I introduced myself.

"You didn't phone. Did you write him?" Her eyes were wide under her red bangs.

"No, you see I didn't get up this morning knowing that I wanted to see him. I had breakfast and I still didn't know I needed to see him. It came over me suddenly."

"I'm afraid that Mr MacIntyre doesn't see people without appointments."

"It's a rule, I guess?"

"Oh, yes, sir. Never as long as I've been here."

"I see. I like a place that stands by its rules. May I borrow that telephone book, just by your elbow, for a minute?"

"Oh, of course." She handed it to me and I flipped to the yellow pages, stopping at *Consultants*. The girl was clever about keeping her sandwich out of sight. It didn't go with the buff marble walls or the framed posters of ancient art shows that hung on them.

"*Plummer and McCullough*. Are they good?"

"I beg your pardon?" she said, looking up at me.

"*Plummer and McCullough, Consultants*," I repeated with a smile. "They're reputable? Sound, in a business way?" Her cheeks went hollow. "Or what about *C.N. Geale, Consultants*? I've heard only excellent things about them. Yes, Geale. It sounds like a name you can trust, doesn't it?" She was sitting like a poker was sticking down the back of her white poplin blouse. She got up without bending the poker or making the chair squeak and asked if I would kindly wait for one moment. I promised.

A minute later she ushered me into the august presence of Tom MacIntyre, who looked me up and down then smiled. He was a man in his mid-thirties, I would guess, but the white hair totally fooled me. He was an albino, or an albino's cousin. His pink eyes looked me over through thick lenses. Then he started to laugh.

"Well, you put the wind up Vicki, Mr Cooperman. You took her in and more power to you. Will you have a drink?" He pulled a bottle from an open tray to the right of his desk and paused, waiting for instructions. The room was full of music. I could hear the sound of penny whistles, fiddles, pipes and a drum. They were busy doing a lilting jig tune in an enthusiastic but none too slavish way. He turned it down.

"That's my brother's group, *The Far Darrig*. This is their second album."

"Nice, very nice."

"And you're drinking?"

"Ah, rye with water unless you have ginger ale."

"I have, and I'll give it to you as long as it's rye you're drinking. My arm wouldn't bend if it was Jameson you wanted the ginger ale poured into. I also have some Black Bush, if you like." I shook my head in the negative. He made a drink for me and poured an inch from a bottle marked Jameson into a glass with his fingerprints on it. The light coming through the large window framed his very impressive head. When we both had had a chance to take a sip of our drinks, he brought the conversation back to business again. "Mr Cooperman, you are not looking for a consultant, whatever you told Vicki Daubney. She's a wonderful typist, and she does usually take care of the tinkers. Are you a tinker, Mr Cooperman?"

"I'm a private investigator, Mr MacIntyre. I've been looking into some property once owned by Larry Geller."

"Then it's a tinker you are and no mistake. Good. I was getting bored sitting around here today. Larry Geller ...ah! He's the one who's flown the coop. What did they say he got away with? A tidy sum, a tidy sum, to be sure. Here's to enterprise, Mr Cooperman. Enterprise and imagination." We both drank to that; I didn't know how to refuse a toast.

"I'm interested in 44 Woodland Avenue. What can you tell me about it?"

"Not very much. I own it and have since Geller splintered his partnership with what's-his-name. Bernstein. It was a two-way real estate deal. No money passed. All very simple, honest and, I'm afraid, dull. Nothing spectacular there, Mr Cooperman. A very dull property, on a dull street and filled with dull tenants who send in post-dated cheques for a full year in advance. I even have a set from..." He stopped talking and looked at the tufts of white hair growing on his pink knuckles.

"You were saying?" MacIntyre got to his feet and stared down at the city from his window. From where I sat, the city could have been London or New York. It didn't seem to interfere with his concentration that he was seeing the roof-tops of Grantham, Ontario. After a minute he turned back to look at me, with his arms leaning back on the window ledge.

"Well, you may be on to something after all."

"How do you mean?"

"Well, your quarry is, or was, a tenant of mine. Has been for several years." I felt like I was running up a flight of stairs in a dream. "Small office," he was saying when I was again able to tune in, "in the back, if I remember. Rents are cheaper in the rear. Silly of me not to have remembered sooner."

It wasn't behind a bookcase. It was a small office on Woodland Avenue. "The false wall," I said out loud.

"I beg your pardon?" MacIntyre was splashing another ounce of Jameson into his glass. I was still sipping on my first rye and ginger ale.

"If Geller gave you a set of post-dated cheques for his rent, how would these cheques be honoured? Are you going to find those cheques bouncing?"

"I don't know, Mr Cooperman. I wasn't thinking about that. Here we have stumbled upon a situation alive with possibilities, and all you can think of is whether I'm going to be out of pocket a few hundred dollars. You mustn't imagine Geller's office in terms of this place or even in terms of his Queen Street location. I've never been to Woodland Avenue to inspect it—I have people who do that for me—but from the outside I wouldn't have high hopes about what I would find up there."

"How exactly did he pay you? I mean was it through a company or what?"

"Look, Mr Cooperman, my brother's the brilliant member of the family. All I know how to do is make money. I'll have to see the ledger."

When he came back into the room, his face was looking like he'd just stepped out of a sauna. He'd been in the file room and I'd heard him speaking with Vicki. I wondered if she thought any better of me. "Here it is," he said, opening an old-fashioned ledger on his desk. "We set it up in this book when the property was transferred. It's been put on the computer, of course, but this is the original of the arrangement. His cheques were drawn on the Bank of Upper Canada. Never any problem with them. He paid his money and I assume he made use of the space."

"Want to take a look?" I asked.

MacIntyre grinned and finished his drink. He replaced the empty glass on his drink trolley.

"I don't want to be caught any closer to 44 Woodland Avenue than I'm now standing. If I'd had my wits about me I would have informed the police as soon as I read about Larry in the paper."

"Who said anything about getting caught? You have keys, don't you?"

"Mr Cooperman, I'm tempted, honestly tempted. But I suspect that the trail is cold. Besides, I'm far too conspicuous to go about doing that sort of thing except in my sleep."

"I see. You wouldn't let me borrow the keys for an hour or so. I'd like to have a look around."

"No doubt you would, Mr Cooperman. And no doubt the police will want the same opportunity. They usually like to arrive first on the scene. In fact they insist on it."

"A little slow off the mark today. They usually do better. I don't suppose you could study that ledger for an hour before tumbling to its true significance?"

"Mr Coop—"

"I was afraid not. I have to play all the angles, you understand."

"And you see that I would be playing a very silly game if I went over there with you. I'll have to telephone the police. But perhaps it can wait until this evening. I do have a great deal to do before I leave the office. Yes, I think I can wait until this evening, when I'm home after I've had a run in my boat."

MacIntyre wouldn't go so far as sharing a conspiratorial grin with me. Instead he began playing with the papers on his desk in a way to suggest that the nub of the interview was over, and that I should begin my farewells. I was backing away from his desk and heading towards the door I'd used earlier, when he looked up from his papers and interrupted my speech of thanks. "Mr Cooperman, why don't you let yourself out the side door? It will save embarrassing Vicki any more." He got up and took my drink from me without making the situation awkward. In my excitement, I'd forgotten I was holding it. "I see you haven't got very far with that drink. I'm not surprised. Ginger ale and rye indeed. You should try a good malt one day, Mr Cooperman. Good afternoon to you."

I went through the door his left hand had indicated and found myself in an abandoned office with piles of papers and open filing cabinets everywhere. On a desk sat a box full of dusty Christmas decorations and next to that one of silver platters and trays. On the far wall hung a large board with bunches of keys dangling. Street addresses had been painted neatly dividing the space logically into the required rectangles, but some of these had been crossed out in chalk or felt pen, sometimes changed several times and new addresses filled in. Near the bottom of the board, off by itself and still legible in chalk, I read *44 Woodland Avenue*. I took the small bunch of keys from the hook and let myself out into the outside corridor wondering why MacIntyre was making this so easy for me.

From the open window of my Olds, 44 Woodland Avenue looked like a building that had gone up the wrong year with too little invested in it and a hard-luck story right from the moment nobody arrived for the sod-turning ceremony. It was a four-storey yellow brick building with a small entrance on the left side as I faced it after getting out of the car. I let myself in with a key when the door wouldn't open for nothing. There was a directory near the entrance and somehow I wasn't surprised that I couldn't find Larry Geller's name on it. I went over the names one by one until I had discarded them all. One looked as flea-bitten as the last. I tried walking down the main corridor to the back. MacIntyre had said that Geller's office was at the back. He'd also said that he'd never been there. I looked at the bunch of keys. The labels were marked with room numbers beginning with 100 and running up to 405. I eliminated the denture-making establishments and the two rare-stamp wholesalers. I discarded the jeweller with the Swiss awards after his name. There were eight back offices and I had already disposed of five of them. Thank God for the invention of dentures. One of the remaining offices, was marked *Lawrence Peyre, R.M.T., Cranio-sacral Therapy*, and the other two doors were unmarked except for their numbers. I tried the one on the top floor first. It was a single room with a desk of the roll-top type, with bookcases on all three walls. A standard typewriter stood on a frail-looking metal trolley in front of a leather-backed swivel chair. An ancient electric fan in a wire cage and an upright telephone on the desk made the whole place look like a scene from *The Front Page*. I could imagine the tenant wearing a green eye-shade and sleeve garters reading proofs.

A closer look at the books lying open and closed on the desk led me to believe that this was the haven of an author of Harlequin romances. The first page of each of the books suggested a similarity of authorship. I liked the names of the authors: Bonita Culver, Samantha Ross and Madras Richardson. I went through the desk but came up with nothing of interest except maybe to other Harlequin romance writers: plot charts and lists of names.

There remained the office on the next floor down, room 304. Here I hit pay dirt. The office contained a desk, swivel chair and a small filing cabinet. The room smelled of burned paper, and I could see flakes of paper ash in a green waste-paper basket. It was discoloured on the outside from the heat. A layer of dust covered the faded green desk blotter. I went over the place from top to bottom, bringing all the textbook tricks to bear short of making holes in the wall. Under one of the dark leather triangles that kept the desk blotter in place I found a torn-off piece of an envelope. On it was part of the name and address of Bolduc Construction on Facer Street. I promised to give myself a medal as soon as I got out of there.

The telephone on the desk was one of the cheap, *Made in Taiwan* types. I lifted it off the desk and heard a dial tone. On the bottom row of the push-button display was a button marked "redial". I tried it. I could hear the seven tones jingle in my ear.

"Hello?" I didn't recognize the voice. But then I seldom do.

"Hello. It's Benny Cooperman here. Who's this?"

"Oh, hello, Mr Cooperman. This is Ruth Geller. What a surprise. Any news?"

"Just checking in. You know that your brother-in-law claims to have heard from your husband? He called me last night."

"Why would Sid phone you and not me? That seems strange."

"It wasn't Sid; it was Nathan."

"Same thing. Although Nathan's a little less predictable. Do you believe him?"

"I don't know. I'm surprised he didn't tell you. I'm naturally suspicious, but all the same I think you'd get to hear all the real news first, don't you?"

"Nathan's trying to put you off the scent, you mean?"

"I'll settle for that. I honestly didn't expect him to help me collar your husband. Still it's strange. The call was supposed to have come from Daytona Beach."

"Nathan knew about our holiday in Daytona two years ago. But why would he...? I mean, that might be where Larry went. At least he knows Daytona better than the rest of Florida."

"I'm sure that Nathan is not trying to close the net around Larry. It's either mischief or he knows something. Naturally, if I go down to Daytona looking for him it's because Nathan knows that Larry's living in a loft in Papertown on canned anchovies and Ry-Krisp." I heard a sigh from the other end. "If he is hiding out locally," I said, "he'd better be careful who's bringing him his meals. The cops aren't completely up the road on this. I'm sure

they know where Sid and Nathan and you have been
since they opened a file on this case."

"I guess you're right. We're no longer invisible. That's
another thing Larry hadn't counted on." She sounded
like she was spiralling down into depression.

"Mrs Geller, this may sound peculiar, but have you
been talking with a man named Wally Moore, a panhandler you may have seen on St Andrew Street? He and his
partner are part of the scenery. Has he phoned or come
to the door?"

"There have been dozens of calls. People threaten-
ing. I hate answering the phone. But I don't remember
him. I hope it's not important. I've got to go. Debbie's
just come back. I'll pass you to her and talk to you later,
okay?"

"Never mind Debbie. Just one thing. Did Larry call
you for any reason that last day?"

"The day he...? No, I don't think so. No, I'm sure he
didn't. Why?"

"Just wondered."

"I've really got to go, Mr Cooperman." I said "Sure"
and she was gone.

So Larry burned his papers and telephoned home
before he skipped out. And Ruth doesn't want me
to know about the call. It wasn't much, but it was
something I didn't know ten minutes earlier. In this business you have to be thankful for mouldy crumbs sometimes.

I sat in Larry Geller's chair for a minute trying to
see things his way, from his point of view. Inspiration
didn't rain down on me from the ceiling, so I got ready
to leave.

Making a mental note to get the keys to Larry's door
and the building duplicated at Coy's, I went out into the
unlighted corridor. The door closed with a punctuating
click behind me. My memory is vague on the subject of
what I was thinking about next. In fact, apart from the

ghost of an idea that I might have been thinking of my supper, things aren't very clear at all about the next part. When I turned around from the door, thinking whatever I was thinking, I was staring into three badly lit mean faces and the open end of a .32 calibre revolver.

Chapter Eleven

"We don't want no trouble," said a voice somewhere above the gun. I wasn't too particular which of the heavies facing me was the spokesperson. The two on the outside moved around both my flanks while my mouth tried to find something to do besides hang on its hinges. I started to turn to the right, the direction of the stairs, when a big sunflower bloomed suddenly behind my left ear. It developed magenta petals and enlarged to fill the whole screen. You read in mysteries that getting hit on the head is like diving into a pool of darkness. Tonight it was like diving into a three-hundred-watt bulb. I didn't even feel myself hit the ground.

Two or three hundred years slipped by without my noticing. I think there were dreams at one point. I remember Ruth Geller was trying to tell me something. Pia Morley was glowering at me over my mud-stained desk. Somehow her car got into the office. I was walking down a line of parked cars and the doors kept opening to block the way. I leapt over one car, then a door opened and Joyce See fell out. She didn't move. Nathan Geller was there fixing the windshield, and he was joined by the rest of the family pointing at the heap on the ground and then at me. They were leering at the gun that was smoking in my hand. I tried to explain; I tried to back up and get away, but true to the nature of dreams, the way was blocked by a pile of Nathan's life-sized statues. A newspaper vendor in plaster of Paris, a balloon salesman in bronze, a traffic cop with his fat hand raised against me. Then it was a dinner-table with Friday night candles burned low and Ma and Pa frozen in an attitude of patient waiting, while the gravy congealed around a cooling brisket roast. Nathan's skilled hands had put worry into both of their faces.

When my senses started coming back, it was the sense of motion that hit me first, I think. I felt short bristles under my cheek, a rug, maybe, and a bouncing movement. I couldn't see anything. I moved and it hurt. My wrist banged against something cool. It was even cooler than I was. Fingers traced the outline of a metal object in the shape of a cross. It felt heavy without my trying to move it. The arms were about ten inches to a foot across. I felt the end of one arm and knew what it was. That was a low moment. Carefully I reached above my head. I was right. There were only a few inches above. The metal cross was a tire iron, and I was in the trunk of a moving car.

I'm not generally prone to feelings of claustrophobia. As a matter of fact I'm not generally prone, period. I could see panic beginning somewhere around my solar plexus and I knew that if I didn't put a sock in it, it was going to come out a scream. I knew that wasn't going to yield much of a harvest except maybe another bump on the head, so I tried to chill the urge. If they wanted me dead, I thought, I'd be dead. I tried to squeeze some pleasure from that. I tried to move around. Each movement was like having your ear-drums tickled with a chisel and mallet. At least there was a lot of room in the trunk. I wasn't being taken for a ride in a cheap imported compact. I could move across to the fender covers, or down into a valley where I found a spare tire that felt new. I could feel little nipples of rubber on the treads that would have been normally worn away within a few miles of driving.

We were on a smooth highway, judging by the even flow of the ride. There were no sudden turns or stops. Another passenger in the trunk with me was a coat, a light raincoat by the feel. I went through the pockets and moved everything I could find to my pockets. I'd like to think it was training that made me do that. It was more likely that I did it just to stop myself from starting to holler. At the very least I would separate one of the hoodlums from his laundry for a while.

Gradually, my eyes began to send weak messages to my brain. At first they were false notions of light in that dark place. I seemed to be able to see a faint glow in one part of the trunk and then in another. Maybe that's what happens when the dark is that thick. I tried moving again and a bright light exploded in my face, forcing me to blink. It was the illuminated dial of my wristwatch. The glow seemed to light up the whole space under my nose and plunge the far corners into even deeper black. "Seven twenty-three" the little figures read. I hadn't been out for very long, then. I kept looking at the little red lines that made up the numbers. Useless information was presented by a damaged mind: I'd get the maximum of illumination at ten-O-eight and the least at one-eleven.

These speculations were interrupted by the smell of exhaust working its way steadily into my moving coffin. Carbon monoxide! I'd be found cherry red in a ditch without a scratch on me. I tried to sniff my way to the place where the smell was strongest, and stuffed the raincoat into the gap of rusted-away wheel cover. Canadian winters are great eaters of innocent metal. The smell began to settle down. I remembered that carbon monoxide is heavy, so I propped my head as high as I could. That meant that I took an occasional thump on the forehead from every pot-hole or dead skunk the car ran over.

I needed to take my mind, or what was left of it, off the panic that had found nesting ground in every joint of my body. I did a survey of my pockets and came up with a ball-point pen, cigarettes and my penknife. I could see myself chipping away at the trunk lid with it until it broke, like Injun Joe in *Tom Sawyer*, with his cheek against the massive door of the closed cave. Then I thought of that new tire without even a mile on its factory-new treads. I took the knife firmly and with what little leverage I could find worked the blade back and forth along the smooth wall of the tire. I was getting a little light-headed. Would it be better to relax and keep still or should I go down with harness on my back? That was *Macbeth*, I think. I think I felt the presence of an old English teacher. We were talking about an essay I'd got a C-plus on. "It's not good enough, Benny. It's just not good enough. I know you can do better. Where's your stick-to-it-iveness? You've got to work like a Trojan if you intend to graduate." I kept moving the knife against the rubber, the nylon cords and then the backing. It was something to do, something to demonstrate to Mr McDonald that I was trying to improve. When the tire blew, I thought my ear-drums would roll out of my head and spiral about like two nickels on a table-top. The air that came out was stale, smelling of dust and rubber. But there must have been a little stale oxygen in it somewhere. It made a nice change from the carbon monoxide I'd been breathing. I was glad to see that the English teacher had vanished. My head even felt clearer, until the car lurched sharply and I was thrown against the left-hand side of the trunk. We'd gone off the smooth highway and were now on a bumpy road. My back took a pounding. Every new bump hit where a sore place was hiding. All body secrets were out in the open. I had to clench my teeth or lose them. Rough road, journey's end. That made sense. Life's happy journey. Dead and red in a ditch.

About then the car stopped and turned slowly to the right. I was swimming in a rough surf. Breakers ahead with sharp barnacles and limpets on the rocks like

Chinese coolie hats to tear at my hands. The car stopped again. I braced for another turn, but there wasn't one. The motor was shut off and I heard the doors open. I had only enough sense left in me to play dead to the world. I was born for that part. My eyes were closed when I heard the keys go into the lock. The lid sprang up.

I guess I'd thought at one time of leaping out flailing the tire iron in all directions, but I realized that I would have to do this after lying in a cramped posture for the best part of half an hour. I could only have made a mess of it.

"He's still out."

"Looks that way. Hey, did you know you got a leak in here?" The second voice came from next to my left ear. "Pee-oo! I bet we finished the bugger with the exhaust."

"Shake him. See if he groans. Is he breathing any?"

"Hold your flash ready. I can't see anything." That was the third voice. It had a trace of Cockney or some other English echo. A true Cockney would have said "torch," but this guy had been helping himself and making free with Canadian ways and customs.

"He's heavier than he looks. Easy, Len, don't blunt him any more than necessary!" I was lifted out by six hands, a very spidery sensation, and carried feet forward along a path that crunched underfoot. The man in front stopped suddenly, and I buckled in the middle.

"Hey!" That was Len.

"I've got to get my keys, chum." I felt my weight shifted, and then heard the scratch of the key making its way into an old-fashioned lock. The knob turned with an audible protest and the safari moved into a room of some kind. They put me down without ceremony on a couch that smelled of mildew.

"What do you think?"

"Well, he's still breathing."

"Yes, I know, but..."

"Come off it. All he needs is air. I'll see to him. Why don't you see if you can get a fire started. It may be July, but I feel cold."

"Yeah, it's like my wife's feet in here. The trees keep the sun off the roof." In a moment I could hear someone breaking kindling across the room, then the unmistakable sound of a stove lid being shifted.

"There's enough paper in there already. Give us a match." I heard the match being struck and almost at once began to smell smoke.

"Did you see to the draft, you clot?"

"What?"

"Christ, he's trying to make smoked salmon of us. You have to fix the draft so the smoke goes up the chimney. Bloody smoke's backing up." I could hear the kindling crackling and snapping in the stove and imagined that I was beginning to feel better. I heard chairs scrape on a wooden floor, and imagined the three of them sitting down at a table near the fire.

"You been here before?"

"Nah, not me."

"I was," said the one they called Len. "Last time I worked for this bloke. A couple of years ago. I was here a week that time. All the guy did all day was play cards with himself. Wouldn't let me take a hand."

Just then we heard a blast like the sound of a locomotive just as it's about to run over you.

"What the hell was that?"

"Steamship going through the canal. Going through the twin-flight locks. Sound bounces off the escarpment. You get used to it. It's scary at first." The boat gave another tea-cup-rattling hoot. "Can't tell whether it's going up or coming down." Under the lingering echo of the ship's whistle I could hear another sound, that of an approaching car. I heard it before they did, and counted four breaths before Len said, "That'll be him. See if you can wake the charmer."

Footsteps coming in my direction, then three powerful slaps in the face. I thought I was ready for them, but I jumped awake and was almost sitting up when the fourth slap was ready to descend. From where it had fallen off the couch I brought up my right arm, making a fist as I went, and hit one of the hoods in the mouth. My hand rang sharply with the pain, but it made up for that tap behind the ear and the bumpy ride.

"Christ, the bugger's awake!"

"He's smashed Gordon!" They were on me in a second. Gordon was sprawled under the table holding his face. I was still only half sitting. I couldn't get up. A fist was raised above me. I closed my eyes for the next shock, feeling both my wrists held fast.

Chapter Twelve

"Stop that, you idiots! What do you think this is?"
We all looked towards the door. There was a man
standing there with an attaché case in his gloved
hand and wearing a light Burberry. Car keys dangled
from the other hand as it rested on the doorknob. "Get
away from him at once! Are you trying to kill the man!"
He took a step into the room, noted the sprawling form
of Gordon on the floor, and set down his case on the
table.

"Glenn, we..."

"Shut up. Help Gordon off the floor." He began removing his gloves like he was at a garden party. He put
them in his cap and placed the lot next to the attaché
case. He kept his eyes on me all the while, watching as I
moved to a sitting position. He walked towards me with
a friendly smile on his face.

"Geoff, see if there's a drink about, will you? I think
Mr Cooperman could use one."

It was Glenn Bagot. I'd seen his slightly puffy handsome face in the paper often enough. It was tanned, and
still looked like it could run forward towards chairman
of the board or back to footloose beachboy. His wavy
dark hair was touched with grey in the usual places. He
wore it rather long making him look a little like a public-
school boy in mid-term. There was something about
those regular features that reminded me of an English

garden that's been rolled every Thursday afternoon for the last five hundred years. But there was a slight droop to his right eyelid. He could have been a banker in the navy-blue pinstripe under his Burberry. I knew now that my execution, if that was what was on the program, would follow from a matter of policy and not from a faulty exhaust system.

"Well, Mr Cooperman, how are you feeling?"

"A little better, Mr Bagot, thanks."

"You know me, then? All the better. No need to beat about the bush." He pulled a chair close to the couch I was sitting on and sat down on it the wrong way around, so that his arms were folded across the top of the pressed-back chair. He smelled of cologne and talcum.

I tried to scan the room for the first time. It looked like the kitchen of a summer cottage, or hunting lodge. There was a sink with a pump in it, the wood stove which was still smoking, and a round wooden table with turned legs and an oilcloth cover. Oilcloth? I didn't think they even made it anymore.

"Mr Cooperman, we are both businessmen in our different ways, so I don't imagine that it will be very difficult for us to come to an understanding."

"I came to listen," I said. Mr Bagot didn't have a sense of humour. He merely nodded like I'd answered an engraved invitation. "What's on your mind?"

"I'll be frank with you. We all deplore what Larry Geller has done. He was a man in a privileged position. A man who went back on a trust. In every civilized society that man stands condemned. Before any bar of justice he would be branded guilty. We have no dispute so far?" He didn't even look at my face to see if I was still awake. He enjoyed language and he seemed to find the words written about a foot above my head on the rafters at the back of the cabin. Gordon was sitting at the table with a wadded tissue pressed to his red nose. I guess

Geoff had given up looking for booze. My host didn't press him. "Further," he went on in his grand court-room manner, still hugging the top of the chair, "we all regret the difficulties that Larry's conduct has forced upon his family. No amount of reparation will ever let them regain their place in the community." I could feel him warming to a "but" and it didn't take long. "But, as they say, life must go on, Mr Cooperman. Life and business must go on." I thought business would come into it. In fact I had the feeling that if we changed places I would be able to read his lines without looking at his script. He wasn't ready to run down anyway. "You may know that I'm president of a cement company. It's a fairly large company, perhaps the largest in the Niagara district. From time to time I've done business with Sid Geller's company. Recently we have joined forces to tackle jobs that separately would have been too big for us to handle. Some of these have been government contracts. Together we've been able to give satisfaction. We've recently bid on a very big job. One which will give a lot of employment to local labour. We know that the tenders are all in and that an announcement of the winning bid will be announced next week." He took a breath and wiped his forehead with a clean handkerchief. His words sounded calm, and I knew that he intended to present himself as a rational man talking to another rational man. But he didn't get the breathing right. I could feel the panic underneath. I had to give him credit, though. He came very close.

"All of this investigation into Larry Geller's past is bad for us. I can't prevent the usual routine investigation by Niagara Regional Police; we have to be willing to accept whatever they turn up. If Geller is found, he will be extradited and put in the dock. We are powerless to do anything about that. But we will do whatever we can to delay matters. We only need a week. By that time the bids will..." He stopped. "I've told you this already.

You see, I can't predict you, Mr Cooperman. A man like you might turn up a great deal in a week."

He had apparently ended his argument. He sat back in the chair as though my lines came next and his next cue was several pages off. I didn't say anything. I was still trying to take in what I'd just heard. When I didn't fill the silence, Bagot tried again. "Mr Cooperman, I've been told you are a reasonable man." He paused to see if I would deny it.

"Look, Mr Bagot, I don't want to stand in the way of progress. Everybody has to live. You, me, even Larry Geller. I don't have any quarrel with you. But I can't see how my digging into Geller's affairs drops bird-lime on your hat."

"It's too complicated to go into."

"Isn't it always. Let's see. Your company and Sid's are up for a government job. Provincial or federal?"

"What's the difference?"

"Well, if you said federal, I might think it had something to do with that canal-widening scheme they've been talking about in the papers. If it's provincial, then my guess is that it has something to do with highways. But whatever it is, I can't see how Geller's game can hurt you. You're not letting me in on the whole story."

"Cooperman, I see that the reports I've heard about you are correct. I've underestimated you. But hear me out. You must see that the very name Geller will be enough to put the wind up the ministry involved. Our tender may be the best in the box, but no government can afford to get mixed up in a scandal. The opposition parties will jump at a mistake like that. The Geller name could be the axe to topple this government."

"But Sid Geller isn't Larry. He's not even Sid Geller, he's something called Bolduc Construction."

"Nevertheless."

"You're not giving me all the pieces to play with. There has to be another element. A second breath of scandal maybe?" That made him blink.

"Mr Cooperman, I'm going to make you a proposition. You have gone to a great deal of trouble in this matter. My associates Geoff, Len and Gordon have not treated you with the degree of politeness that I would have suggested under the circumstances. I don't know who you are working for, but I would like you to come to work for me. I have here..." and his hand went into his breast pocket and came out with a wallet. He took from it a handful of new bills, "...five hundred dollars for you as a retainer. Treat it as that. Treat it as payment for the insults that you acquired in coming here. What do you say? Is it a bargain?"

This was one of those offers Mario Puzo used to write about, the kind you can't refuse. I couldn't see any way of getting any more out of him. Five hundred was a hell of a lot more than I could expect to get from the rabbi and Mr Tepperman. I remembered the excuses I tried to give to them, all the reasons why the cops are the right people for digging into matters of this kind. They may not get results fast, but a private operator can't honestly expect to get results at all. I'd been working on the case since Wednesday. This was Friday. I said I'd kick it around for a few days and I did. I didn't owe Rabbi Meltzer or Saul Tepperman another hour on this case. I reached out and took the money.

"Excellent," said Bagot, and as soon as I'd pocketed it, it felt anything but excellent. I felt like Damon after saying "Pythias who?" Or like I'd just taken Kogan's last dime from him. But there wasn't anything about my feeling that I thought I could share with Bagot.

"Car coming, Glenn." Geoff went to the window and lifted one side of the green blind. "I can't see who it is." He opened the door and went outside. By now I could hear the motor. My hearing was sharper when I wasn't on the take. If there are ever any Jewish monasteries, at least one will be called Our Lady of Perpetual Guilt.

"It's the Audi," Geoff announced over his shoulder as he returned to the cabin. Bagot let out the breath he'd been holding. He got up and walked to the door. Geoff, moving back to give him room, rejoined Len and the still bleeding Gordon at the table. It was like a film director was rearranging the groupings before bringing new characters on stage. The only new character was Pia Morley. She was wearing a rust-coloured suit that was supposed to add a casual note, but once she'd seen me the grin she'd been offering around to the boys closed its shutters for a moment.

"Well, hello, Mr Cooperman." Then she gave Bagot a pouting look.

"It's all right. We've had a little talk, Pia, and Mr Cooperman's agreed to be cooperative." Bagot knew the right words to make me wish I had thrown his five hundred into the stove. I wonder whether soldiers who never volunteer for dangerous missions go through life being put off by all sorts of imagined references. Are they embarrassed by every passing birthday? But when you're bought, you're bought. You have to take the insults that come with the wages.

"I still don't think I like it, Glenn. He's too cosy with the family," she said, talking about me like I was a spot on the wall the paint wouldn't cover. "He could tell them things he doesn't even know he knows." Bagot looked from me to her. He reminded me of a judge I'd seen. Was Bagot giving a fair hearing, or was he going to believe his five hundred dollars? Pia went on, "He's been talking to Alex. He's been seeing people all over town."

"The boys picked him up outside Tom MacIntyre's and followed him to a place on Woodland Avenue."

"You shouldn't have brought Tom into this, Mr Cooperman. He plays both sides of the street." I tried to shrug to show her that I was just a beginner in such things. Bagot had put his arm around Pia's shoulder.

"Pia, calm down." She leaned into his embrace and began straightening Bagot's tie. She did everything but purr.

"Glenn, you know you can't pay him enough to get him to leave this thing alone."

"He sees things differently now. We had a little chat. I'll find something else for him to do. We will have rights-of-way to negotiate eventually. He can help out there." That was all I needed: to end my active life searching titles in the registry office.

Pia Morley came over to me trying to read me like a poster. I got up and used the opportunity to move a few feet closer to the door. I gave her my best smile. She wasn't buying it. She had a way of moving so that the outfit, while it remained unruffled itself, gave a hint of a great deal of movement within.

"You wouldn't listen to me, would you, Mr C?"

"Just doing my job, Mrs M. Are these boys some of Mr B's retainers, or are they borrowed for the occasion?"

"You might ask him yourself, now that you're on the payroll."

"Sure, once I've found out about my duties. Do you think they'll include being lent to friends and colleagues, Mrs Morley?"

"I hate the way you say that. It's like 'Mrs Morley' was something you were hitting me with."

"The only weapon to hand. Sorry." She turned back to Glenn Bagot, and I edged another few inches further towards the door. "It's up to you, Glenn. I've said what I think. And you know that Tony doesn't like loose ends. Of course," she turned to me for this, "as for me it's a matter of complete indifference." I wondered, as I continued my soft shoe towards the out-of-doors, where she'd bought her low opinion of me, and was it always this low or had it been marked down from something higher.

Now Gordon was watching me. I tried to lean into the wall and become part of the decor. It didn't work. Gordon got up, and breathed a word into Geoff's ear without taking his eyes off me. Glenn and Pia kept nattering at one another, but now I couldn't hear them as well. On the whole I think I preferred hearing their hostility. All of this whispering sounded dangerous. I went over to Gordon, deciding to beard the lion in his den.

"Sorry about your nose," I said, in a voice that came out a little more squeaky than it left my head. "But, in the circumstances, you understand."

"Sure, I understand." And to show there were no hard feelings he offered me his pack of cigarettes. They were Rothmans and I didn't quite see Gordon choosing that brand. Geoff offered matches while Len looked on. I didn't much like being looked at that way. I felt a bit like a condemned murderer being watched by his death-house guards. Everything I did they found remarkable, from blinking to blowing a cool smoke-ring over the centre of the table.

"That's a nice cigarette," I said. "Does Tony still smoke Rothmans, Gordon?" I knew I couldn't make it sound casual, but I couldn't help trying either. What the hell, I thought, I had the five hundred.

"Sure he does," said Gordon. "He..."

"Shut up, Gordon. And you get back over to the couch where we can see you." Before I could get moving, Bagot came over and the boys looked attentive like he was going to make an announcement. I didn't think it was going to be about sending out for Chinese food.

"Len," he said with easy authority, "we're going to try to make Mr Cooperman comfortable for a day or two. See what you can fix up for him in the back room." With a look that didn't quite meet my eyes he said, "We can't let you go back to town just yet. I've got to see somebody and then I'll want to talk to you again. It'll save your coming out here a second time." We both smiled at the inadequacy of his explanation, and he shrugged and went on. "I think the boys can make you reasonably cosy in the meantime." I nodded and returned to the couch showing all signs of an agreeable, easy-going nature. Meanwhile, I was trying to think of ways in which I could have planted a letter in Pete Staziak's hands to be opened in case of my sudden disappearance or death that might implicate all of these people. In the movies detectives get out of tough spots like that all the time. I'd even seen it work for me once. But that night I don't think I could have found words a two-year-old would have believed. My getting picked up by this bunch was not something I could have had in my appointment book. Even if I kept an appointment book. To tell the truth I wasn't up to giving a performance. I could see my desperate face reflected in the eyes that didn't quite meet mine.

Len came over and with a toss of his head told me to follow. There were two doors at the back of the kitchen. The one on the left led to a small sitting-room with a studio couch that opened up into a sleepless night. There was a rack of shot-guns on the inside wall, which Len removed from the case. I shrugged as if the last thought in my head was of escape. "That window," Len explained, "drops straight down forty feet into a dry lock in the old canal. I wouldn't try anything unless you're good at landing on limestone. You can doss down here comfortable enough. I've done it and lived. One of us will be right outside your door in case you want a glass of water. If you need a john, there's a tin bucket in the cupboard." I heard the door lock behind him after he'd finished showing me around.

The view from the window didn't get me any confirmation of Len's story, but I was inclined to believe him. I found the bucket in a closet that was set in the inside wall of the room. The rest of the furnishings were simple, a couple of shooting trophies on a bureau, a lamp made out of a winebottle with a twisted shade and some framed photographs of hunters, who stood with dangling waterfowl displayed and their shotguns bent to the open position. One group stood in front of what I took to be this building. If it was, Len was right. It looked like it might have been a lock-keeper's house. It certainly overhung the lock in the picture. Perhaps it had been moved there from a little farther away. From the picture I got an idea of the size of the place. The room I was being kept in represented about half of the space at the back of the lodge. I'd been thinking of it as a shack, but the mounted antlers over the front door made me move it up a notch or two in my architectural hierarchy. The angle of the photograph told me that there was a window that looked over solid ground in the room next to mine. I looked in the closet again. A piece of mock-wood wallboard separated the closet in my room from one in the neighbouring room. Without breaking my penknife I managed to remove the partition about the same time I could hear the motor of one of the cars starting up. Two fists less to contend with at the very least, I thought.

The cupboard on the other side was divided by shelves, so that it wasn't going to be easy to take possession of this second room. I got the look of the back ends of more shooting trophies. I had the time, so I removed them and set them behind the studio couch. It was awkward insinuating myself through the shelves and I got stuck half-way when one of them decided to come away from the supporting wall brackets. I retreated to the couch, moved the winebottle lamp closer, then lifted off the closet shelves as I should have in the first place.

The other room was about the same size as the one I'd just left and I wouldn't have insisted on changing for the fun of it. The window was similar to the one in the other room except for the wire grill outside that kept vandals out and me in. There were more hunting and shooting pictures on the wall. One showed a grinning face over a torso so loaded down with lethal hardware I thought he must be inadequate in bed. That's the first thing I thought of. Silver trophies mounted on plastic bases occupied a series of shelves on the outer wall. I nearly yelled "Bingo!" when I found another rack of shotguns, this time with boxes of suitable ammunition. I tried to match shell to bore and picked out a stylish pump-action beast that looked mean enough for my purposes. I set the loaded gun on an overstuffed chair and listened at the door. I tried the knob. It opened. I could see Bagot with his cap on at the front door.

I worked my way back through the closet to my room. I was wondering why I was identifying with this prison cell when I heard Bagot's car start up. For the plot that was distilling in my head, I thought that the window with the forty-foot view (straight down) had better be open. I ran the window-sash up as far as it could go. Good, it jammed and stayed open. I listened with my head out the window to the sound of Bagot's car growing fainter on the night air. The engine noise blended with the night noises like a black cat vanishes under a fire escape.

I knew that my way out of the lodge led through the closet, to the next room then out the front door. But how was I supposed to get by my guards? I didn't like the shot-gun in the next room. I didn't trust myself with it, and I didn't know how I could stop three men with two shells. I knew one of them at least was armed, but I couldn't remember whether it was Geoff or Len. If I could make some kind of noise, I could get the three of them to come into my room. That would be tidy. I liked that.

I went through all the drawers in the room looking for an idea. I came up with a sewing basket, three paperclips and a rubber band. A little more looking brought me a dirty toothpick. Then it hit me. It might just work.

I placed the tin bucket upside-down close to the bureau with the lamp on it. I put a piece of lath normally used to prop open the window on top of the bucket. It reached within an inch of the bureau top. I raised the bucket with a few lurid paperbacks. There were four spools of thread in the sewing basket, the strongest looked like black linen, the kind my brother Sam used to manipulate his marionettes when he was twelve. I tied one end to the lath, and balanced the lamp so that it teetered over the bucket but was held up by my strut of lath. When I pulled the thread, I thought, the lamp would crash down noisily on the bucket. I ran the thread behind the couch so that it wouldn't be the first thing the boys saw when they heard the noise and came in to investigate. I led the thread into the cupboard and into the adjoining room. Then I put the wallboard back in place and took a minute to catch my breath, get used to the dark and prepare myself for whatever was going to happen next.

Like the old nursery rhyme, I set things in motion. The thread began to pull the strut, the strut began to upset the lamp, the lamp began to make a racket, the racket began to worry the boys, the boys began to search the house... I heard them open the bolt on my door. And as soon as the three of them were in there, I slipped out and slid the bolt on the door behind them. I was running out the front door with a shot-gun under my arm before I heard them yell for the first time.

Chapter Thirteen

When I got into the bush that ran along the side of the canal, I tried to orient myself. I had never been totally familiar with the territory, but my teenage memory gave me some encouragement. The black mass ahead of me was the shadow of the Niagara Escarpment. At the top I could see a light in what must have been a watchman's hut at the quarry at the rim of the cliff face. Below I thought I could make out the metal girders that formed a railroad bridge. I knew the bridge, and seeing it, or even imagining I saw it, made me feel better. Somewhere out to my right, I guessed I was facing south, ran two rights-of-way, two generations' ideas of where the canal should run. They crossed like a double cross a mile below where I was standing. If I wanted to get back to the city, I was going to have to find a way across the old canal and the new one.

I didn't hear the door being broken down, but it couldn't have taken the boys very long. The night was still noisy with my own breathing, and a feeling that somewhere out there great ships were moving heavily through dark waters. I tried to think. Well, to be honest it wasn't thinking. At times like this I get more intuitive than thoughtful. Sometimes I can't tell the difference. I knew that I couldn't cross the steel bridge. They would be waiting for me there. At least they would if they knew the territory half as well as I did. I stopped and listened.

Nothing. Through the dark, looming up at me was the grey form of a discarded lock on the old canal. It looked like a dry bone, with all the wooden and metal works removed from it. I headed south, towards the escarpment and the railway line. There wasn't much cover, but at least there wasn't a moon to give me away. On the top of the first lock I came to I sat on an ancient bollard and could make out the rope burns along the limestone facing at the edge of the lock. The lock gates had disappeared years ago, so there was no way across the canal here. I pushed on, keeping the canal to my right.

Faintly, I could hear a car motor. That would be them, heading to cut me off. Once they got to the tracks they could cover a fair stretch. I'd have to cross where the bridge crossed the canal or head east until I was out of sight. I could see the criss-crossing girders closer now, and for a moment they were swept by headlights. Then to my right the deep whistle of a lake boat nearly lifted me by my belt into a stunted sumach that had grown between blocks of limestone. I could see the slow progress of the ship's riding lights as it moved into position at the bottom step of the twin-lift locks. The old canal took twenty-five locks to lift boats in the 1870s up the escarpment. The present canal did the same job for ships three times as big, in eight huge cement steps.

I could now see the railway embankment. There was no way I could slip by under the bridge without being seen. And the embankment was high enough so that I'd be seen clambering up the slope. I kept to a fringe of sumachs that began in a depression that ran east, parallel to the railway. It suited me, so I went along with it. From the edge I could still see the bridge, and now I could make out a flashlight beam running up and down the rails. My comfortable, well-shaded depression turned towards the tracks, and just as I thought that we might have come to the parting of the ways, I could see that it was running straight for a culvert that ran under the tracks. It was made to order. It was even dry until I was within fifty feet of the entrance, then I felt both feet go wet at the same moment.

It was a narrow squeak through the culvert. Ahead of me something scampered close to the ground. Things brushed across my face, and my head banged into the overhead arch every time I tried to give my aching back a break. As I eased through, it sounded like a pipe-band rehearsal; the sloshing of my feet through the muck between the stretches of water nearly deafened me. I was glad when I came out the other side. By now I was very close to the base of the escarpment. If I had to escape to the south, that meant I'd have to go straight up.

I looked back towards the bridge. That was when the beam of light caught me. The glare blinded me and I heard the sound of the bullets cutting through the branches of the trees before I heard the echo of the shots bombarding off the face of the escarpment. I turned the shot-gun on them and let them have one blast. When I stopped running I was at an intersection of depressions. The one I was in turned east, the larger one, like a track for oxen, moved south-west. That was roughly towards the new canal, and gave me the feeling of doubling back on my pursuers, so I took it. It went low, lower than the other stream-bed, and the longer I followed it the more it seemed like an abandoned road or trail.

By now the track had continued in a gentle curve moving in the direction of the old canal. At the same time it was cutting deeper into the ground, giving me complete protection on both sides. My feet slipped in and out of muck and tripped over stones as I went. By starlight I could only see a few feet ahead at a time. For some reason, I trusted this trail. I kept moving. There was a dark round spot ahead. I was almost on top of it before I could see that it was the handsome entrance of a tunnel. I could make out a curve of well-matched stone blocks over the arch. From where I was standing, it looked enormous, although it couldn't have been much more than about twenty feet high and fifteen or sixteen across.

It hit me at last. I'd been walking along the old right-of-way. Now the old canal was crossed by the black iron bridge I'd seen, but at some earlier date, the tracks went *under* the canal.

I moved in, holding to the middle and trying not to think of the creatures of the night that used to haunt my bedroom when I left my clothes in an untidy tangle on the chair when I was a kid. The tunnel curved gently, continuing the arc of the graded trail. The middle was mush. There was no sign of ballast or railway ties anywhere, and the place smelled as dank as a sewer. It seemed to go on forever, but it couldn't have been more than an eighth of a mile until I saw an arched section of magenta light ahead of me. It got bigger as I slushed on. It must be the glow above the foundry that had located off the St David's road. In fact, I could hear the distant thump of drop-hammers through the night.

Once out the other side, I turned north for just long enough to let the embankment over the tunnel reach a reasonable grade. As soon as it looked no steeper than about forty-five degrees, I scrambled to the top. To the north I could see the present line of track with the steel bridge almost shining in the dark. That's where I'd last seen the boys. There wasn't any way that I knew of for getting to where I was faster than the way I came. I had the old canal between us now. I was kneeling on one of the oddest pieces of man-made engineering ever made: the spot where an abandoned railway tunnel passes under an abandoned canal. I'll have to think of that spot again sometime when I think that Grantham is moving into the twenty-first century too quickly.

Half-way down the embankment again, where I'd half slid, half fallen, I heard a distinct rattle among the sounds of slipping feet and stones. I moved my feet quickly

before the rattlesnake of my nightmare struck at my un-
guarded ankle. I must have been hallucinating. I didn't
see anything, and whatever it was it was gone without
another sound. Over my shoulder I could see lights from
the flight locks and I could hear the faint hum of motors.
Beyond the other-worldly twin locks with their regular
light standards lifting the buff planes out of the darkness, I could make out the pale glow of Papertown on
the other side.

I kept hiking along the ghostly railway track, knowing that it would eventually lead me back to the main
line from which it had separated years before I was born.
I kept pushing the pace. "Before I was born," as though
that's a measure of anything. It was like my asking when
I was six if the ocean was over my head. The universe
was divided into what was over my head and what
wasn't. Not a fair division at all unless you happened to
be six. Ahead I could see the present canal's surge tank.
It looked like a gigantic car muffler on end. It must have
stood two hundred feet in the air. Right beside it ran the
railway right across the new canal. The bridge was down
so it was easy over and home free for Papertown.

Chapter Fourteen

"What do you mean, 'Can I put you up for a few days?'"

"Just that, Martha. I'm on the run. If I show up at my office or at the hotel, somebody's going to lean on me pretty hard. It's just for a few days. I know you've got a spare room."

"Yeah. You fixed it so that it's been spare ever since..."

"I'll pay rent, Martha. I don't mean to take advantage."

"That's the story of my life: nobody ever takes advantage."

"I'll keep out of the way. I never cook in my room."

"M'yeah. I know the type. Taco chips in your briefcase, milk cartons on the window sill."

"No. Honest. I'll fill up your refrigerator for you. Nothing in the room but me. You've got my word on it."

"Benny, you don't seem to realize that I'm a maiden lady and maiden ladies don't invite strangers into their homes without at least three weeks rent up front. And even so, on this street, I'll never hear the end of it."

"Thanks, Martha. You'll never regret it."

"M'yeah. I regret it already. How soon will you be moving in?"

"I'll hail a taxi and be right over. Bye."

"Tonight? Cooperman—" I pretended I didn't hear her and hung up.

Martha Tracy has more things to do with her life than keep a rooming-house. She'd lost a paying guest once when I started digging up the past. But in the main she'd been helpful to me in my work six or seven times. Nobody knew this town the way Martha did. She worked for Scarp Enterprises, a big real-estate firm. She knew where all the bodies were buried in Grantham and who buried them. I've had more free advice from Martha than I like to remember. She lived in the western part of the city in a house that backed on the tracks that came from Hamilton and were on their way over the Eleven Mile Creek bound for Niagara Falls. I noted the neglected privet hedge as I went up her walk to the green porch.

"Well, you didn't waste any time, did you?" Martha gave me a heavily leaded smile and pushed open the door farther to let me pass. "I've got the kettle on," she said. Martha doted on instant coffee. Sometimes she got her hot water from the chrome kettle, but often from the hot-water tap. She was blonde, stocky and met the world with a Churchillian jaw.

"Martha, I'm not going to tell you about the trouble I'm in. The less you know about it the better."

"Library chasing you for fines again?" She dropped into a kitchen chair as she passed a mug to me, and then straightened the hang of her housecoat. She regretted her gag about the library and moved the conversation to the practical matters of towels, the availability of hot water, the broken bottom step and the quirky radio that suddenly increases in volume when you least expect it. I gave her some money which she put into a drawer bursting with coupons.

"Martha," I asked, after I'd emptied my mug and cleaned the ring on the white enamel table with a dishcloth to show my clean living habits, "what is the biggest engineering project now going on around town?"

"You mean us or the other wheelers and dealers?"

"Not Scarp. I mean a big government contract going to Bolduc or to Bagot Cement."

She lifted a red-marked palm from the table and leaned her cheek against it, while staring out the back window to the maple tree by the railway fence. "Bolduc is building the new fire hall on the Queenston Road end of St Andrew Street. As usual they are building condominiums in about six different locations around town. But nothing big, nothing special." I returned the dishcloth to the sink. "Cooperman, have another cup of coffee and don't jump up and down like that. You make me nervous. Let me think. You want bigger than that, don't you?"

"Yeah. Something with government money in it. Something with rights-of-way that need buying."

"Now you're making it easy. The Feds have called off the work on the canal, so that leaves the province. What they are up to is this: a new major superhighway is going to be built to help the Shaw Festival at Niagara-on-the-Lake. As it is there are so many switchbacks and traffic circles on the last part of the trip from Toronto that half the potential audience for the plays ends up in Lewiston or Niagara Falls, New York, wondering what went wrong."

"I know that road. You have to double back to the Skyway bridge to make connections with the road to Niagara-on-the Lake."

"Well, the province," Martha said, lowering her voice just perceptibly, "in its wisdom, is going to build a four-lane divided highway from the Niagara end of the bridge all the way to the Festival theatre without getting hung up in the traffic of hamlets like Virgil and Homer on the way. It's big money and Bagot and Bolduc are the only local developers big enough to handle it."

"That sounds like the one I'm looking for. When it's finished the festival will be able to run all year round and the sale of fudge along the main drag in Niagara-on-the-Lake will double our sugar imports."

"Don't knock it, Cooperman. My brother-in-law works in the bar at the Prince of Wales Hotel. Think of what he'll make in tips alone. What's going on, Benny? Dirty work at the projected crossroads?" I didn't want to do my guessing in public, so I dodged the question and showered some thanks in Martha's direction. "What am I here for?" she said. "Don't leave a ring in the tub if you love me and don't tell any of your friends that phone after ten at night that you're shacking up here. Now, let's have a little drink to make it legal, Cooperman. I've been thinking about you lately." Martha unscrewed the top of a bottle of Crown Royal, the last of the Christmas bonus, she said, and filled two tumblers well beyond my limit. I knew there'd be a price to pay for dropping in on Martha like this, but it seemed steep only when she'd pulled the cork of a second bottle. This time it wasn't a brand I was familiar with. When I stopped coughing, I told her I wanted to go to bed. She looked at me to be sure of my meaning, then she got up and reappeared with a pair of pyjamas, which she poked at me. I had the tact not to ask where they came from. After all, I was a guest under her roof. Who was I to judge? She gave me some clean towels, a wash-cloth and told me to leave my shoes and pants outside the door and she'd see what she could do for them.

"Your shoes look like you've been running through a sewer."

"In a way, I was. I've been playing games over by the old canal. You know where the Showers is?"

"Teach your grandmother to suck eggs. Patrick Oliver Tracy, my grandfather, ran lock eleven and the Homer bridge for nearly thirty years. Where'd you get your feet wet?"

"I found a tunnel running under the old canal."

"That'd be the old Great Western tunnel by lock eighteen. There's a road tunnel between sixteen and seventeen. I'm not sure whether it's still there. I haven't been out that way since I was a kid. But, hell, I'd wear my Wellingtons if I went anywhere near there. You've got to be careful. My cousin got a bad bite looking for the road that Laura Secord took trying to warn the British of some coming battle or other."

"What bit him?"

"Her. Iona Tracy. Iona Lloyd she is now."

"Martha, what bit her?"

"Massasauga rattler. She said it was a yard long. Got her on the leg above her boot. You can't be too careful."

"You mean there *are* rattlesnakes down there?"

"One of the few places in the whole province. You get them in the Niagara gorge too and up on the Bruce peninsula."

"Martha, I'm going to bed." And I did that.

Next morning I got up to the sound of bacon frying in a frying pan. I'd heard that sound before, in fact I've been hearing it all my life. The world's chief occupation it sometimes seems to me is the baiting and setting of bacon traps. Sometimes I can walk around them, sometimes I can jump over them, and sometimes I fall into them like a tiger into a tiger trap. I wondered how I was going to meet this challenge as I moved stiff legs over the edge of the single bed to the uncovered floor. In the no-nonsense bathroom I tried to simulate a toothbrush with the wash-cloth. In my head I was making a list of things I would need if I was going to stay clear of my room at the City House. I owed my mother a call for missing Friday night dinner. I wanted to talk to Nathan Geller again about his miraculous telephone conversation with his missing brother.

When I was looking as fit as I could manage in shoes and trousers sponged into passable condition by my land-lady, I joined Martha at the kitchen table. "I hope you aren't one of those morning talkers," she said, stifling a friendly "Good-morning" before I'd got my mouth open. I drank reconstituted orange juice and tried to outstare the crisp rashers on my plate. I chewed on some cold toast and watched Martha spread peanut butter on hers. In the end I ate the bacon. I always do and I always pay for it before the month is out. Like the time I nearly got drowned under a swimming pool's nylon cleaning net, after eating bacon out Pelham Road a few years ago. I know these things are related.

When Martha disappeared into her bedroom, I phoned my Ma. It was early, too early to bother her under normal circumstances, but I knew she would be worried about my skipping out on Friday night dinner. It was one of the things I should have mentioned when Geoff, Len and Gordon extended their kind invitation to join them at the gun club.

"Hello?"

"Ma, it's Benny. Sorry to wake you so early, but I wanted you to know that I'm okay."

"You're okay, Benny? That's fine. Goodbye."

"I knew you'd be worried when I didn't show up last night."

"What time is it?"

"Time? Well, it's just after eight. Eight-thirteen."

"Benny, you shouldn't call so early. I was up till all hours last night with Chopin, George Sand and Paul Muni. I love that music. Chopin wasn't Jewish was he, Benny?"

"I don't think so."

"That would explain the nuns at the end all right."

"I'm sorry about last night, Ma."

"No, I liked it. It's one of my favourite movies."

"I mean about missing dinner. I was held up, couldn't get away. I know I should have called."

"To tell the truth, your father asked where you'd got to. You usually come over. We had a nice brisket and roast potatoes. Your favourite."

"So, you weren't worried?"

"No more than usual. Should I have been?" I heard a yawn come over the wire with the words.

"Course not."

"There you are then. Well, if that's all, Benny, I'll turn over and see if I can get back to sleep on the other side. I don't want to hear the phone ring until the crack of noon. Goodbye, dear."

After I put the phone down, I picked it up again and called for a taxi, then watched for it out the front curtains. Martha's living-room was full of overstuffed furniture. A television set held pride of place on a fumed-oak tea-trolley. Above the small fireplace was a huge portrait in oils of a bearded man who looked like he thought he was a somebody in the last century. He watched me watching for the taxi. I picked up a copy of *Time* magazine from under the trolley: "Should Germany Rearm?" I replaced it.

When the taxi came, I had him drop me at the station, where I rented a car. I folded the receipt in half and placed it carefully in my wallet. There's nothing so impressive on a progress report as an expense with a matching receipt. I'd forgotten to get one from the cab. That dampened things. I started wondering, as I drove the small Ford up the gentle incline to St Andrew Street West, who exactly my client was on this Saturday morning. I thought I'd better confirm that one way or another right away.

The congregation of B'nai Sholem worshipped at the corner of Church and Calvin, a fact that amused several of my Protestant friends. It was a textured red-brick building with twin garlic-shaped cupolas on top that failed to make it look like a postcard view of the Kremlin but more like a double dollop of Dairy Queen soft ice-cream. There was a wide stairway on the Church Street side leading to an open double door. I'd parked the rented car three blocks away with the cars of others in the congregation. The local reading of holy scripture didn't prevent members of the shul from driving on the Sabbath, but simply it forbade parking within sight of the synagogue.

I felt a little bogus as I went through the doors into the back of the synagogue. I hadn't ever been there without my father, and felt both shy and foreign. I borrowed a yarmulka from a cardboard box on a card-table near the door. Although I knew most of the men seated in the pews arranged around the bema, as I took a place in back, I felt all of twelve years old and sitting between my father and Sam (with my mother up in the balcony behind the brass rail with the women).

The place hadn't changed much since my bar mitzvah. The long pews were stained the same walnut brown as the wood trim of the cream-painted walls. The skylight still showed symbolic beasts painted in a reedy style in faded yellow and green on the four sides of the rectangle. The ark at the front was closed and covered with a wine-coloured velvet curtain. On the bema, Mr Hecht was auctioning off the privilege of opening the curtain and carrying the Torah from the ark to the bema, a privilege for which the merchants of St Andrew Street often paid big money. I'd seen some highly competitive scenes between several of the leaders of the Jewish community as they fought it out for the right on a hot Saturday in the autumn during the high holy days, while the rest of the congregation took side bets on who'd give up first. At the back, on the same wall as the ark, Rabbi Meltzer could be seen sitting at an old-fashioned slant-top school desk. Under the lid he kept his bound copies of the books, so that he didn't have to pull out the Torah scroll just to establish the correctness of a citation or conduct a bar mitzvah lesson. The big moment towards the end of preparations for a bar mitzvah was the day when the student got his first chance to read from the scroll just as he would on the big day itself.

Rabbi Meltzer was sitting at his desk watching, but not with particular interest, the fact that Mr Belkin, the jeweller, and Mr Hirsch, the druggist, were trying to out-bid one another, but the incremental rise at each bid was not large enough to catch the attention of everybody.

"Benny," the rabbi called, giving me a warm unshaven Saturday morning smile. "*Gut shabbas.* What brings you out on a Saturday? Have I ever seen you on a Saturday? I don't think so." He cleared a place beside him and I sat down. We both watched Mr Hecht's large eyes as magnified by his thick glasses. He looked for an advance on fifty dollars from Mr Belkin. Mr Hirsch went up a dollar. "It won't hit sixty," the rabbi said. "Belkin's courage always fails him around fifty-five or six. What can I do for you, Benny? I expected to hear from you."

"Is it all right to talk?" I asked. "Here, I mean?"

"Why not? I can't get away, Benny. If you want to talk this morning, this is where I am." I'd been more concerned with the correctness of talking sordid business in shul than simply having the rabbi to myself, but I let that pass. Rabbi Meltzer waved his hand and mimed something to the right-hand side of the congregation, and shortly we were joined by Mr Tepperman.

"Good-morning, Benny. Is your father here?"

"Morning, Saul. No, he's home and in bed where he is most Saturday mornings." The sun coming into the synagogue glinted for a moment on one of Saul's gold teeth. There was silence all around us. Hirsch had won the auction, and the rabbi was now needed. He got up and the service continued. Mr Tepperman let me look at his prayer book as various members of the congregation were called up to the bema to read a small portion. It all seemed to be building up to something, and then it hit me: I recognized David and Lou Gorbach beaming up there. Then the rabbi called out in his familiar sing-song for Lou Gorbach's boy to come up to the bema. A nervous thirteen-year-old in long pants went up the step and took his position, like he was over-rehearsed. He read the blessings in a strained voice that carried up to the balcony where his mother was sitting. "*Vilosechi h'oretz eschem...*" The musical decoration was simple and repetitive. I remember that the musical clues were written on the text, curlicues like accents above the words which indicated the next sequence of notes. The boy's voice cracked a few times, just enough to bring tears to the eyes of most of the women in the balcony, and when he finally came to the end he became the centre of a hail of tiny paper bags with candy in them. Nothing changes in Grantham. I remember scrambling with the younger kids to collect as many of the bags as I could when I was little. Then I remembered that as I stood there on the bema in my first pair of long pants after reading my *mafter*, suddenly I was a man, too old to scramble for candy. I knew then that there was such a thing as dignity and I didn't think I liked it.

The Gorbach boy didn't pick up any candy either. It was a coming-of-age ceremony, and as such things go around the world, relatively painless. The only hazard in my day was getting my cheek pinched by the old rabbi when I got something right.

"My dear rabbi, beloved grandparents, relatives and friends..." The little so-and-so was now giving my speech. He got a few things different and changed some of the details because he'd read a different part from the Torah, but the thrust was the same and so were the lessons to be learned from the text. I felt violated by a thirteen-year-old. I picked up a small bag of candy that had landed at my feet and began feeling better right away.

"Nathan Geller has had a call from his missing brother," I said to Saul Tepperman. "At least he says so." I added that to show that I didn't believe it was necessarily true. "He says that Larry's in Florida. Daytona Beach."

"And you believe he's anywhere but Daytona Beach, is that right, Benny?"

"It doesn't make sense that he would tell me where his brother is hiding." Saul Tepperman licked his lips and ran his finger over his moustache as though he was confirming that he still existed. "Look, Saul, he could be downstairs for all I know. I've talked to everybody in sight. It's like running a stick against a picket fence. One piece makes the same noise as the last. This thing with Nathan, well, I don't know. I'll go see him."

"You mean you'll stay with the case?"

"I said I'd look around for a few days. That was last Wednesday. I don't know, Saul. To find out where Larry's gone will take a bigger organization that I can offer."

"Look, if you could stay with it until next week." He turned his head making a helpless gesture.

"In the meantime I'm not making a living, Saul. I've got a licence that has to be renewed and I don't have the five hundred dollars it takes. If I don't get renewed, I'll be just another interested amateur." I said this, then remembered Bagot's five bills in my wallet. The way I was thinking, it wasn't the same as real money. I knew I wouldn't be able to relax with my debts until I'd put the money in an envelope addressed to Glenn Bagot.

"We're meeting on Thursday," Saul Tepperman said. I didn't see how it followed.

"Eh?"

"The committee. I'll tell them what you've done and at the very least they'll pay you for the time you've already spent." I wondered what he imagined was the most that the committee might do for my sagging affairs, but I let it pass.

"Saul, who in town, apart from his legal friends and his family, was closest to Larry Geller?"

"Apart from them..." he stroked his moustache between his thumb and the knuckle of his first finger, the one I used to call Peter Pointer. (The others were Tom Thumb, Toby Tall, Reuben Ring and Baby Finger.) "Apart from them I don't think there was anybody. Close, you know what I mean. A family man, that's what he was."

"Or appeared to be," I added, and once I'd said it, the more I liked the idea. The rabbi had now rejoined us, having quietened a dispute at the back over a procedural wrangle. On these occasions he can shut everybody up with the single word, "Sha!" spoken in a loud stage whisper. I asked him the same question I'd just posed to Saul and got the same answer with this addition: "Why not ask Nathan some further questions. If I had to guess which of his brothers Larry was closest to, I'd say it was Nathan not Sid. Sid was more like a father to the two of them. Talk to Nathan. God forbid we shouldn't get to the bottom of this thing." I said "Amen" and left the synagogue as quickly as I could, congratulating the Gorbachs at the door and dodging their invitation to join them downstairs in the vestry rooms for a small kiddush.

Once back behind the wheel of the car, I felt like myself again. There was something about religion that made me nervous. It was too closely connected with childish nightmares to leave me feeling wholly grown up and driving my own car. After an hour in the shul I felt an urge to turn over a new leaf and become a better person. It was the bacon in my stomach giving me heartburn and not God's interference in my life that made me stop the car and buy some antacid tablets. That took care of my metaphysical speculations for about ten minutes.

I parked the rented car where I'd parked the Olds a couple of days ago, at the side of the two-storey warehouse where Nathan Geller did his sculptures. The green garbage bags had been collected but it looked pretty much the same apart from that. The bell still didn't work, and the door was still open. I went in.

Sunlight warmed the brilliant white figures I'd seen on my last trip. The late morning light made the Mountie stand all the straighter and the tourist with the camera appear to have been frozen in the act like bodies found at Pompeii frozen in lava. I called out, and heard only the sound of my own feet echoing across the floor. I had just reached the stairs to the balcony, when I heard a car starting up. I ran to the door and saw Alex Bolduc rapidly backing his car away from the studio then heading back to town in a hurry. His face looked as old as his father's.

Upstairs I quickly found the reason for Alex's quick exit. Nathan Geller was lying in a heap on the floor in front of his colour television. A distorted image was running up the screen and reappearing at the bottom again. Geller was lying with his knees bent and his arms wrapped around his stomach. His sleeves were red with blood and his eyes were open in disbelief. I lurched my way to the toilet before covering the telephone with my handkerchief while I dialed for the police.

Chapter Fifteen

Chris Savas was an old friend. From the moment he came into Nathan Geller's studio I started to feel better. It wasn't because the sergeant was considerate of my feelings, far from it. He always gave me a hard time. When he'd finished with me, after a couple of hours of close questioning, barbed sarcasm, and taunting comments on my line of work and personal foibles, I felt I'd been taken to the cleaners and hung up and dried by one of the best. No, it was even better than that. I felt like I'd been put in a crucible and exposed to white heat. There was nothing left but a fine grey ash. As a chemist, Savas was top of the line.

We were sitting in his office at Niagara Regional. Paper cups of coffee with floating corpses of cigarette butts littered his metal desk. The floor had the same rust marks I remembered from last time. The venetian blinds were still dusty and the windows still looked out on the parking lot next to the city's market square. I could see the old court-house with squadrons of wheeling pigeons circling the geranium which was annually planted in the memorial fountain to commemorate something or other.

Pete Staziak had wedged his large form into the doorway a few minutes before to see what stage we were at. He and Savas exchanged looks and Savas broke down and gave me one of his cigarettes for a change. Staziak had briefed Savas about my activities, judging by the bite of his questions. He's taken me over the scene of so many crimes in the last five years that I'm going to get them all into one big mulligan stew of who did what to whom. I looked at the bastard sitting across from me, even as his old partner was examining him from the doorway. I wondered if what we saw was the same man.

Staff Sergeant Chris Savas was a hard man and a good cop. He'd been named after a Cypriot painter and on occasion had tried to show a few friends what Greek cooking and drinking were all about. He had a face like a slab of beef, with eyes that could become as cold as steel ball bearings. He had a voice like the sound cardboard makes when you rasp it across a desk. He also had an instinct for when enough was enough.

"You think young Bolduc did it?"

"Christ, Chris, I told you. He was there when I got there. That's all I said. If I thought you were going to make him the corner-stone of your investigation, I wouldn't have bothered mentioning him. How do you know he didn't stumble into it the way I did? Hell, if I got there and thought I might become a suspect I might think twice about sticking around, especially if I heard somebody driving up and turning his motor off. I think he panicked, that's all."

"Yeah, you could be right, and you could be wrong. You've got a sentimental side, Benny. You always see the roses and never the thorns. When we have the medical report we'll be closer to knowing which of us is right."

"You need anything, Chris?" That was Staziak. Just his way of saying that his shift was ending and that if Chris didn't need him he was going home to his wife Shelley.

"No, we're okay, Pete. See you tomorrow."

"Goodnight, Pete."

"Night."

We listened to Pete's footsteps echo down the corridor and heard him say good-night to somebody else. When that was all over, and it hadn't amounted to much, Chris took a deep breath and let it out with a satisfying noise. It was supposed to divide what we'd just gone through from what was coming. The second part always had more of a human face on it, even if it belonged to Chris Savas.

"You still saving things, Benny?" He continued to stare at a marksmanship trophy over my shoulder.

"I told you what's germane to the best of my knowledge. I haven't burdened you with theories or speculations. I've given you a blow by blow account of my activities since last Wednesday. If I know something that you don't know, I don't know that I know it."

"Don't bother piping that through again, I got wet the first time. Are you going to make a fuss about Bagot and his boys?"

"What's the point? What can you get them on? They didn't try to extort money from me, they didn't hold me for ransom, and in the end I walked away. The best you could get them for would be molesting me. And at my age that sounds disgusting. Besides, I'm sure that they would find witnesses who'd say they were watching a cement-pouring derby or something, and I don't have a single witness. Nope, I'll have to pass on that one. But, I wouldn't mind feeling safe to go back to my room."

"Give it a day," he said, nodding. "I'll appeal to Bagot's better side. But that depends on your keeping your bib clean from now on. If you get rattlesnake poisoning after today, be it on your head for monkeying in this business."

"I hear you."

"I know you hear me. Damn trouble is you aren't listening. And for Christ sake will you take that silly thing off your head."

"Silly...?" I felt my head and pulled off the yarmulka I'd been wearing since I'd visited the synagogue in the morning. I must have been cutting an impressive figure all afternoon. I buried it in my pocket, promising myself, under my breath, to drop it off at the shul when things settled down a little.

"Now, look, Benny, we've been sitting across from each other before. I remember that on these occasions you sometimes forgot to tell me things. You got a little forgetful, and I end up coming along just in time to save you going over Niagara Falls or something. I hate that stuff, Benny. Let's play it my way this time. You empty out your pockets on the whole schmeer and then nobody will need to set you afloat in a barrel. It's simple as pie. Don't get me wrong, I'm not saying I don't believe you when you say you've told me all you know. I know that funny memory of yours too well. What I'm saying is you know my phone number if you remember something."

Savas sucked at his teeth, like he thought that some missing piece would come unstuck from his molars and it would unlock all the sealed doors in this case. I saw the pile of files on the left side of his desk and wondered how often he could put any of these away for keeps. I wondered whether he followed his cases through the court-room phase into the appeal courts and up to the Supreme Court. Did the nuts and bolts of what was happening on the streets today put practical limits on his interest in the cases that had started in his office but had gone on out into the big world of experts and mistakes in charging the jury? He shifted in his chair and turned back to face me. I put paid to my speculations. "As far as I can see this time, Benny, you don't have a chance in hell of getting anywhere on this case. You got no organization. Come on now, you're outclassed on this one."

"Well at least we agree that Nathan's death is related to his brother's disappearance. That's a bond between us."

"I may think that, but I've got to check it all the way around the weather-vane. Who knows, it might be somebody doesn't like statues kept inside where it's warm.

Benny, there are a lot of strange people out there that never kill anybody. Spare a thought for the ones that do."

Before I promised I'd behave myself and not get into deep water without an attendant policeman, Chris told me that I could redeem my Olds from the police parking garage by paying towing and storage on it. I asked him to lend me an envelope, thanked him, then borrowed a piece of paper which I used to wrap around the five hundred dollars I was having trouble living with. Savas looked like I hadn't been listening to him, but I still walked out of the NRP headquarters a free man.

I stood on the broad limestone step, under the shade of a limestone overhang, and looked across at the convent and thought of the girls in black stockings I used to see when I was in high school. Later on at the theatre workshop under Monty Blair or Ned Evans, black stockings were almost the rule. Those convent girls were the first Bohemians in town, even if they never knew it. I addressed and posted the envelope.

"Hey, Mr Cooperman!" I looked over my shoulder. It was Kogan with his blazer buttoned up and looking very spiffy for Kogan. "I'm glad to see you. I just come from viewing the remains. Poor Wally." He wiped his eye with the corner of a polka-dotted bandanna. "Well, he's in a better world I guess. Ain't that right, Mr Cooperman?"

"Well, Kogan, I don't know whether it's right, but it sure would be fair. How come you just got around to identifying your pal today?" Kogan rolled his head instead of answering quickly. "I couldn't be reached," he said. "Hell, I owed it to him. He would have done the same for me and then some."

"I'm sorry for your trouble, Kogan. He was a nice little guy, Wally. I'll miss him."

"Yeah, and he'd just come into money. Like I told Priam this morning, your money's a thief in your pocket. The only way to survive is to stay broke. I tried it both ways and I know."

"Priam who?"

"Priam Phelps. We went to school together. We were on the same football team."

"You're a friend of Magistrate P.B. Phelps?"

"Yeah and I'm the only one left who remembers what the B stands for. Ain't tellin' either. Old Priam didn't know Wally so good, but we had a few nights together, the three of us. Priam's an awful one for the drink sometimes. Only thing'll straighten him up is a nip of Aqua Velva. I'm a drinking man myself, Mr Cooperman, but poor Priam lets himself go to extremes. It's steady family life that does it. It ain't civilized. Hell, if I couldn't take it, then it's a wonder anybody can. Just as hard on the women and kids. I'm no reactionary."

"I didn't say a thing. Where did you and Phelps play football?"

"Cranmer College, across the creek. I never had the weight for the line, but I was fast. Priam was big and heavy even back then. We goin' to stand here all day, Mr Cooperman, or should we walk over to the Harding House?"

"Sure, Kogan. It's hot enough for a beer."

We walked along Church Street to James and then up James to the Harding, where I found my old theatrical friends Ned Evans and his pals Jack Ringer and Will Chapman ensconced with a table of amber glasses in front of them. They hailed me loudly, and pulled us over to the two tables they had spread themselves around.

"Ned, you know Kogan, don't you?" Ned blew air between his teeth and his upper lip to properly evaluate the question.

"Know? Who really knows anybody. You may think you know somebody, and then..." Ned left the phrase hanging in air hoping that one of us would pick it up. Jack and Will didn't do it and neither did Kogan or me.

"Kogan here's just come from identifying his best friend in the morgue."

"God's blessing be upon you," said Ned.

Will, who was slipping out of sight in his chair, replied, crossing himself, "And on all Christian souls, I pray God." They both sounded like they were overdoing it, and they'd climbed into some play script to protect them from something as real as death. I wished I had a page of that script myself.

The room was warm and busy with men wandering towards the john or the potato chips rack. Waiters slid like beefy ballet dancers with their short aprons and full trays between the tables. The air was salty with beer and heavy with opinions. Jack Ringer tugged at Will Chapman and between him and Ned they were able to delay Will's inevitable sliding off his chair. Jack was Ned's uncertain stage manager, who listened to Ned plan a new theatrical production every night in the beverage room at the Harding.

"Oh, he had a good life," said Kogan, redirecting the conversation. In the bidding in the game of life, death is trumps and so the floor was his. A mere projected production of *Henry IV—Part I* couldn't compete. "Yes, a gentle soul," he said drinking the second straight draught since he'd sat down. He had his theme and we were all waiting to hear him expand on it, to eulogize his friend, to erect a monument to him among the emptying glasses. But he didn't. Kogan was no great talker so Ned wrote an end to the chapter to allow the afternoon and the drinking to proceed.

"God be at your table, and there's an end." He banged his fist on the table.

I put down some money and the waiter skirted by, dropping ten glasses and removing the empties. He gave change from his apron without looking and accepted the tip I pushed after him without acknowledgement.

"How did your frien' die?" asked Jack Ringer, who didn't always take his cues from Ned.

"Stabbed with a shiv," said Kogan. "Murdered by person or persons unknown. He was a saint of a man. That's what Wally was. He got shot at Carpiquet airport, but he wouldn't let the dressing station send him back to England. Wound the size of a silver dollar through his shoulder. As fine a blighty as you ever saw, but he wouldn't let them send him down the line. Me, I went right through to the last day without a scratch. I got to be so unlucky nobody'd stand up next to me. Soon as I'd talk to somebody, they was for it. Took Wally longer than most, poor bugger. Poor little bugger." While he was saying this he brought out a small metal badge. He turned it around and around in his hand as he talked.

"A ruptured duck!" Ned said, "An honest-to-goodness ruptured duck!"

"What is?" I asked.

"Thing Kogan's holding. Army discharge pin. That's what the Americans call 'em. I still have mine somewhere, but nobody wears them any more except panhandlers. Funny it should come to that, eh, Benny? Funny. That's what we used to call 'em when we were on the inside wanting out. I never saw anything as beautiful in my life as the one they handed me. Better than the Victoria Cross."

"Poor old bugger," Kogan said.

"They give you that at the police station?" I asked.

"Eh? This? Nope. They wouldn't let me even see his stuff. Just his face on colour TV."

"Then where did you get the duck? Is it yours?"

"Please have a little respect, Mr Cooperman. I'm wearing mine." We all looked and there it was on the lapel of his blazer. Kogan gave Ned a dirty look for what he'd said about panhandlers. "This was Wally's. I'd know it anywhere because of the way it's worn at the bottom. That's from openin' beer bottles. I told Wally that's no way to treat the symbolic tribute of a grateful country, openin' beer bottles, but Wally just laughs and flips off another cap."

"Okay, it's Wally's duck. Where did you get it? Did he leave it where you were staying?"

"Are you kidding? Wally wouldn't go out without it. Even if the safety catch was broken. See." He turned the back of the badge to show the broken catch.

"Kogan, I'm going to bounce a glass off your head if you don't stop splitting hairs and tell me where you found that thing."

"You know I told you where Wally used to work?"

"Yeah, you said on St Andrew Street near the Loftus Building."

"That's right. He worked the front of the Loftus building because..."

"Because the workers coming on and off the job were good marks and so were the carpet workers at Etherington's."

"Marks? I never said that." I picked up my beer with blood in my eye. "Okay, he was usually around there, across from where they're building the new fire hall. Well, I was worried about Wally. I missed the son of a gun. So, I went lookin' for him all around that area. I found it on the fire-hall site. It was right in the dirt. I could of easily missed it, but there it was shinin' up at me like a quarter in the gutter. I got a trained eye, you understand. I knew it was Wally's right away. But what was it doing on a Bolduc building site?"

"That, Kogan," I said, "is the answer to a lot more than you think."

Chapter Sixteen

The authorities refused to release Geller's body to his family, so that it was impossible to hold the funeral until the coroner was finished with his investigation. It gave poor Nathan a chance to cool off before beginning his eternal rest. In most cases a Jewish funeral is over before the body's lost all its heat. Even in a small town like Grantham a paid-up member of the shul can sicken, die and be buried within twenty-four hours. It must be an old-country tradition. Me, I'm not in favour of lying around in state for a week or so, but I guess I'm against an unseemly gallop to the cemetery.

First thing Monday—I won't bore you with my gin rummy games with Martha on the weekend—I collected my car from the police garage. It cost me an arm and half a leg to get it back. I gave the guard a dirty look; he seemed to expect it; then drove to Niagara Regional on Church Street. The desk sergeant told me that Savas was out but that Staziak was in and would see me.

Pete had a file open on his desk when I came in, but he closed it against the temptation of helping out the struggling private sector like I knew he would. I hovered on the threshold for a minute, then we went into the usual song and dance about what he and his wonderful kid did together on the weekend. If Pete was to be believed, his boy was a genius. I hated to admit it, but he was a good chess player. I tried to bring the conversation back to business, but Pete wasn't helping.

"What is this, Pete? Some new policy? It won't break your mother's back to tell me when the bugger died." I tried grinning, but it didn't work. Pete put a pained grin on his face to give it an overworked and I-have-no-time-for-triflers kind of expression.

"What do you want to know for, Benny?" he said rubbing the back of his neck with a big hand. "This is out of your hands now. It's a murder investigation, not just a runaway embezzler. Come on, Benny, you don't want any part of this."

"Look, Pete, I'm part of it whether I like it or not." Pete shifted his bulk in the swivel chair in my direction. I took it as a hopeful sign. I kept talking. "I can't go back to my hotel, I'm even taking a chance driving my old car. Come on, I came up clean when Chris went over me. I'm not keeping half of what I know under my mattress. You know what I know, and you wouldn't have anything in that file if it wasn't for me. Damn it, Pete, you know I'll only find out anyway."

"Okay, okay! Spare me the guilties. I got enough of my own." He opened the flap of the closed beige file and cleared his throat: " 'Medical report on Nathan Geller, deceased of this city...' Most of this is garbage. Did you know he had cancer of the prostate? Did you know that he had been a drug-user? Did you know that his aorta was pierced by a pointed, long, thin blade?"

"Stabbed? No wonder I didn't smell powder." Pete thought that was pretty funny. Let him try unwinding dead arms wrapped around a bleeding body. I couldn't do it. "Now the big question: when did Nathan get him his grievous hurt?"

"That's from Miss Lutman's English class, right? Tennyson?"

"Tell me about Nathan first."

"According to this he died ten or twelve hours before you found him, which was around noon. Both rigor and lividity were present. 'The subject was not moved post mortem.' He died where you found him. What else can I do for you, Benny?"

"Well, I guess I can't ask you what Alex Bolduc was doing at the scene of the crime?"

"That's right. You can skip that one. Privileged information. Next?"

"Okay, let's change the subject. What about Kogan's friend? Is his a more open file, since he isn't a solid citizen?"

"You're working your way through that door, Benny. Don't push too hard. Pimps, pushers and bank presidents go through the same routine around here. It's your only true democracy. We tie the same tags on the big toes of every stiff comes our way. We ain't particular. As for your friend, Wally Moore, he was plain John Doe until Saturday morning. Your other prosperous pal came in and did his duty."

"Yeah, I know about that. He was stabbed? That's what you told me last week."

"Let me find the damn thing." He played with the paper on his desk, lifting up several files and several loose pieces of paper. Pete and I used the same vertical filing system: everything in the same pile in the middle of the desk. Pete had more stuff, that's all, and most of it was recent. My stuff went back for months. "Here it is: 'Bamfylde Moore, a.k.a. Wally Moore, indigent of no fixed address...' He was found on a park bench in Montecello Park near the bandshell. According to the post they did on him, he was killed someplace else and dumped on the bench. Patrol car found him midnight Thursday. When they did the post on Friday morning, he'd been croaked for forty to forty-two hours."

"Just a second! Let me walk that back along my fingers." Pete smiled since he was holding the answer in front of him. "So, Wally was killed around one or two o'clock Wednesday afternoon."

"Looks that way. It's the lividity of the body that says he was moved, and that would have been any time after the first six hours, if you're taking this stuff as holy writ."

"You don't see me arguing with it, do you? What about the wound, Pete?"

"What *about* the wound?"

"Was it similar to the one that killed Nathan Geller?"

"Sweet shit, Benny! You have the tidiest mind in town. What makes you think there's a connection...more than a connection...between the one and the other? You're saying they've a common killer. Come on, Benny, not even you can tie these things together. They're different flavours of people: social, economic, geographic, any way you want to look at them. What possible motive can connect a low-lifer like Wally Moore and a fancy sculptor like Geller. They weren't both pansies or something, were they?"

"It's something Kogan said. He talks a lot of bull most of the time, but he may have been telling the truth for once."

"Well, it won't hurt to get those guys in the morgue to test your theory. A different guy did each of them, so it's not unusual that there wasn't a connection made on the Geller post-mortem. We still have both of the bodies."

I decided to try to make a fast getaway. I had done Pete a favour and it didn't pay to let him thank me for doing it. It was more negotiable the other way. I heard him calling after me but I kept going.

Montecello Park isn't the biggest in town, but it's the most central, the oldest and the best kept. It fills most of the smaller angle where Lake Street meets Ontario. There was a rose garden in the middle of the six- or seven-acre retreat, with a slightly over-the-hill display of pink, red and white blooms climbing their thorny way up the white trellis arches. Over all hung the heavy green branches of the oldest and tallest trees in town. Most of them were maples, but there were a few surviving elms among the oaks and lesser breeds.

Squirrels jumped back and forth in the high branches. Their nests were clots of dark leaves. There were two roofed structures under the trees, both red-topped: a bandstand, looking like a puff pastry with a dome perched on six arches, and a large Victorian pavilion, which Ned Evans used in his summer staging of plays by Shakespeare. He told me that it had been built on the unfinished foundations of the home of the son of the chief canal entrepreneur from the mid-nineteenth century. The son died young and the foundations were eventually used to support this whimsical fretwork structure. Underneath were indifferently serviced rest-rooms which were usually locked except when not needed. I'd been in Ned's production of *A Midsummer Night's Dream*, so this was familiar territory.

I circled the area near the bandstand. The grass was starting to get a high summer sheen. It was damp underfoot. Park benches were occupied by mothers with baby buggies, couples and singles. People were taking time-honoured shortcuts across the park on the wide paths and paved sidewalks. Around one of the park benches signs of the police investigation were still in evidence. A string with waving pieces of masking tape dangling encircled the bench; a fairy ring, twenty feet across. The bench was about the same distance again from Ontario Street. At night it wouldn't have taken two people long to take the body out of a car and leave it to be discovered. And at night you could get away without anyone asking silly questions. I went through the roped-off area and like I expected, didn't find anything. I sat down on the bench to catch my breath. A squirrel came by, wafting its grey tail in the air, another panhandler like poor Wally. And I was fresh out of nuts.

Two heads had been watching me around the corner of the pavilion. At first I thought it was a couple of kids. Whenever I looked up in that direction, I could see either one head or both out of the corner of my eye. Then, I thought that Gordon, Geoff and Len had caught up with me again, but they wouldn't have played such a foxy game of it. I wanted to get a good look at them and it took me a minute to figure out how. I got up, put the bandstand between me and the pavilion and headed towards Ontario Street. I didn't dare turn around to see if they'd followed. Once across Ontario, I crossed the street and sauntered up College Street. As soon as I thought I was out of their sight, I turned on what speed was available, ran to the end of College, cut up Yates, and came back in the direction of the park along Norris. This put me near the Lake Street end of the park with a clear view of the other side of the pavilion.

As I walked towards the pavilion I got my first sight of my quarry walking side by side from the bandstand towards the white lattice arches of the rose garden. One was a bearded beanpole of a man in a navy turtleneck sweater and dark trousers with a tattered denim vest over his shoulders. The other was a short, wide figure with a baseball cap and the flapping remains of someone else's three-piece suit. I'd seen the short fellow before. The beanpole was a stranger. They went on to the corner of the park where Duke Street intersects Lake. That's when I sat down to catch my breath. I didn't have to follow them any further. When I wanted them, I could enlist Kogan's aid. It was about time he gave me more than an inverted headache.

Back on St Andrew Street I scouted for Kogan. He wasn't at his usual Queen Street stand by the *Stop Me and Buy* French-fried potatoes truck and he wasn't resting in the shade of the bank on the other corner. I walked down Queen Street and up to Larry Geller's office. The place was closed. There was a legal notice in the window about the situation. "Would all creditors with legitimate claims please consult Ms Joyce See of Bernstein, Carley, Grella and See..." Nice to be able to put a face to a public notice.

From there I scouted the Harding House, the Russell House, the Murray and even my own hotel, the City House. I felt silly dropping around to my place after being away, but darting in and out was different from sleeping there at night. I'd been awakened from a deep sleep too many times at night in the past. With Martha Tracy's help, for the time being at least, I had things under control. But there was no Kogan to be found, not even loitering in doorways along the shady side of St Andrew Street.

I saw Pia Morley's Audi parked across from the Radio Lunch. I couldn't imagine her trying to tuck her long slender legs under the Arborite counter in there. Maybe she was planning another visit, just to warn me, in case I'd missed the point of her earlier visit and had forgotten all about my trip to the old lodge on the edge of the abandoned canal.

But when I got to the office it was Kogan who was waiting for me, not the attractive Mrs Morley.

"Don't you do no work here any more, Mr Cooperman?"

"I've been trying to neglect it. I've been looking for you though."

"Small world. Great minds and all that."

"Kogan, I want you to do something for me." Kogan looked dubious and I told him about the two characters from the park. I described them and suggested that I wouldn't be surprised if they knew something about Wally Moore's death. He knew the short guy in the baseball cap at once and thought he'd seen the bearded beanpole.

"The short guy's a Hungarian named Blasko. He's decent enough. Don't think I'll have any trouble finding them." He looked at me under the brim of his fedora. "Do you think you can let me have something on account, Mr Cooperman?"

"On account of what?"

"On account of me being an operative in your employ."

"Kogan, you've got more *chutzpah* than six deadbeats in Vegas with somebody else's wallet. Get out of here before I throw you downstairs. Who's Wally Moore in the first place, your friend or mine?"

"Okay, chief, I'm going, I'm going."

Chapter Seventeen

Debbie Geller lived in the biggest house on Francis Street, which was not much of a street apart from her place. It was too close to Welland Avenue's heavy traffic ever to be a posh address, and the rest of the pebble-dash and frame houses with either open or closed-in verandas were closer to the beau ideal of the neighbourhood than Debbie's overgrown Victorian monstrosity. The house sat crookedly on the street as though the street came by after the house had settled. The little bungalows running down the street made a rather smug comment about the proper way for a house to address the street it lived on. Debbie's place was brick with elaborate wood trimming around the gables, porch and windows. On the left side, as I faced it, a tower ran two and a half storeys above the regular roof, looking like an octagonal bell with fancy round windows near the top, a widow's walk and large gabled windows below that. The garden in front was kept from running off by a wrought-iron fence with pagoda-like red stone posts. On the front steps rested a blue plastic pail full of water and a sponge and towel.

I'd just come from Nathan Geller's funeral in the small Jewish cemetery off Queenston Road. It was an orthodox service with the near relatives helping to fill in the grave by taking turns. I made sure I pocketed my borrowed yarmulka as I followed the small crowd back towards the parked cars. I saw my Ma and Pa, but I didn't get a chance to talk to them. Debbie and Ruth stood close together. Sid stood farther away near the rabbi.

It was around three-thirty, still a rather dull Monday, with a chilly wind following from the cemetery as I washed my hands at the pail before going into the house of mourning. Wisely they had decided not to hold the *shiva* at Ruth's. Recent associations would have prevented Nathan getting a fair send-off in that setting. You can't throw stones through the windows on one day and then drop in to partake of the funeral-baked meats the next.

The crowd divided itself into family, arty types from out-of-town, and local friends of the family. The out-of-towners looked a little cowed at a *shiva*, but quickly found that there was plenty to drink. The locals, family and friends alike, descended on the refreshment table and consumed quantities of smoked meat, rye bread, pickles, potato salad, herring, smoked salmon and, for the old-timers, baked carp. A smoked turkey had been sliced and laid out, but I couldn't get close. I saw a couple of hired hands with trays, but I was always too far away. Eating after a funeral is serious business. It's a reaffirmation that the living are still living and the dead are out there beyond the pail and sponge on the porch. A tweedy arm reached under my nose and pulled back with a pickle. When I turned, I saw Pete Staziak taking a bite.

"Where do they get off calling these kosher dills, Benny?"

"You don't see them called that anywhere that knows dills."

"My old aunt makes dills like this and she's as Jewish as your average Cossack." He nibbled farther, advancing on his thumb. "They're good, though, for commercial pickles."

"Why don't you make a pinch so I can get near what's left of the pastrami? I'd do it for you, Pete, honest."

"Trouble with you, Benny, is you're always abusing your gut. I never saw anybody in my life eat as terrible as you do. You want to look after yourself or you're going to get into trouble."

"What are you talking about? I eat in the best restaurants in town. If they don't know their business, what can I do about it?" A short fat man pushed between Pete and me, giving him an unfair time to reflect.

"Look, kid, you always order the same garbage no matter where you eat. I don't think I've ever seen you when I couldn't guess what you was going to order."

"Well, if you mean that I don't order meat..."

"Come on. I know it's not the meat. You eat spaghetti, don't you?"

"Sure, with tomato sauce."

"And no meat in the sauce? Come on, Benny, I don't buy the bit that you only eat kosher. What about that pig-out Savas arranged? There must have been every kind of strange meat on that table you can imagine."

"We can't eat cormorants or owls, you know. They're out."

"Glad to hear it. What about bats?"

"Only the kind with feathers if they have cleft feet and chew their cud."

"Does that mean you can't eat venison? Deer chew their cuds and have cloven hooves."

"Well, you'd have to have a *shochet* who could throw a fast knife, I guess. Can you get near the turkey? Let's move in that general direction."

"Hell, Benny, I'm stuck. I can't move in any direction. It's lucky this coleslaw isn't moving as fast as some of the other stuff."

"Instead of feeding your face, Pete, why don't you tell me what happened when you got them to compare the wound in Wally Moore with the wound in Nathan Geller, may he rest in peace?"

"I'm not feeding my face. I'm trying to look inconspicuous." Pete grabbed at something on a tray. He landed one. I tried at the same time and missed. He stopped chewing long enough to grin at me. "The wounds could have been made by the same weapon. That's all they'll say. They are consistent with having been made by the same size and shape of blade. Make what you will of that."

" 'Consistent' is one of their words."

"Yeah. Forensic people."

"That way they can be expert witnesses and sit on the fence at the same time."

"It's like reasonable doubt, Benny. They only want to say exactly what they know and no more."

"I don't see the connection with reasonable doubt, but never mind. Are you really worried about my health?"

"Naw, it just makes conversation. As long as you're happy, that's what counts. You know most of these people?"

"The ones from town I know. His artistic pals from out-of-town don't light up any bulbs."

"The tall guy with the long hair and beard is from *The New York Times*. Writes on the arts pages of the Sunday edition. I was talking to him and he says that Nathan was very well respected." The man Pete was describing was working on a very stiff drink judging by the deepness of the amber in his glass. He was talking to a large woman with upswept hair and designer bifocals.

"A real loss to the art community," I said.

"The guy from the *Times* said it was a good career move." I heard a high-pitched laugh from across the room. It came from a member of the bereaved family. The *Times* man looked shocked. Sometimes cynicism's not even skin-deep. A row of relatives sitting knee to knee with paper plates full of potato salad and smoked salmon didn't even look up.

I moved through the crowd towards Ruth Geller. She was nibbling at a cocktail frankfurter on a toothpick with some blue cellophane trimming.

"Oh, hello," she said. "I saw you at the cemetery. Did you ever meet my brother-in-law? Oh, yes, he was here last week. I mean at my house."

"I was at the studio too," I said, watching someone trying to slice more meat from the turkey carcass.

"In spite of everything, he was very dear. He cut himself fixing the windows." She dabbed at her right eye with the knuckle of the hand holding the frankfurter. "Are you going to stay for the service?"

"I'm not much good at this sort of thing, but if you're short of the tenth man for a minyan, I'll come back." Ten was the minimum number for a quorum in the holding of group prayers. In fact it was the minimum number for starting up a synagogue.

"But why are you doing this? You're not part of this family? Do you think that one of us will tell where Larry's hiding? Do you think he'll come up from the cellar when nobody's looking?" Ruth was looking for a place to deposit the empty toothpick. I took it from her; the least I could do, and added it to an ashtray with cigarette butts and chewed-up salami skins.

"Thank you, Mr Cooperman," she said, as though I'd just done something important. I guess she was still in a daze. Funerals are hard enough to take when you are unacquainted with the dear departed. "You said you'd seen his studio?"

"I liked what I saw. I'm not surprised that these out-of-town art critics or whatever they are came. Your brother-in-law made powerful figures." I wasn't happy with the way it came out, but I'd promised myself I'd say something along those lines to one of Nathan's relations.

"You called here the other afternoon. I forget what it was you wanted," Ruth said, making conversation.

"I asked you about that call I'd had from Nathan saying he'd heard from your husband. You didn't by any chance talk to Nathan after that call, did you?" She switched her eyes from my face to the view over my shoulder. "We can talk about that some other time," I added.

"I remember now," she said. "Just before Debbie came back. No, I never spoke to Nathan about that call. It was probably like you said: something to put you off the scent."

Debbie was wearing a black dress that both squared off her shoulders and made her look vulnerable. She was busy talking to one of the out-of-towners, with a tall drink in her steady hand. When her eye caught mine, she frowned, as though she never thought that an open society would ever include me standing in her living-room. It was the Welcome Churlish in anybody's register, comparable to saying "How do you do?" while biting down hard on a noisy celery stalk. In cases like this I simply assume it's not me personally who's unwelcome, simply the profession I represent that's unwholesome. I went back to the table and found an opening in front of the corned beef. There was a lot of plate showing through the cold cuts, so I took advantage of the circumstances, making a sandwich which included the possibility that I might not make it to the platter again before it was empty. I'd just taken a bite and had my mouth full when Debbie planted herself in front of me. I chewed my way towards being able to defend myself.

"Mr Cooperman, I won't say I'm glad to see you. I've tried to form the words, but they won't come out. Never mind. This is my first *shiva*, and I hope it's the last."

"Me too. Why did *you* have it instead of Sid or the immediate family?"

"Always working, aren't you?"

"Curiosity's not confined to business hours. I just wondered. You don't have to answer." I bit into a black olive and found it had no taste to it. Debbie was rolling her glass between her long-fingered hands.

"Well, to be honest, Sid as the older brother should have had it at his place, but his place is the apartment that he rents as a convenience. In practice he lives with Pia Morley. Have you met her yet? I should think you'd get along. You know that Sid's mother and father are dead. Over there's a brother of my former father-in-law and next to him are the brother and sister of their mother. Did you imagine that Nathan's death would tempt Larry home for the funeral?"

"The thought flickered in my mind, but it didn't last. I can see why Ruth didn't have it at her place."

"Yes, that would have been something to see. It's not a huge family, and most of it out-of-town and getting on in years. Is that your mother and father talking to my father, the man eating the piece of honeycake?"

"Right. I haven't had any honeycake yet. You have all the traditional things."

"Not my doing at all. You know that at a *shiva* things just arrive. I don't even know who sent most of this stuff. It will be like this all week. Sid's already put on his slippers."

"Isn't that a little awkward for you?"

"Not in the least. He won't actually be staying here. Pia doesn't understand about our ancient customs. She once saw a *mezuza* by somebody's front door and remarked that she thought it was 'cute.' But I've tried to do what I could. I've covered the mirrors. But I hope nobody looks too closely in my fridge. There are some necessities of life that I won't give up. And I'll be damned if I'll cover up the paintings. There are too many of them for one thing, and what a farce that would be considering what poor Nathan was."

"I liked the work I saw in his studio."

"Oh, he was going to be wonderful. I don't want to think about it. Do you think you can get through traffic and get me a Scotch with a little water, Mr Cooperman?" I nodded and tried braving the crowd. She wasn't hard to take, Debbie, when she stopped sniping for a minute. The crowd thinned out as I got farther away from the food table. The bar was nearly deserted.

"Benny, this is a fine way to spend your afternoon!" It was my mother. I hadn't seen her dressed up in a Paris Star suit for many months. One thing about Ma: she always knew when and whether a lady should wear a hat. I never saw her caught out. It must be radar or something. "I mean, Benny, did you even *know* young Nathan?"

"Ma, this week the Gellers' troubles are my troubles. I'm sorry for their loss, and I only had a cup of coffee for breakfast. Have you tried the turkey yet?"

"You go around half starved, Benny."

"What about I come over for dinner tonight?"

"I think your father's got a meeting."

"Well, it'll just be the two of us."

"Benny, have some more of the turkey and I'll see you Friday night as usual. At my age I don't need first-of-the-week surprises. *Guess Who's Coming to Supper* with Sidney Poitier I don't need and you I can wait for."

She disengaged herself from me and began talking to one of the older Gellers. The last I saw of her that afternoon was when I caught a fleeting glimpse of her in a corner conversation with the man from *The New York Times*.

Sid Geller was standing at the makeshift bar. I asked the young man in a white coat and yarmulka to pour a Scotch for Debbie. Sid leaned over to me smiling sadly, "You can walk out of here, Cooperman, and go run up the flagpole at the Collegiate. I don't want to see you standing there gorging yourself, you understand?"

"I wasn't planning to spend the night, Mr Geller. If you'll excuse me, I've got a drink for your former wife." I didn't rub it in about it being her house and not his. I didn't want to find myself rediscovering the world through the ice-bucket. Debbie had the house, Sid had the mortgage, I guessed. I don't think that gave him special privileges. But he had at least seventy pounds on me, and it was his brother we'd just buried, so I shut up and carried the glass back to Debbie.

"You're getting friendly with my ex," she said, nodding her thanks for the drink. "He doesn't often get along that well with people of your sort."

"Well, I'm more than usually cunning for my sort," I said. "When are they holding the minyan?"

"Just before dark. Isn't that the normal thing?" She looked just the least bit confused. "The rabbi's coming to start things off; or so I was told. I don't see him."

"It's not half-past four yet. It won't be dark for hours."

"You're right. I don't know what I was thinking of. This hasn't been one of my best weekends, Mr Cooperman. There were a lot of decisions that had to be made, and I ended up making them."

"What about Sid?"

"My dear ex-husband was unreachable for the first day and then he was inconsolable, which is another way of being out of reach. Oh, Ruth helped, and so did Aunt Hazel in Toronto. But the feeling I'll take to my grave is that I did it all myself."

"It couldn't have come at a worse time," I said. It sounded all right to me, but she shot me a warning with her eyes. I started to back away, but she grabbed my elbow and stopped me. It was a mimed apology, and I let her hang on my arm and lead me over to meet the senior relatives sitting on the treasury bench of this gathering with refilled paper plates balanced on their knees. I met the uncles and aunt. I met Morris Kaufman, Debbie and Ruth's father. I explained twice that I had no connection with medicine or Toronto General Hospital. I wonder if my brother Sam is telephoned in the middle of the night by people wanting their wayward spouses followed. I should wear a medical alert bracelet saying that I'm not Sam under any circumstances.

Before I left, I thought I'd have another shot at Sid. He had been joined by Pia Morley and Glenn Bagot had arrived to bolster Sid's side of the room. They were being eyed by the aunt and the uncles. Bagot looked like he had dressed for the Toronto Stock Exchange, not a *shiva* on Francis Street in Grantham. You couldn't fault an item he was wearing, but it was all wrong, like a surgical mask at a wedding. Bagot got my eye before I reached Sid. Something struck him as mildly amusing.

"Well, Mr Cooperman, the athletic Mr Cooperman. Will you have a drink with me? I think you'll remember Pia?" I bobbed my head twice and watched what the lad in white put in my drink. Another trip in the trunk of a car and I'd be ready for the rubber room for good.

"I don't have any time for you," Sid glowered at me over the rim of his glass. He'd been putting a lot of rye between himself and his grief.

"Oh, Benny's all right," said Bagot. "He won't misbehave in Debbie's house." Pia hadn't said anything. She was wearing flamboyant mourning: black satin, black crepe, black nylons. I wondered if she'd had her Audi painted for the occasion.

"Poor Nate," said Sid. "If Label knew about it, he'd be here. We are brothers after all. He wouldn't care that..." Here he snapped his fingers perhaps more noisily than he'd intended. "...for the consequences. And him," he wasn't pointing at Staziak, "*him*, with the gall to come in here and eat our food."

"Steady on, Sid. He's just going. Aren't you, Mr Cooperman?"

"You have paid all the respects you intend to pay, haven't you, Mr C?" Pia looked very fetching even when adding her vote for rejection. I couldn't do anything but leave after that. I took a look at the newly arrived cold cuts they were standing in front of, and beat my retreat for the door.

The place was still humming with mourners. New ones on the porch weren't of the crowd from the cemetery. They were mourners who disliked funerals. They were washing up on the porch as I tried to remember where I'd left my car.

Chapter Eighteen

The old man was nowhere in sight when I banged on the Bolduc front door. Inside I could hear the professional tones of a TV host cajoling a husband to tell all about the first time he was alone with his wife. A give-away show. Lots of laughs. I banged on the door again, but either the viewer inside was caught up in the program or the set was running unattended. I tried the door: not only wasn't it locked, it opened to a little prodding.

"Alex!" I called, and the studio audience laughed. The living-room was empty, but the velvet cushions looked appreciative and reflected the colour of the TV screen. I called for Alex again, and got no more than an echo in reply. I let myself out the front door and wandered around to the back of the house. A spade was standing up in the garden where the old man had abandoned it. The ribs of the abandoned home-made canoe made the yard look bigger and emptier than on my first visit. I followed the garden hose around to the front of the house, and got back in the car.

Alex was the next person I had to talk to. I might as well wait. I lit a cigarette and checked the glove compartment for something to read. I found a murder mystery I'd been working on for the last nine months: nothing special, but it was good to have something on hand when you couldn't get away to restock on cigarettes, sandwiches and newspapers. In theory I always kept an extra pack of Player's on hand in case I was pinned in the car. In practice I used them up to prevent them going stale. A book was harder to consume in that way, so I'd often gone hungry and smokeless, but this old dog-eared mystery with the stub of a parking ticket serving as a bookmark went on forever.

One of the things I liked about reading mysteries was the way things happened bang-bang-bang one after the other. Nobody in print ever sits around listening to the shadows growing longer. It's like in the movies when the scene where the detective is waiting disolves to the same scene four hours later and there is the hero just as fresh as he was in the last shot. I wish I had a dollar for every hour I've wasted in the front seat of my car waiting for the shot to dissolve.

Old man Bolduc was coming up the street with a pack of beer in each hand. He was moving slowly, with the left foot dragging a little. He slid away a piece of green lattice-work and put the cardboard cartons under the porch. As he moved the lattice-work back into place he looked up and down Nelson Street to see if any of the neighbours were watching. He didn't see me slouched down in my seat.

I gave him five minutes, and then I walked up on the porch and banged again at the screen door. I heard the old man stir and then slowly, maybe even suspiciously, make his way to the front door. "Yes?" he said, keeping the screen closed between us. "You lookin' for Alex? His shif' not finish yet. Come back later, mister."

"Mr Bolduc," I said, and he turned back to look at me with his washed-out blue eyes. "Could I talk to you for a minute?"

"I got nothin' to say about anythin' around here, mister. Alex says you're some kind private police. Whatfor you bodder my son? Alex's a good boy. He no mix up in nothin' crooked. You understan'?"

"Your son's in no trouble, Mr Bolduc." He looked at my face like I'd just said the opposite.

"I think you go 'way from here now. I don' want to talk about bad things Alex get mixed up in. Mister, you come back when Alex is here. Hokay?" I went back to the car and slouched in my seat again wondering what the old man was so frightened about.

An hour later, Alex drove up in a blue Dodge that made my ten-year-old Olds look good. The winters had eaten big helpings from his fenders and the bodywork under the doors. A woman in a dark coat over a white uniform got out from the passenger side and went up into the house. Alex drove the Dodge into the garage and closed the door on half-empty paint cans, a rusty bicycle and a collection of back issues of the *Beacon* for the past ten years. I hailed him from my open window as he crossed the grass to the porch and he came over.

"Benny! Hello. Glad to see you. Will you come in and meet the wife?" He said the words but he wasn't putting much into them. They zipped away over his shoulder like deflating balloons.

"Thanks, Alex, but not today. I was just passing. But I do want to talk to you. You must have been spending some time talking to the cops over the weekend, and I guess you've got me to blame for it. I got there just as you were leaving."

"I thought it was you, but I couldn't be sure. But as far as the cops go, no sweat. I guess it was wrong for me to take off like that. I panicked, that's all."

"Sure," I said, "I've done the same thing in my day." I was beginning to sound like Pete Staziak with a suspect. He can make a suspect feel secure by agreeing with him about everything from poisoning grandpa to burning down City Hall. He's even tried that line on me a couple of times. "Now who hasn't wanted to get the jump on the cops from time to time," he suggested, trying to make it easy for me to spill my guts. But I saw it coming and bit hard on my tongue. Now I was using the same technique.

"They sure do ask a lot of questions, Benny. I even got so I didn't know whether I was telling the truth myself. Everything sounded made up."

"Why did you go to Nathan's?"

"I can't tell, Benny."

"I understand. What did you say when they asked about finding anything at the scene of the crime."

"I just said I didn't, that's all."

"Good. That was the right thing to say. But you could still get into a lot of trouble."

"Why, nobody saw anything. You weren't even there yet. So how come you think you know so much, Benny? I was on my way out when I heard your car."

"When you heard the car, Alex. But you didn't hear me earlier when I came on foot."

"Tell me another, Benny. You can stick-handle better than that."

"Look, Alex, you're a bright character. You know that the cops have determined the time of death and that puts you in the clear. The coroner has made it easy for both of us. The cops aren't going to bother with either one of us. I figure you picked something up at the studio. You've got incriminating evidence that you lifted from the scene. It's highly illegal, but you see it all the time on television. The tube shows us what's right and wrong these days, not the letter of the law. Come on, Alex, I've done the same thing in a good cause. Was it to protect a lady's good name by any chance?" Alex gulped while his Adam's apple shifted like a wary defenceman near his own net.

"Okay, Benny. I'm not trying to get away with anything. But supposing I did find something?"

"If you keep it to yourself, you're likely to end up the way Nathan did. We're both mixed up with people who don't think twice about killing. Look at poor Nathan.

He knew a secret too many, and now look where he is. If you know something, and you want to go on breathing, I'd tell as many people as I could. It's the only guarantee that your breath won't be interfered with." Alex creased his brow as though he imagined that useful thoughts would begin to flow automatically to his brain.

"Suppose I did find something?"

"Then you're as good as dead right now."

"Hell, you're kidding me, Benny. Who'd want to kill me? Why would anybody want to hurt a broken-down hockey player?"

"Somebody's done in a sculptor and a panhandler in this town. Maybe there's no connection, but secrets can be deadly company, Alex." He thought a minute, then went to the porch where he shouted something through the screen door. Returning, he came round to the passenger side and got in.

"Let's drive around the block, Benny." We did that. A couples of times, Alex looked over his shoulder to see if we had won a popularity contest. I didn't see Geoff, Len or Gordon in their car following in the rear-view mirror either.

"What exactly did you tell the cops?" I asked. It seemed a reasonably low-key beginning. I turned into Welland Avenue and headed west. We passed Tarlton Avenue and Albert Street in silence. Somewhere in the block between Woodland and Francis he started opening up.

"I didn't lie to them. I just said I went to see Nathan. When I found him dead, I got scared and left. That's all."

"Why did you say you picked Saturday morning to pay your visit?"

"I told them I was on the company entertainment committee, which is true, and I went to try to talk him into giving a talk at the PPA."

"The what?"

"Paper Producers' Association. It's a joint management-union thing. Arranges Christmas parties and a few cultural events every year."

"Then they asked if you touched anything and you denied laying hands on anything but the doorknob on your way out."

"Something like that. I told them how shocked I was, and then, when I heard you coming, I went out the back way as fast as I could."

"I'd believe you though thousands...Never mind. Now tell me what you took with you." I kept my eye on the street, but I could feel him staring at my profile.

"I never said I took..."

"Alex, this is me, Benny, you're talking to. Remember what I told you about secrets."

"Well, I..."

"Just tell me what you took and why you took it. I don't need names. Not at this point."

"Okay. I got a call Saturday morning from a friend of mine. This friend told me that Nathan was dead and that...this friend had left something with initials on it at the scene of the crime."

"This must be some friend for you to stick your neck out like that for her."

"I didn't say it was a woman."

"You didn't but all those 'shes' you avoided told me plain enough. Besides, I can't see you going back to cover for a guy. It had to be a woman. What was the object? The one with the initials?"

"It was a lighter. Fancy job. Easily traced, she said."

"How do you know your friend didn't ice Nathan herself?"

I felt that look again on the side of my face as I pulled up to the stoplight at Welland Avenue and Ontario. I turned and he suddenly found the white house on the corner, where the rabbi used to live, much more interesting.

"How do you know anything, Benny? You just think you know people, that's all. People don't change when you've known them, just because other things change." He was now looking along towards the Hôtel Dieu Hospital, and added, "My mother died in there. Three years ago. My old man's drinking had a lot to do with it." He was moving away from the target area. Is it something about cars that makes people ramble in their thoughts? I thought about that myself for a few blocks, sparing a moment to Wally Moore as I passed Montecello Park.

"You knew Pia Morley pretty well. Do you think she's changed much?" I thought I'd slid her name into the conversation with skill, but Alex's head spun around like I'd pulled out a fingernail.

"Huh? Pia? She doesn't have anything... You don't think I've been talking about...? Benny, she doesn't know anything about this business. Keep her name out of this."

"I told you I'm not interested in names yet. I meant it. But she does own an initialled Dunhill. Probably just coincidence. Doesn't matter. When did this unnamed female friend call you?"

"Saturday morning. As soon as she told me, I got dressed and picked it up. It was on the coffee-table. I didn't like to leave...Nathan like that. But I could see there wasn't anything I could do."

"You returned the lighter?"

"Yeah. Must have been nearly noon."

"Did she explain herself?"

"Didn't want to talk about it. She thanked me and said she'd call me in a few days. That's the truth, Benny, I just acted as a messenger boy."

"For auld lang syne, right?"

"Yeah. For auld lang syne."

"One more thing, Alex. Why is your father frightened?"

"What do you mean? I haven't noticed..." He broke off like he's just discovered he was talking to himself. His expression shifted and he changed the chewing rate of his jaw on a wad of Spearmint. "Come to think of it, he has been acting strange. And jumpy, like the last thirty seconds in the penalty box. I wonder what's got into him."

"Could it have anything to do with Pia?"

"Naw. He didn't like me running around with her years ago, but he took that out on me not her. He always liked her. He's got good taste, the old man." Alex smiled at me and we started in talking old times again. He remembered the time I played the guard in *The Valiant*, a one-act play in which I said "Yes, sir" seven or eight times and then went offstage to be ready for my curtain call.

After I dropped Alex, I returned to Martha's house in the west end. On the way I bought a dozen eggs at Carrol's grocery store and a few other things including Martha's favourite brand of instant coffee. She was nowhere in sight when I plunked the two bags of groceries on the counter. I washed out a few dishes and dried them while my eggs bubbled on the stove. I found the toaster and was nearly in business when Martha came in the door with bundles of her own.

"Okay, I always knew you could boil eggs, how are you at making a martini?" She told me what to do, and didn't complain when she tasted my maiden effort. "I usually make a whole jar of them and keep 'em in the freezer. If they freeze, I know I used too much vermouth."

I made two sandwiches, toasted on white, and washed them down with coffee. I stayed away from the martinis. In fact, I didn't really need to eat at all, I was still stuffed from Nathan Geller's funeral.

When I'd cleaned up the kitchen, including Martha's discarded coffee mug from the morning and her ashtrays, I went into the bedroom to change out of my good suit. I wore it for funerals and weddings. For bar mitzvahs I had developed a more informal approach. I intended to make a fast visit to my office to see whether anything negotiable had come through the letter slot since I'd last looked. But as I was cruising with the one-way traffic on St Andrew Street prospecting for a parking spot under a street light, I saw a familiar shape walking along the sidewalk in the same direction as the cars. I was having trouble finding a parking spot anyway, so I didn't mind the distraction. I think I'd done away with the notion of parking behind my office. Too many dark places and long shadows back there. And there was the alley to negotiate coming and going. No, better to stick with old Luc Bolduc ambling along the south side of the street with a small case of beer in his hand. The light turned red against me so I stopped and watched him move east up St Andrew.

When the light changed, he was passing the Capitol Theatre. I crept along at less than fifteen miles an hour until the car behind me honked. I let him by and turned down Chestnut Street. I pulled over next to a union headquarters, turned off my lights and locked the car. Bolduc was still in sight when I regained St Andrew Street on foot. I stayed well to his rear, wondering whether this was one of the cases he had hidden under the front porch of his house on Nelson Street, or whether this was a second lot to be used for some other purpose. He walked past the Presbyterian church and the Lincoln Theatre and continued along towards the point where St Andrew ends abruptly by sending out three streets like branches from the main trunk. Queenston continued the curve along the canal, while Geneva and Niagara started off in two straight lines that would both finally stop at Lake Ontario.

Between Geneva and Niagara, not far from Etherington's Carpet Works, lay the site of the new fire hall. It was a triangular piece of land surrounded by a green wooden fence. On the Geneva Street side there was a high gate, hinged on a stout post that rose high enough to attach a wire which supported the swinging end. Bolduc walked directly to the gate and fitted a key into the lock in the chain that held the gate closed. He slipped through, closed the gate again, but did not reattach the chain. As soon as he was out of sight, I crossed the street and approached the gate.

There was one street light near the entrance, and from this bright spot, the shadows began. I crept through the space between the fence and the gate without either moving the gate or even sucking in my breath. Inside I was in the lee of the light. Only the unshaded light bulb now burning in the construction hut competed with the shadows of scaffold and fence.

To an architect or an engineer, a building site has a logic and a geography to it that make sense, but to me it just looked sloppy. I recognized the construction hut on the ground level and the ramp that led down a steep grade to the bottom of the excavation. Here and there stakes were planted with the tops painted red. In one place the stakes even had string running between them. It was loose and looked about to be blown away. Would that matter? I didn't know. From where I stood looking down I could see a little more logic showing. On the right were wooden forms filled with metal rods waiting for the cement trucks to arrive in the morning. Next to these stood several footings with the wooden forms still intact, but with hardening cement oozing through cracks in the wood. Beside these stood columns rising from the footings that had been poured some time ago. Here the wooden frames had been removed, and on the cement, when the available light hit the curved surface at an oblique angle, I could see the grain of the wooden frames etched into the cement surface.

With a light burning in the hut, I felt free to move about. I knew that if Bolduc was inside the hut he was concentrating on his beer, and the light in the shack would turn everything out here into blackness. I worked my way down the mud ramp and came to the bottom of the excavation. Here I got a new perspective on the footings I'd been looking at. I mean, if you're walking around at night in an excavation, what are you going to look at? I must have been thinking about that, or about some other deep thought, when I blundered into a stack of steel rods. They seemed to jump out at me. In changing directions, I hit a wheelbarrow and it fell over on me, emptying itself of some noisy pieces of metal. I cursed under my breath, and ran through a puddle down one of the unused footing frames.

"Hey, down dere! Wally? Is dat you? I got a beer for you, you old son-uh-ma-gun." Bolduc shouted down the ramp and sent his flashlight beam into the shadows where his voice melted. "Son-uh-ma-bitch, Wally, it's me. Don't be scare." He was coming down the ramp. I pressed myself as close to the curved piece of wood as I could. My wet foot felt almost chilly, as Bolduc came closer.

I hadn't tried to imagine what Wally Moore had been doing down in the excavation the night he lost his discharge pin. Was he sleeping off some Old Sailor close to my hiding place? Did he have some nook that he preferred? As I looked around the end of the frame, I could see where Bolduc's light was picking out muddy cement-truck tire marks, piles of lumber and pipe, my overturned wheelbarrow. He made his way directly to a spot where a canvas tarpaulin was stretched between two piles of lumber. His light picked out some old clothes, pieces of blanket and newspaper. It looked like a downy kip from where I was watching. Except in the worst of the winter, Wally could have made himself comfortable. He didn't have exacting requirements as far as I'd heard.

"Well, bugger you, Wally. I'll drink de beer my own self." Bolduc turned and began making his way back up to the ramp. The street light poked bright fingers through holes in the fence, and the moon could be seen looking up out of a puddle and shining on idle machinery, oxyacetylene tanks, power generators and stacked piles of picks and shovels. The place already smelled like an underground parking garage. Bolduc's feet shuffled in his dirty yellow boots. Then he stopped. I looked out again to see why. Bolduc was shining his light at one of the new cement footings. The light hit the curved surface just above his head. He slowly approached the column like the column might back away or run off if he came on too fast. He kept the light on the same place. "Son-uh-ma-bitch!" Bolduc said, and dropped his flashlight in the mud.

For a moment, I couldn't see what was going on. The fallen flashlight pointed straight at my hiding place. When I next dared to look out, Bolduc was dragging a wheelbarrow over to the footing. Back near the base of the ramp he uncovered a long shallow trough. The tarp made a slapping sound as he flicked it back. Then, muttering just audibly, he took a spadeful of the cement from the trough and applied it to the footing while standing in the wheelbarrow. With a plasterer's skill he smoothed off the new cement on the old, so that the added part blended in as well as possible with the lighter dried concrete. When he had finished, he stepped out of the wheelbarrow and surveyed his handiwork. He returned the spade to a pile of tools, re-covered the cement trough, and retreated back up the ramp, still grumbling to himself. I heard the door of the construction hut open and close before I dared come out of hiding. Before I did, I listened to the distant sounds of traffic and the snapping of plastic sheeting in the wind somewhere above me. Water was dripping behind me. They were the sounds you only hear when it's quiet.

I crept out of hiding. Bolduc was still inside. Occasionally I'd hear him banging around up there. I went over to the column that he had been working on. Except for his bit of redecorating, it looked like the rest of the columns rising from the footings. I found a stick and began to clean off the newly applied cement. What was Bolduc up to, I wondered. Was he trying to hide cracks in the structure before an inspector catches them? I couldn't guess, and further speculation was stopped when I literally got an eyeful of fresh cement. I dabbed at it with a moderately clean handkerchief until the tears stopped. It took about two minutes to clean off the cement. When it became fairly clean, I polished the surface with an old vest found in the pile of rough bedding in Wally's nest. It did the job all right, but I wasn't in a position to see what was to be seen. The light available didn't tell me more than the fact that there was no gross or obvious flaw in the column. I lit a match and cupped it in my hands. The brightness nearly made me fall off the wheelbarrow, but I held on to my balance and the match. I ran the light up and down the darkened wet portion of the surface. At first I saw nothing. Then I found a square darker area about a half inch on all four sides. There was a pattern in the centre. I rubbed the square with my fingers until the match burned down to my fingernail. The second match showed that the square I was looking at was red, that in fact it was a gem stone, a polished gem, probably a ruby. While I was trying to understand how a ruby, a ruby with some regular marking on it, had found its way into a cement column, I could see two more things which answered my question and made me forget about the match burning dangerously close to my fingers. The ruby in the column was set in a ring and the ring was worn on a finger.

Chapter Nineteen

I climbed slowly out of the wheelbarrow, my head a little light on my neck. Somewhere in my brain I was going through the words to that old campfire song "The head-bone's connected to the neck-bone, the neck-bone's connected to the shoulder-bone..." Whoever it was, he was in that column. All of him, part of him. I didn't want to think about it.

From the construction hut, I could hear Bolduc crashing around. Somehow I didn't care whether he heard me any more. I had some questions for him that were forming in my head. I climbed the ramp.

Back on ground level, the increase in light at first startled me. The night sky was looking magenta behind the dark silhouettes of the scaffolding and surrounding fence. Far away I could hear the thud-thud-thud of drop-hammers in the steel plant several miles away. I could smell the paper-mill on the night air. Was Alex Bolduc working his shift? Was he worried about being involved in Nathan's death more than he indicated?

I crept over to the side of the shed and looked through the window. Inside, on his hands and knees, Bolduc was putting his case of beer through a hole in the shed's floor. It was a good hiding place, and judging from his motions alone I could see it was one that he'd used many times. The hole was slightly larger than the case of beer, and hidden under a work-counter against the far wall.

Once the beer was beneath the floor, he moved a heavy tool box over the hole. Normally, when the tools were needed, the box could be pulled directly out from under the counter, still masking Bolduc's secret.

A high beam of light caught the corner of the construction hut; I got out of sight as a dark Cadillac drove to the gate and stopped its engine. I heard the rattle of chain and a moment later, footsteps. I peered around the corner carefully and saw Sid Geller about to enter the shed.

Once more at the window, I could see Bolduc smiling, still on his knees but quickly getting to his feet. They shook hands. I wanted to hear what they were saying, but I couldn't. Was Bolduc about to report on what he knew about the column down in the excavation? It would make sense, but there was no way of telling until it happened. I watched their expressions. Bolduc had said something about Nathan's death. Sid nodded heavily acknowledging the greatness of the loss. That seemed right. But Sid wasn't there to exchange chit-chat. He didn't seem to be dipping into family memories of the good old days. He was soon on his hands and knees, pulling out the case of beer from under the box where Bolduc had hidden it a few minutes earlier. Sid was on his feet now and he was not friendly. He was shouting at the old man. I could hear the force of his tirade through the window without being able to make out separate words. I decided not to be backward about coming forward. At least that way I'd get to hear what was going on. I came around to the door of the shed. "Anybody home?" I shouted in an innocent voice. Both men looked around. Sid's right hand remained stuck in the air in the midst of a gesture as he turned.

"Who the hell is that? Is that you, Cooperman? That's all I need." Bolduc was forgotten for a moment while Sid's heavy eyebrows met in a frown that had nothing to do with Bolduc's beer consumption. "What brings you out at this time of night? You following me or something?" Luc Bolduc looked relieved by my timing and let a half-grin slide across his face as he stepped past his boss to the door and waved a flashlight at the two of us by way of explanation: urgent business on the site. Sid didn't pay any attention as the old man left. He motioned me to a nail keg and I sat down. He moved his compact no-neck frame into a battered swivel chair with yellow foam rubber sticking out of the seat. Instead of answering him, I flashed my Player's and he shook his head. I lit one for myself and stared at the clean black shoes of my host. Sid Geller took one of his own home-made-looking cigarettes from a pocket, and tapped it against the top of a messy desk to tamp down the tobacco. Once lit, he didn't bother taking the cigarette from his lips to get rid of the ash, he simply blew out of the corner of his mouth until the ash vanished.

"I haven't been following you," I admitted rather lamely, and added "I haven't been following anybody," as though that made me an innocent man. I'd been wrong about my interruption; it hadn't got me closer to the action, it'd stopped it. Now I was into something else. Whether I could turn it to account remained to be seen.

"Cooperman, you're an oddball. I can't get a make on you. Whenever I look around, you're underfoot. It's only because I got a lot of respect for Rabbi Meltzer that I give you the time of day." He was looking at me like I was expected to explain myself in a topic sentence and a tight paragraph. I just shrugged.

"You're visiting the fire-hall site pretty late to see much activity," I said. Geller pulled at his earlobe and thought for a moment.

"For what it's worth, I'm just checking up on the old man. He's alcoholic and he's been hitting the booze again."

"You feel responsible?"

"Hell, no! I paid to have him dried out half a dozen times. I'm not his goddamned keeper."

"But you've known him for a long time."

"Yeah, too long. Luc was with me at the very start. Showed me the ropes. But it's been downhill for him for the last fifteen years."

"I heard he was dry."

"Yeah, I thought so too. He knows what I told him would happen if I caught him drinking himself silly again. He thinks he's got some God-given right to make me feel guilty about not making him a partner. Somewhere in that thick skull, he's got the idea that I cheated him. I don't know where he gets the idea. It's not from Alex. He knows the score."

"Is he disappointed that Alex didn't make more of himself?" Sid looked at the rolled blueprints standing up in a metal-topped cardboard bin.

"Why would he be disappointed in Alex? Alex was one of the fastest juniors in the league. He's a good kid. Hell, I wish I had a kid like that. Alex is all right. I see what you mean, though. He's not a world-beater these last few years."

"Did the old man have ambitions for him?"

"Look, I've known Luc for twenty years, and I'll be damned if I know what's going on in that head of his. He knows that for all the noise I make about his drinking and wandering off the job, I'll never really let him go. He's part of all this. Hell, the yard wouldn't be the same without him. He's part of me and my life. It's his name, for God's sake. What am I going to do about it?" I shrugged, which was the expected answer.

"Do you know what set him off this last time?"

"No more than I know why it didn't rain today. You can't tell with him. And he knows that he's got more than his job to worry about. He's got health problems. It's going to kill him if he doesn't stop." I didn't say anything. I was trying to add up what Sid was saying and match it with what I already knew. Sid noticed the pause and filled it. "Look, Cooperman, I'm sorry about this

afternoon. I was edgy after the funeral. If I said anything
...I'm sorry. You rub my girl-friend the wrong way. But
Ruth told me you'd been a help to her." He cocked his
head to one side awkwardly and smiled. "I'm not the
most sensitive guy around, you know what I mean? I
call a lot of shots in a day, and I don't call them all right.
I know you got your job to do, and I guess it's dirty
work. Ruth and Debbie say you haven't been making a
pest of yourself. And I'm glad you came to the funeral."
He looked at the floor and over at Bolduc's cache of
beer. "You want a beer?"

"No thanks."

"Come on, split one with you." He reached for the
beer and brought out two bottles. He used one to pry off
the cap of the other. He handed me the frothing open
bottle and returned the other.

It was quiet in the hut, sipping from the bottle and
passing it back and forth. Sid Geller wiped off his mouth
with a run of knuckles after each sip. He didn't bother to
clean the rim of the beer bottle with his hand. "I've enjoyed talking to your friend, Pia, this last week," I said
to Sid Geller. It seemed a good idea; the sort of talk for a
construction shed. "You're a lucky guy." Geller closed
his eyes and lowered his head slowly shaking it from
side to side.

"She's a pain in the neck half the time, but the rest of
the time it's...I don't even know how to describe it, it's
so good." He looked at me with the broadest grin I'd
seen on him since I walked in on him four days ago.

"You're a lucky guy," I repeated, trying to put on a
look that would inspire confidence. I didn't know what
Pia could tell me about the missing Larry Geller, but I
didn't think I'd mind hearing about Pia Morley even if it
had nothing at all to do with the case.

"She's got the loudest laugh of anybody I know, and I
know some wild types. She can handle all of them. Buck
Corelli takes bottle caps off with his teeth, but for her

he's running out and buying pantyhose 'cause she's got a run in the pair she's wearing. Hell, she can drink any three men under the table."

"She get that from her last husband? Glenn Bagot?" Sid took the bottle between his thumb and forefinger and finished it off. He reached into Luc Bolduc's carton and fished out another. He had the top off before I could lodge a protest with my embassy and he gave me first swig. You can't be fairer than that. I took a sip and passed the beer to him. He gulped down a third of what was left. He looked like he was trying to let the answer to my question bubble up to the surface.

"Glenn's got a lot of class, but he's a prissy son of a bitch. He doesn't like you. I'll tell you that for nothing. He gets his guts from his family connections. I mean he'll go anywhere, walk into board meetings, visit cabinet ministers without writing or phoning." He paused for the length of a thought, then added, "She's a lot like that. Nothing scares her. I saw her light into a guy on her street once for hitting his own kid. Now I got a lot of brass, but I probably would have kept on going. She's got the right stuff. With Glenn, now, he's more a back-stairs type. He gets in there, if you know what I mean, but he doesn't make as much noise doing it as Pia does."

"She sounds like she would get along with Tony Pritchett." I threw in the name Alex Bolduc had mentioned to see what would happen. I'd already been thrown out of a house by Sid. This might be my chance to get thrown out of a shed.

"Pritchett? We both keep as far away from him as we can. He may be trying to look like a modern business-man these days, but he's got some nasty habits that die hard. I wouldn't want to bump into him or his boys after dark."

"Yeah, Gordon and Geoff can cut up rough when they want to."

"Sure, and they're the tame ones. No, we steer clear of that bunch. I got enough problems just coping with the games City Hall thinks up for me. Look at those plans up there on the table. It took weeks to get each of those signatures. Nobody'll just let me get on with the projects. That's the only thing I'm good at."

"How well known is it that you and Glenn Bagot have put in a bid on that Niagara-on-the-Lake highway project?"

"Nobody knows about that, Cooperman. You don't and I don't. It's up to Queen's Park in Toronto. I'm holding my breath until I hear who's been awarded the contract. I think we made the best offer, but you never know. This stuff about my brother Label isn't helping. Believe me it isn't helping."

"But this isn't your first government contract? There've been others."

"Sure. But that was small-time stuff compared to this. A lot of those jobs were so small they didn't even ask for tenders. We got them because we were closest and didn't have to learn how to read blueprints." Sid was quiet for a minute, looking at me like he was trying to read my thoughts. Then he changed the subject. "I wonder where the son of a bitch went?"

"Nathan said he was down in Daytona Beach."

"Not *him*. I mean Luc. You think he was drunk when he left?"

"He looked like he could take care of himself. What was he doing here anyway?"

"He promised me he was through with booze, so I told him to keep an eye on our sites here in town. He does his rounds like a watchman. It takes him hours to do it, because he doesn't drive a car any more."

I began to get the feeling that as I was running out of questions, Sid Geller was beginning to think of some, like how did I happen to pay this social call at this time of night. I declined his offer of a third beer, and I got up

and brushed myself off. We made our courteous farewells and I headed back towards my car. Waiting for me
under my windshield-wiper was a bright yellow parking
ticket.

As I got into the car and started it up, I thought, when
I considered what might be waiting for me, I wasn't so
unlucky after all. Sure, I had returned five hundred dollars of Glenn Bagot's money. It might have distracted
me from the affairs of the Geller family. I was even saved
from searching titles for properties along the right-of-
way of the new highway. Maybe I should be getting into
the act and begin to look out for my old age. Information about that right-of-way must be worth something
on the Rialto. I thought about that as I drove along
Geneva to Church and then down Church as far as Ontario Street. With me thoughts like that don't get very
far. I have an instinct about making money that keeps
me poor. It goes against the grain of my nature even to
seek out the gas stations where there's a gas war going
on. I can't remember saving a nickel on a coupon or
taking advantage of a once-in-a-lifetime money-saving
ground-floor offer in the tons of junk mail I get every
day. If I wasn't going to take on a deal where I could get,
at a fraction of the cost in stores, a genuine reproduction
of a Shaker night-table, how was I going to get involved
speculating in farm property. I sometimes think you have
to have brains to be a crook. In my line of work, I just
get by on what I have.

Coming around the corner of Montecello Park for the
second time in not so many hours, I saw three familiar
faces and what went with them sitting on a park bench
not far from the bandstand. It was dark, but I was sure
of the faces. I made an illegal U-turn and parked the
Olds. I got out and started walking towards the bench.
The two bums, Blasko and his gangling friend, took off
when they heard me. Luc Bolduc slumped down on the
bench.

"Mr Bolduc, are you all right?"

"Eh? All right? Sure I'm all right. Havin' little talk dat's all. Breakin' no law I know, mister." He said this trying to straighten up and open one or other of his eyes. He got the left one to open half-way and then both eyes were looking at me, watery, washed out, but wide awake. "Oh, it's you. I got nothin' to say to you and dat's fer sure."

"Come on. I'll give you a lift the rest of the way home."

"Some udder time. I don't trust nobody. Wanna stay alive, me."

"I was just talking to Mr Geller. He's mad at you for drinking. But he's had a few of your beers and he's not so hot at you any more. I'm not hot at you at all. If you want the lift, the car's leaving." I started back to the Olds, hoping that he'd follow. I didn't have a plan for what I'd do if his independence was made of sterner stuff than I was prepared for. For a long time, I heard nothing coming from behind me. I had my hand on the door when he called out: "Okay, hey, you wid the Oldsmobile. You'll drive me to Nelson Street?"

I got in on my side and leaned over to unlock the door on the passenger's side. I tried to remember who was the last passenger I'd had in the car. I sometimes go for months without unlocking that door. Then I remembered that it was Alex, Luc's own son.

Luc Bolduc got in and sat as close to the door as he could. I felt like I was driving home my brother's babysitter instead of an old goat who was my father's age. "You take me straight to Nelson Street, hokay?" I nodded as I again passed the intersection of Ontario and Welland. I headed north out of the area of old mansions turned into doctors' offices to the industrial north end.

"Were your friends telling you the bad news?" I asked.

"What kind bad news? I don't need no more bad news. First Mr Sid's one brother goes away, den his udder brother gets hisself killed. That's too much for one small town."

"And they told you about the panhandler? Wally? From the building site?"

"Oh, dat's what dat was hall about. Dey say somebody get stab. I been drinkin' too much, me. Found him in the park. Dat's bad business. I don' like."

"Mr Bolduc, I had a long talk with Alex earlier. He's worried about you."

"Me? Whyfor should he worry 'bout me?"

"Because you're frightened of something. What is it?"

"I'm not scare of anyt'ing. What you mean, mister?"

"I can tell when a man is frightened, Mr Bolduc. And you are a frightened man. You're worried about Alex..."

"Sure, dat's hit. I'm worry about Alex." He looked a little relieved. But I spoiled it.

"...but I know that's not all you've got on your mind. I was telling Alex a little while ago that secrets can make deadly company. Look what happened to your friend, Wally. He knew a secret and now he's going to keep it until the dead shall be raised incorruptible." I was running away with myself. I think I heard the words on an LP somewhere, something with music, but I could see they were shaking old Luc up a bit. That or the booze.

"Wally saw something happen, he kept it to himself, now he's dead. You saw something happen. You know something about the footings in that excavation. Don't deny it. I know you know there's something in the cement that shouldn't be there."

"Stop the car! I gotta walk! I gotta t'ink!" I did what I was told both because I was told and also because we had arrived in front of Alex's small bungalow on Nelson Street.

"Here we are," I said, leaning across to open the door for the old man. But he just sat there, like I'd clubbed him with a gunny sack of wet sand.

He didn't speak for a long time. Finally he looked across at me and in an almost childish voice he asked, "You know about dis t'ing too, mister?" I nodded slowly. Again he didn't speak for a minute. Finally: "Alex not do this. I know he not do this."

"I believe you, Mr Bolduc. But you must tell me why you think people might think Alex did this bad thing."

"Because on the phone I hear him talk to a very bad man. I know dis man for many years. And I know he only trouble for my family."

"And you heard Alex talking to this man?" Now it was Bolduc's turn to nod. And I nodded my understanding. And we sat for a long moment.

"Is this man Tony Pritchett, Mr Bolduc? The one who talked to your boy?"

There were tears in the old man's eyes, when he raised his face to look at mine. "Yes," he said. "That is the man."

Chapter Twenty

I felt silly eating Martha's toast and jam the following morning. What was I afraid of? Wasn't I drinking beer with Pia's boy-friend last night? What did I have to fear from Pia's other friends? Then I remembered the ride in the trunk of that car. Martha had a good assortment of jams and marmalades. We had exchanged a silent greeting an hour ago when she stepped out of the bathroom, leaving the mirror steamed up and loose dental floss in the hairbrush. I didn't mention any of these things, but I began to ruminate about them as I got a slap in the face from the errant leg of a pair of pantyhose thrown over the shower-curtain rod. I had a brisk shower and felt the better for it. By the time I came out of the bathroom, Martha was on her way to work.

I put myself together, even got rid of some of the mud on my shoes, and drove to the office. I still had a feeling that using my regular parking place was a mistake, so I pulled into the lot next to the Diana Sweets, paid for a day's parking, and went into the Di and ordered coffee. I didn't know the crowd at the counter here as well as the gang at the United Cigar Store. It was half the legal profession in town on their way to or from the court-house. Ray Thornton smiled at me from the other end of the counter. I hadn't seen him since that business in Algonquin Park was cleared up last year. The smile told me we were still speaking to one another. That was the first good news of the day. I was thinking of moving my coffee down to see if he had any legitimate work to throw my way, when Joyce See pushed a cup to the spot next to me.

"Hi, there. Good-morning." She looked fresh and trim, ready to do battle with crown grants, easements, and bars of dower rights down at the Registry Office.

"Good-morning," I said, trying to think of a dozen things I'd forgotten to ask her at our last meeting. She settled in beside me resting a large briefcase next to her feet. She was wearing light leather sandals.

"Is this all you eat for breakfast? You're courting an early grave, Mr Cooperman."

"Please. Call me Benny. But don't you start on my eating habits, Joyce. I got a lecture from Grantham's finest yesterday."

"I didn't mean to be rude, Benny."

"I know. Don't worry about it. I take my not taking food seriously seriously. I had toast and jam before I came downtown."

"I jumped to a conclusion. I'll make a bad trial lawyer at this rate."

"Is that what you want to be?"

"Naturally. Conveyancing properties will make an old woman of me if I keep at it. There's more fun in law than you find in the Registry Office."

"I want to thank you for the information you gave me on Friday. It helped."

"Good. I hope you find him."

"Thanks. Joyce, what kind of check is there on what the provincial government spends on, say, highways and other public works?" Joyce took a sip of her tea then set the cup down in the saucer before she spoke.

"You must be thinking of the Public Accounts Committee of the legislature. Is that what you mean?"

"I don't know yet. Keep going."

"The committee plays watchdog on all government spending. Makes sure that there are no crooked deals and that everything is both fair and looks fair on paper."

"And is that how it works? No corruption in high places?"

"Less than some high places I could name. But the committee operates under rigid guidelines, which are well known. So that a government department, knowing that contracts above a certain amount have to be put up for tendered bids, sometimes divides the contracts up into smaller separate contracts and that way avoids the committee altogether."

"You mean they pass on small contracts without looking at them?"

"Oh, no. But they are looking for different things. You still can't let your brother-in-law have a contract and not hear about it. If you're found out, it hurts you, it hurts the party, and everybody remembers at election time."

"I see." I'd finished my coffee, and I could see that Joyce had put down her tea for the last time. "Thanks, Joyce. I'm beginning to understand things."

"I should start charging you," she said with a smile as she got up and hefted her briefcase.

"Just think of yourself as part of my vast network of operatives."

"Will that pay the rent?" she asked as she turned to leave.

Ten minutes later I'd climbed up the twenty-eight steps leading to my office. The toilet was running as usual. Frank Bushmill's waiting-room was filling up, and Kogan was waiting for me in front of my locked office door.

"No wonder you can't afford me on your payroll. You can't call these office hours?"

"Kogan, you're breaking my back. Cut out the cracks."

"I just came to report, chief." If he'd saluted, I would have thrown him downstairs. Instead he looked earnest while I opened the office door and collected the morning mail from the floor. Nothing of interest except the bills my past is measured in. I threw the junk into a pile of older junk and sat down. Kogan sat in the client's chair, pinching the imaginary creases in his trousers as usual as he settled.

"Well," I asked, "what have you got?" Kogan leaned over towards me.

"I found that guy Blasko I was telling you about. The Hungarian."

"Yeah, I remember. They were in the park."

"The other's named Frank Secker. The tall one with the beard."

"And what did they have to say for themselves?"

"Nothing. They wouldn't say nothing to start with."

"Come to the bottom line. Forget the subtotals."

"Well, after I went back a second time, and told them how Wally was my buddy and how we went through the war together and all..."

"What did they admit finally, Kogan?"

"Blasko wouldn't admit anything. He..."

"And Secker?"

"Finally, he admitted that he and Blasko had moved the body outside so that the cops would find it."

"Outside? Where did they find it?"

"It was in the cellar under the pavilion in Montecello Park. They went in to kip and they found Wally. At first they ignored him, but when he was still lying there when they came back the next night, they found they couldn't wake him up. They were afraid to get involved with the police, so they waited until around eleven then carried him to the bench where he was found."

"Cops were on the job. They found him an hour later."

"Probably thought he was sleeping."

"You're a cynic, Kogan. Tell me, when did Secker say he and his pal first came across Wally?"

"They don't know the exact time. Neither carries a watch. But they think it was between nine and ten on Wednesday night."

"So they didn't suspect anything when he was still there in the morning, but when they came back the second time and he hadn't moved, they investigated."

"I just said that."

"I'm just getting things straight in my head. What else did you learn from Secker?"

"They described you hanging around in the park yesterday."

"What else that is useful, I mean."

"I told you everything."

"Try again."

"Okay, they took forty bucks off him before they carried him outside. They're entitled. Even if I was Wally's sole heir, I figure they had it coming. Wally didn't need it."

"Did you know that Wally knew about the cellar under the pavilion?"

"Come on, Mr Cooperman. Everybody in town knows about that place. It's shelter, dry and away from the wind. If it gets a little high in the summer, it's only because the school kids use it as a bathroom. None of the guys sleeping rough use it as a john."

"Are you surprised to hear that Wally was probably killed in there?"

"First of all, I ask myself, who'd want to kill old Wally in the first place."

"Kogan, I know. Try to answer the question." I was losing patience again, and Kogan was squirming because he had trouble doing anything in a straight line. He thought a minute.

"I never went there with him. I never heard of Wally going there. Wally didn't like the smell and I don't blame him."

"And you knew nothing about the forty dollars."

"Hell no. And he had fifty the day before. He hadn't had a wad like that in ten years. Not since we found a bunch of arrowheads and told a guy up at Secord University. He gave us a hundred dollars to split. Found them at the bottom of the escarpment near DeCew Falls, framed and mounted in a glass case, but we took 'em out and..."

"Never mind about that. Do you remember telling me about Wally getting that fifty from Ruth Geller? Wally told you on Tuesday."

"Yeah, we'd just cut into a can of..."

"Forget the cat food. Try to remember what Wally said."

"He said...Hell, Mr Cooperman, I told you once. I don't remember any more. Just that we were coming into money. He mentioned this Queen Street lawyer's wife. The one who's disappeared. Not the wife, I mean the lawyer."

"Kogan, you've been a lot of help."

"And I don't care about the forty bucks those guys ripped off. I mean, they found it, didn't they?"

"Kogan, you've got the heart of a capitalist under that necktie somewhere."

"Of course I have. You think I'm some sort of Commie bum?"

"Get out of here, if you want me to hold on to my sanity."

Kogan got up and walked to the door. Here he turned and asked, "You got any more assignments for me, chief?" I threw an outdated copy of the Pocket Criminal Code at him but missed.

Chapter Twenty-One

Pia Morley's apartment was in a high-rise at the north end of James Street. In Grantham, a high-rise is anything over five storeys. This had eight and I pushed the button that carried me up to the penthouse. If the word penthouse once meant something special, I couldn't read it in the layout of Pia's place. It looked like every other apartment I've ever seen in Grantham: the usual low ceilings and galley kitchen. I suspected that there wasn't much room to entertain in the bathroom. There were compensations however: the balcony space looked generous and I counted lots of doors leading somewhere. Even if half of them were closets, it was a bargain. As soon as I saw the furniture in the livingroom, I knew it was going to be tough going back to either one of my rented rooms.

Pia let me in when I rang from below and got the door when the elevator deposited me. She was wearing a velvet housecoat that looked tied with a belt but probably wasn't. She motioned me to the chair that had flowers embroidered on a blue background. It was like sitting on a work of art. She settled into a generous couch with a large floral pattern. Behind her on the wall were framed pictures of classical building façades. There were three on each side of the fake fireplace, one above the other. The gilt mirror with an eagle on top gave the final blow. This was a very interior-decorated room. And when I

thought about it, I couldn't imagine Pia giving the required time to swatches of fabric and patches of paint. I
wondered whether she could even give me the name of
the chocolate-bar colour of the walls. I'd seen brown
walls in a garage once, but never in a fancy apartment.

No sooner had she sat down than she was up again
getting me a rye and water, weak on the rye and heavy
on the water. She poured a mineral water for herself and
sipped a Grand Marnier on the side. She sat down again
and lit a cigarette with the piece of evidence Alex said he
had removed from the scene of the crime. I didn't know
where to start, but I was getting used to that. I never
seemed to have a list of questions percolating in my head.
I knew that a couple of hot tap-water questions would
hit me as the interview got going. I hoped.

"It's good of you to see me, Mrs Morley. I'll try not to
overstay my welcome."

"Let's cut the crap right at the start. Call me Pia, and
you're Benny, right? I heard that they call you Benny."

"People of my generation. People like Pete Staziak,
people like Alex."

"Okay. I know you knew about that. You want to
know about me getting molested by my camp counsel-
lor when I was nine? Or should we keep to the present?
You want to know about when I was a drug addict for
two years? If you've got the time, I got the time."

"I'd like to know why you went to see Nathan Geller
last Friday night."

"Is your drink strong enough? There's hardly any rye
in there." It was a straight evasion, but she did it with
polish. "I'm glad you're not the type who waits for the
yard-arm to come over the poop deck. I'm a true demo-
crat about drink: I'll drink anything, anytime." I gave
her an appreciative grin made specially for the occasion
and was about to try again when she tried another line:
"I thought you were being paid to uncover Larry Geller's
whereabouts. Are you taking on the whole family now?"

"You don't think Nathan's death and Larry's taking off are related?"

"It only happens that way in books. In real life the strangest coincidences are just coincidences. It makes for a tidy world when everything is related to everything else. That's why people are so frightened of strangers; there's no chance of coincidence with them." I didn't follow what she was saying, but I was of half a mind to ask her to explain, when it hit me it was just talk to keep me from business.

"I don't know about that. But, maybe you can help me to get unconfused about your name. Who was Morley and where does Pia come from?"

"Pia? It's Italian. My family's Italian. At least my father was. Morley comes from Barry Morley, my first husband. I married him when I left Alex. Like I told you, I spent the next two years in orbit. I was stoned all the time and when I finally came down I landed on my derrière and a decree nisi. Unless I think about it, I can't even remember what he looked like. I was not all that discriminating in those days." She lit a second cigarette with the restored monogrammed lighter and blew smoke at the imitation fireplace. I joined her. "Then, I met Glenn. He helped me straighten up my act. I'll always love him for that. But I couldn't live with him. Sometimes I think I shouldn't live with anybody." She was watching the smoke drift between us. "I was straight with Glenn. I told him up-front, 'I'm a mouthy, aggressive, angry woman. Don't think you'll change me, because you can't.' He married me anyway and found out I was right. Sid's the only man I've ever known with balls. He's like an old ad in the magazines for piston rings or something: 'Tough, but oh so gentle.' That's Sid. When I moved in with him, I never thought it would last. I gave it three weeks. I said to myself, 'Live it and see what happens.' I'm still here and I can't wait till he gets home."

"And what about his brother? You got along with Nathan?"

"Sure. I like his stuff. He was totally different from Sid. Like they came from different planets. You have a brother or sister?"

"I've got a brother on Mars."

"I didn't have a brother or sister. We were a very talked-about Italian family when I was young."

"You say you admired Nathan's work?"

"God yes. Didn't you? Or did you ever see it? He was so wonderfully clear-headed."

"He tried to pass himself off as a little simple in a social way. Claimed not to notice things. Does that ring true?"

"Nathan noticed what he wanted to notice. You've seen his stuff. You can't do that sort of thing without being an observer all your life. Gosh, I hate to think about Nathan. I mean it's so bloody depressing. When you think of all the bums without any talent. Without even any talent for living. You know what I mean?" I nodded and she was off again. I'd had a rough beginning with Pia Morley, but now I was on to her. Her natural mode was talking. This time it was about Nathan getting reviewed in American papers before his work was written up in the Canadian papers. Then she was on about prophets in their own country which I didn't follow. I tried to lead her gently back to my investigation.

"You talked with him on Friday. He called you?"

"What? Oh, yes. Nathan called me. He sounded worried and he usually came to me with his worries. He and a dozen others. I tried to tell him I needed a break, right? That I needed some space, but he sounded so pathetic, and I'm the world's greatest sucker. So I agreed to drop in at the studio as soon as I could get free. Nathan was practically the only person I ever smoked dope with any more. We used to do that a lot, now we do it for old times and giggle. Would you like to share a joint, Mr

C?" She opened up a box on the table-top and in with the cigarettes were half a dozen expertly rolled joints of marijuana. I shook my head and she closed the lid, like it was jellybeans she'd offered me. I tried to pick up my end of the interview.

"Around when was that?"

"Was what? Oh, when I got free. Well, I was out at the gun club with you until after dark. It must have been around ten or ten thirty when I got back here. Sid was wondering where I'd been and I had to tell him something credible. Then we played gin rummy for an hour. Sid had to go out around 11:30. I had a soak in the tub then went out for cigarettes. When I got to Nathan's studio it was somewhere between midnight and one. He looked so pitiful lying there, all doubled up. I don't want to think about it. I won't sleep."

"The coroner says that he died between midnight and two in the morning. If you saw him dead in the hour between midnight and one, that narrows our time for when the murder was committed."

"That's great. I mean good for you. But what about me? I found him during the critical time. Doesn't that make me *numero uno*? Top suspect?"

"You could have done it, then asked Alex to see what you left behind. The cops like a neat package like that."

"Shit. All that stuff went through my head when I was standing there in his studio. If I'd called the cops, they would have crucified me."

"Did you touch the body?"

"I had to see if he was still alive. He was still warm, but I knew he was dead. I mean you don't recover when you get stabbed with a knife like that. It must have been a yard long."

"What!"

"Well, I'm exaggerating a little. But it was more than a foot."

"Are you saying that the knife was lying there?"

"Sure, I'm not a total incompetent at telling a story."

"But, what I mean is, the knife wasn't in the studio when I got there. There was no murder weapon found."

"But it was right there on the floor."

"Until somebody picked it up and carried it away."

"I've got to have another drink. You want one?" Pia got up and poured a generous belt of Scotch into a tumbler and gulped it down standing there. She didn't move in the direction of getting me another drink. Maybe she could sense what kind of drinker I was. Holding on to the glass with both hands, she came back to the couch. She didn't say anything for a long time. Then: "Benny, are you saying that the murderer came back for the knife?"

"Not necessarily, Pia. The murderer could have still been in the studio when you came in."

"Oh, my God! He was *there*?"

"How long were you in the studio altogether?"

"I came in, closed the door, and called Nathan. He didn't answer so I went up to his apartment on the second floor. I didn't like spending time with the statues at night any more than it took to walk by them. At night they were scary. Upstairs I found... You know what I found."

"How did you happen to leave your lighter? Did you have a cigarette?"

"I'm vague on the details after I found the body. I remember thinking... No, it wasn't even thinking. It's what you do instead of thinking when panic sets in. I remember the telephone. Wondering should I use it. I don't think I had a cigarette. I wasn't there long enough. I think I just arrived, looked at the body, then got confused and left. I came right home and got into the tub. That's the only safe place in the world."

"Then how did you lose your lighter?"

"It must have fallen out of my bag when I put it down to examine Nathan. I don't know. I only remember that in the morning I didn't have it, and I knew where I didn't want to have it found."

"You didn't have a cigarette before going to bed? What I mean is why didn't you notice that the lighter was missing after you got back here?"

"I guess I used the table lighter. When I've got both I use either one. I don't know. And there is such a thing as matches. All I know is that I didn't really start to worry until morning. And that's when I called Alex."

"Did Alex answer the phone himself?"

"Yes. He tried to calm me down. I was next door to going out of my mind."

"Did he call you by the name he used to call you in the old days?"

"You mean did he call me Toni? Sure. He always calls me Toni. It's from Antonioni, my family name." She looked at me strangely, like I'd just correctly identified the name on the label of her brassière. "What has this got to do with my lighter?"

"Nothing. Everything. I don't know yet. Okay, I'll return to that. You're sure you have no recollection of putting it down?"

"No." Pia was sitting holding on to herself. Her right hand was holding on tightly to her left elbow and the left hand was clutching her right upper arm. This resulted in a pucker of breast showing at the V-neck of her housecoat. It was a nice effect. She could tell I liked it.

"Think, now. You didn't leave the lighter on, say, the coffee-table in Nathan's apartment?"

"I wasn't near the coffee... Oh, Benny, I can't think any more. I can't remember what I remember. I don't think I put it down anywhere. But that's the word of an idiot."

"Okay. Don't strain yourself. Is it possible that you didn't lose the lighter at the studio? Could you have left it someplace else earlier? Don't answer now. Think about it."

"What are you going to do now, Benny?"

"I wish I knew. I feel like I'm holding on to a bundle of rope that's all tangled up. So far I've found at least six ends. I don't know if I'll ever get it straightened out."

"Benny, I want to say how..."

"Forget it." Pia got up from the couch, and I put down my nearly untouched drink. "Look, Pia, I think I know that you live a fairly complicated life, and that there are parts of it that you don't want anybody going into. Things you don't want Sid to find out about. I understand about that. I'm not here to make things difficult for you either domestically or in business. But to find out about Larry's disappearance and Nathan's murder, I have to ask tough questions."

"I think I understand. I'll try to help, if I can."

"Well, at least that makes two of us." We moved towards the door of the penthouse. In a minute I'd be in the elevator on my way back to the street. I wanted to make these last few questions count. "Pia, am I right in thinking that Sid knows nothing about Tony Pritchett's part in the Niagara-on-the-Lake highway plan?"

"Right now he doesn't. I don't think we intended to keep him in the dark indefinitely."

"Why wasn't he involved in that part of the planning?"

"Because he's so up-front, so straightforward. He doesn't realize that we needed Tony to get the proposal underwritten. Once the tenders are chosen and we have the go-ahead, then it doesn't matter any more. But Sid wouldn't have gone along if he suspected that Tony Pritchett and his connections were involved. To Sid, Tony's a crook, a mobster, a character in a Mafia movie. He doesn't understand that in his business investments, Pritchett's as honest as any other investor. He doesn't need to use pressure tactics or strong-arm methods."

"That's why I got an engraved invitation to that meeting at the gun club." Pia lowered her eyes. I got angry with myself. Here I was trying to score debating points instead of digging out as much information as possible. "Sorry, I didn't mean to take cheap shots," I said, and she smiled.

"I guess some of Tony's boys are slow learners. But Glenn tried to make it up to you. Against my advice, remember."

"Was Larry involved in this business with Pritchett?"

"No. As far as I know he doesn't even know Tony. And he and Glenn didn't get along. They were chalk and cheese. No, I think that's a dead end."

"Okay. I think I've just run dry. If I think of anything else..."

"Just call me."

For a fairly short visit, I thought as I went down in the elevator, I'd learned quite a lot. Furthermore, I was already looking forward to my next meeting with Pia Morley.

Chapter Twenty-Two

" Benny, is that you?"

"You were expecting maybe Minerva Pious?" I'd let myself into the town house with my own key. Ma was in the rec room watching TV. Next to reading, it was her favourite occupation.

"You're too young to remember the Fred Allen show. Who're you trying to kid? Your father went down to the club to play cards. I hope you've eaten?"

"I had a bite downtown," I lied. Ma hated surprises, especially at mealtimes.

"Was it yesterday I saw you? At the *shiva*? It's getting so I can't keep the days straight in my head any more. She has a nice house that Debbie."

"Kind of big for one person."

"It's all she's got. No kids, no husband. You want to take away the house too, Benny?" I sat down in the mate to the leather chair Ma was sitting in. I tried to keep my eyes off the TV. When I get hooked, I'll watch anything that moves. My only defence is total abstinence.

Ma was wearing a green housecoat over her night things. Her day wasn't properly started yet. Her morning mug of coffee was sitting coldly on the coffee-table.

"Did you talk to anybody at the *shiva*?" I asked.

"Nobody in particular. It was nice to see Morris Kaufman again. He's got old since the last time I saw him. He used to be such a handsome man. Funny the way men

210

get littler. Oh, I did talk to that Englishman from the newspaper who was there. He was with *The New York Times.* Clyde his name was. Or Trevor. Something English like that."

"Yeah, he was the one who admired Nathan's sculptures."

"We didn't talk about that. He was telling me about growing up in the east end of London and how hard it was to get out of there. He sounded like the autobiography of Charlie Chaplin. I could practically hear that theme from *Limelight* or was it *City Lights* where he eats the flower?"

"Who ate the flower? The *Times* critic?"

"In the movie: Charlie and the blind girl. Aren't you listening? I was telling you Clyde or Trevor had a terrible time getting out of the east end. His father wanted him to run a barrow in Petticoat Lane. But he couldn't wait to escape the smell of cooked cabbage and post-war rationing. At first he was talking down his nose at me like I was a housewife from the sticks, the next minute he's telling me he eats smoked salmon in private, like it's against the law or something. What is it, Benny, you can't be a critic and Jewish too? Anyway, I thought he was kind of cute. Especially when I told him I'd never heard of him. He thought I was trying to pull his leg. But why should I? Have you ever heard of him?"

"Me? I've never heard of anybody. Just Mrs Nussbaum and Minerva Pious."

"Well, I think he kind of liked me. The way he opened up like that. Once he got started, there was no shutting him up."

"Who else did you talk to?"

"I didn't hear where Larry Geller is hiding, if that's what you mean. I heard that the kids are living in Toronto with a relative. They should all pack up and make a new start someplace."

"You've known those girls all their lives practically, haven't you?"

"The Kaufman girls? Sure. I remember their birthday parties and their first long dresses. I remember the way they used to scrap when they were teenagers. You wouldn't believe two pretty kids could quarrel like that. At each other's throats over boys or records or clothes. Honestly. You boys didn't fight like that. And they say girls are easier than boys. I don't believe it."

"You mean they disliked one another?"

"I mean their father, Morris, was a good furrier but a lousy social worker. He made trouble between the girls without even trying. Morris is a sweet man, but he doesn't have your father's sense. Morris never had sense, so he had a noisy house. And when his wife died, that Pearl from Chicago, I think, it didn't help. He needed a resident psychologist to sort the three of them out. Sigmund Freud would have thrown up his hands."

"Sam and I used to fight, and we turned out all right."

"So, who's saying the Kaufman girls didn't turn out? I just said they used to fight a lot. Like you and your brother."

"Somebody should write a book on how to be a sibling. I think Sam and I needed lessons."

"You? You'd never read it anyway. Mysteries is all you ever read."

"I'm working on Dostoyevsky. I'm coming along."

"You started *Crime and Punishment* when I started *Anthony Adverse*, ten, fifteen years ago."

"I get interrupted. I have to make a living, Ma."

"Let's not get into *that* on a nice day like this."

I gave my mother a peck on the cheek and went up to the room my mother still called "the boys' room" to get some summer clothes from a bottom drawer. I put them in a shopping bag, gave Ma another peck on leaving, then beetled back to Martha's place. It was decidedly hot out. I could feel the sun burning through my shirt

warming my shoulders. The backs of my knees began to
itch with the heat. The sun stood out on the hood of the
Olds in spite of the accumulated grime of the city. As I
walked up to Martha's front door I saw ants busy with
their hills between the cracks in the sidewalk. A whole
safari of them was making its way from the smudge that
used to be another insect. I thought of a wasp I'd killed
on the screen of my hotel room a year ago. The buzz
annoyed me, so I killed it. My mind is a whole grave-
yard of tombstones like that: the lake trout I caught but
didn't eat, the bugs on the windshield of the car, the
snake on the railway tracks when I was a kid. I don't
know what it is. Sometimes I think I'm too sentimental
to be in this business. Take Kogan, for instance, and his
pal Wally. To most people in this town they're no better
than the wasp or the snake. They walk around demon-
strating to people that you don't have to work for a
living; just hold out your hand and the Lord will pro-
vide. Granted that He supplies infrequently and when
He does it is either Old Sailor or 9-Lives. Kogan and
Geller have a lot in common. Both are on the take, but
Kogan at least waits for the hand-out. You have the op-
tion of ignoring his outstretched hand. Geller doesn't take
chances. He doesn't put out his hand at all. It's in your
pocket without your knowing about it. It's easy to think
that the difference between them is one of imagination,
with Geller getting higher marks for having thought up
the bigger scam. But I don't keep score like that. Kogan
never hurt people, never picked up a quarter that hadn't
been abandoned or offered without strings attached. Besides, I liked Kogan.

Martha wasn't home from work yet, so I boiled two
eggs without scorching the bottoms and toasted some
bread. I cracked the eggs and mashed them with some
bottled mayonnaise, added salt and pepper and I was as
good as restored to health. I put the works on a plate
and brought it to the enamel-topped table. I poured a

glass of milk from the blue carton in the refrigerator. Meanwhile my mind was guttering on aspects of this Larry Geller business. This was Tuesday. For six days I'd been playing around with the case and not making friends or influencing people while I was doing it. I could have gone down to Daytona Beach on Nathan's suggestion. I might not have turned up Larry Geller, but I could have got some sun and maybe even some swimming. Everybody I know gets to go to Florida for one reason or another. This time I could have written the whole trip off as a business expense, but some still small voice inside me doesn't like the way it bounces, so I tell Nathan to shove it, and stay in Martha's back room. At least in Daytona Beach I'd be able to retire to my own hotel room. Still, small voices should bother other private investigators once in a while.

Back in my car, I headed down across the old canal instead of across the high-level bridge. I parked near the short bridge and sat in the car looking at the three colours of water running under the span. There was the green water from the creek, brown from the pollution works in Papertown and a white scum that held the two other streams apart. It was like Neapolitan ice-cream designed by a madman with a perverse sense of humour. Above the water-line, the red-brick foundry was belching out dark smoke from the tin smoke-stack. The smoke was blowing under the high-level bridge and getting lost among its dark girders.

Ruth Geller was not expecting me. In fact I wasn't sure myself how I got there. I'd been mooning about for over an hour without any clear direction. My mental processes, if they can be called that, were keeping their thoughts to themselves. I was just the driver. I parked the car at this still exclusive address on Burgoyne Boulevard. As far as I could see, property values hadn't plummeted. There were no "For Sale" signs visible on the surrounding front lawns. No additional windows had been broken at number 222 nor was there an accumulation of rotten fruit on the lawn.

"Mr Cooperman! This is a surprise." Ruth Geller looked honestly taken aback as she saw me standing at her front door. I'd rung the bell twice and was just wondering about a third strike and out when I heard steps approaching the door. "What brings you to this neighbourhood today? Don't answer that; I just remembered. You never sleep. Will you come in? I was just going to make some tea." I followed Ruth through the lush hall with the deep-pile broadloom to the immaculate white kitchen. She had more white gadgets than a hardware store. The stove and sink were hard to locate. I finally found them in an island in the middle of the room. The stove was so integrated into the rest of the decor that you practically had to leave a kettle showing just to keep your bearings. Gummed fruit stickers and magnetic letters dotted the refrigerator with spots of colour that the designer hadn't called for. It was the sort of kitchen where one dirty cup on the counter embarrassed all the clean dishes wherever they were hiding in their knobless cupboards. "I'll put the kettle on," Ruth said, and pushed something that looked like it would transport both of us to the command deck of the USS Enterprise. "I hope you don't mind decaffeinated tea? I've had to give the real stuff up because I'm not sleeping very well these days." I nodded approval and she found a box of cookies and put some on a plate. Her milk was from a carton of two percent just like Martha's.

"I should have telephoned first," I apologized. "The fact is I didn't know I was coming here. I just ended up parked outside your front door."

"You looked a little lost when I opened the door. I thought it was just my surprise." In spite of the welcome mat and her smile, Ruth was edgy. Her hands trembled.

"There are a couple of things I remembered I hadn't cleared up."

"Sure. A couple of things. There are more than a couple of things I'd like cleared up. Like 'What the hell are my kids going to do for a father when they get home?'"

"Sorry, I didn't mean to get you started. The kettle's boiling. That's a fast kettle." She ignored my diversion but got up to make the tea. I was surprised to see that decaffeinated tea came in bags just like nature's own. I'd expected a pale blue powder.

She made the tea and we sipped in silence only broken by the munching I was doing on a cookie. It had almonds in it. They had almonds in them, as I found out on further exploration. After a few angels flew by, I picked up the dropped thread again. "Mrs Geller, do you remember on the telephone last Friday, I asked you about a man named Wally Moore?"

"I honestly can't recall that, Mr Cooperman. But if you say so, I'll believe you."

"Wally was a bum, a vagrant, a panhandler, a regular feature on St Andrew Street."

"I still don't..."

"He was a little guy, with a Charlie Chaplin bamboo cane, and he walked with his feet pointed in different directions."

"I'm sorry. Wally doesn't ring any bells. Is it important?"

"Yeah, it's important. According to a witness he paid a call on you and you paid him off for information or silence or to keep off your grass. I don't know why you paid him off, but we know that he came into money. For him, a fortune. And he said that you were the lady bountiful behind it."

"Well, this man is just not telling you the truth. I pay a gardener. I paid the man who fixed the front window. Maybe he was trying to pull your leg, Mr Cooperman. You look very serious just now, but you might be susceptible to the man's blarney."

"Wally isn't pulling legs any more, Mrs Geller. He's on his way to a grave paid for by the city."

"You mean he's...?"

"Yes, Ma'am. He's dead. That's why what we know about him is important. He could have made up the story, but he couldn't have made up the money. Only you can shed light on this."

"But I told you. I've never seen the man. I don't know him and I never paid him off. I suppose I'm sorry that he's dead. I want to be honest, so I shouldn't pretend that I'm terribly upset."

"He didn't just die, Mrs Geller. He was murdered."

"I'm sorry! I'm sorry I can't help you. But I can't see what it has to do with Larry's leaving town."

"He might have seen something he shouldn't."

"He might have seen them driving in the direction of the city limits."

"Them? Who do you mean, them?"

"I meant Larry. I don't know why I said them."

"Mrs Geller, you've just made a slip. You know something you haven't told the police. You'd better tell me before anyone else gets hurt."

"I've told you all I know. I haven't any information I didn't have last week when you came."

"You've lost a brother-in-law since then."

"Nathan? What has his death got to do with Larry? You've got me confused. Do you mean that it was a revenge killing by some...some...?"

"Former client of your husband? Could be. But my money's on secrets. Nathan knew something about Larry, and it was worth the risk to make sure Nathan didn't spread the news."

"I didn't think about that." She was quiet for a minute. She looked at her decaffeinated tea growing chilly on the white counter. Her hands were trembling.

We were perched on chromium and white leather stools. All we needed was a bartender on the other side wiping out glasses and hanging them up to dry. What kind of secrets would Ruth tell a bartender after a couple of drinks? "It's secrets that do it, Mrs Geller. I've been telling everybody this week. Secrets lead down the long dark hall."

"Are you still harping...? Damn it, Mr Cooperman, I don't know this man you're talking about. I've tried to be up-front with the police, and they won't tell me a thing. I've been straight with you, and you couldn't find beets in a bowl of borscht." She was leaning on her arms propped on the counter. Her head was held in the palms of both hands. I couldn't see if she was crying. I thought that she might be. I felt a nickel worse than somebody who felt like two cents. But I felt like that when I arrived, so I didn't pack up and leave.

"Mrs Geller," I said, trying to make my voice stand up as tall as a Mountie in a musical, "you know that Larry had plans to leave town. You know that he didn't plan on leaving without company. Will you tell me now who he went away with?"

For a moment she didn't move. Her eyes were shining when she looked at me with an expression that I tried to forget in a hurry. Her hand shot out and pulled open a drawer. It fished about among coupons like those in Ma's kitchen drawer and came up with a photograph. At first I was disappointed. I'd been hoping for a hotel reservation or an airline schedule with a destination circled. I think you can't improve on neat arrangements like those. But what Ruth was holding out to me was a colour photograph. Smiling Larry was holding his hands over the eyes of a woman. In spite of the covered features, I was sure from what I could see of the smile that the woman was Pia Morley. It was a party photograph and the light in Larry's eyes was pink. "But Pia didn't leave town, Ruth," I said, forgetting to be formal in my inquiry.

"She went missing the same day Larry did. She doubled back, that's all."

"Did Larry double back with her?"

"God, don't you think I've been asking myself that? How could she do it? And while living with his brother! What is that woman made of?"

"Try to stay calm. When did she get back to Grantham? How do you know for sure that she went with...?"

I didn't finish the sentence. There was something else in the photograph that suddenly grabbed me by the tie and shook me around.

"What is it?" Ruth asked, looking at my sagging jaw, I guess. "Mr Cooperman? Are you okay?" She was gone for a moment and then came back to the counter. "Here," she said. "Drink this." I took a glass from her and felt the heat as I swallowed something straight and alcoholic. I never asked about the brand name. But it was the right medicine for what ailed me that day. "Is that better?" Ruth asked, the tone of worry in her voice as genuine as I remember hearing from anybody.

"Mrs Geller," I asked as soon as I could locate my tongue, "where did your husband get that ring he's wearing?"

"Ring?" She looked puzzled. "Oh, you mean in the photo. Why that's his ring from Osgoode Hall, the law school. They all have them, all the lawyers who go through Osgoode. The crest is usually in gold, but I had this cut specially for Larry's birthday three years ago. Why do you ask?"

I still felt like I'd just taken a beating, like my stomach had been removed and the local anaesthetic was just wearing off. I didn't know what to tell Ruth Geller. What I heard myself say at length was, "Oh, I've always been an admirer of fine rubies."

Chapter Twenty-Three

I suppose I should have headed straight to Niagara Regional with what I'd just found out. At least I'd have been taking some of the advice I'd been handing out all over town. If everybody passed on his secrets, nobody'd be sent for a post-mortem because he knew too much.

I hadn't stayed at Ruth's for more than another few minutes. I'd not confided my suspicions to her, but I did hit her with one more big question before I left. It was the one that had been bothering me since the day I'd been snatched coming out of Larry Geller's bolt-hole.

"Mrs Geller," I'd asked, "why won't you admit that Larry called you on the day he disappeared?" She looked blank, but still managed to smile vaguely, like it was through a fog or mist.

"You've asked me that before. Why is it so important? He didn't call. I had no contact with him after he left that morning. Nobody here spoke to him. I checked."

"I'm sorry," I said. "I'm not sure why it's important, but what I have amounts to evidence in a way. It's the sort of evidence that doesn't lie."

"Well, Mr Cooperman, maybe it doesn't, but then maybe you aren't reading it right. Have you thought of that?"

Since leaving the Geller place, that's what I'd been thinking about. The evidence of the phone call. By pushing the redial button I was automatically connected with Ruth. We'd talked about Nathan's midnight phone call to me about Daytona Beach. At least I wasn't imagining things. I pushed the button and the phone made the connection. I didn't dial her number, the memory in the machine dialed the number. Then it hit me. It could have been from the day before or the week before. But she'd told me that he never called. Not for weeks. Who was I going to believe: the redial button or the wife?

Pete Staziak wasn't working that night. He was in the middle of his long narrow backyard trying to get a charcoal fire started with his vacuum cleaner. That's where I found him and he went a little red when he saw me coming over the newly mowed lawn. "Hi! You looking for a chess game with my kid? He's out. Pull up a lump of charcoal and sit down. Shelley's inside getting a salad together. You'll have a hamburger, Benny? When I get this going?"

"Be careful you don't electrocute yourself."

"Nuts, I do this all the time. It's the quickest way. It's a little more bulky than using Shelley's hair dryer, but I cracked that. This works very well, when you hook it up backwards so that it blows instead of sucks." I walked closer and showed an interest in the arrangements. I hoped he was using grounded wires, that's all. He turned the vacuum on again and the sparks shot out of the middle of the bed of coals. In the centre they were red going on yellow. It looked as hot as a blacksmith's forge and smelled about the same. Pete added another load of charcoal from the sooty blue and white bag. Once this lot began to burn, Pete made himself busy handing me the blackened racks to the hibachi and a wire brush. He didn't try talking over the racket made by the vacuum cleaner. At first I thought that working the brush over the racks would be very satisfying, turning the soiled, carbonized grease-covered metal grates into silvery gridirons, but it was hard work and unrewarding. There was no transformation even after I'd gone over them twice. So, I gave up at about the same time Pete turned off the vacuum cleaner. I handed the grates to him and he fitted them into the black holders. He unplugged the vacuum and reeled in the cord. "Don't let me leave it out here all night. That's the sort of thing that brings on a midnight downpour. Will you have a beer, Benny?"

"Sure." Pete went into the house to explain the unexpected visitor and returned with a tray with four bottles and one glass.

We didn't speak until we were a quarter-way into our first beer. It was Pete who broke the silence: "Well, you might as well tell me now. Let's get it over with. I want to eat with a clear head." I gave Pete a fast rundown of what I'd been doing since Nathan's funeral. The highlight was the ring in the fire-hall footing.

"Unless I miss my guess, we just located Larry Geller."

"You're sure about the ring?"

"Ruth says it's a class ring from Osgoode Hall, only she had the crest engraved on a fair-sized ruby. Can't be too many of those around."

"So, you figure, if it's Larry's ring, it's Geller's finger, et cetera, et cetera, et cetera."

"Seems a reasonable assumption. Unless he lost it in a crap game to our John Doe in the column. But that's looking for complications. Let's see what the forensic boys tell us."

"You tell Ruth?"

"Give me some credit. I'm not a half-wit."

"Let's not quibble over fractions, Benny." Pete gulped down the last of his first beer and opened another. He tried to make it as a steel-edged cop through and through, but I could see that it was at least partly an act. Pete looked at the hibachi and not at me. He was figuring out whether the coals were ripe yet. He decided that we could talk for another five minutes or so before he had to tie on his apron. "I'll phone in a call to the station and they can get cracking on the job of removing the body overnight. They'll have to get an engineer to judge about what it does to the structure. That means Sid Geller will have to know about it soon, I mean before we have an identification that we can go to court with."

"Sounds good to me."

"So, Geller didn't run away after all?"

"Looks possible."

"Who gets rich out of that?" Pete was looking at me, and I shrugged the fact that it was anyone's guess. Who's to benefit is the time-honoured question we're supposed to ask ourselves in an investigation. Who's to benefit? Who in a town with a population of fifty thousand could possibly make use of two million dollars and change? The faint shadow of suspicion settled on everybody from Papertown to Port Robertson, from Louth to Niagara Falls.

Pete went into the house through the aluminum door with a floppy screen and returned in five minutes with a platter of fat generous hamburgers ready for the fire. He hadn't put on an apron, probably because I was there, or maybe he never used one. He put the burgers on the grill; they began to sizzle and snap at once. Pete let them alone for a minute, then turned them over. "That seals them," he said, then added: "I talked to Chris. He'll look after things at the fire hall."

We both watched the hamburgers turn from pink to brown, saw the juices run into the fire and ignite a lump of charcoal. The dripping sizzled like the tick of a slow clock.

In a few minutes Pete's wife, Shelley, appeared at the back door with a friendly greeting and a basket of buns. By now the backyard was pungent with smoke. Shelley split the buns and placed them around the darkening meat. As soon as they were cooked on one side, Pete turned the patties over, and meanwhile we practised small talk without showing much aptitude for it.

An hour later, I parked outside the Woodland Avenue building. It was dark and quiet. I'd been carrying the keys to the place since last Friday, and they'd been getting heavier in my pocket every day I ignored them. I'd intended to have them copied, but like my other schemes I realize only about fifty percent of them. I climbed out of the car and opened the front door.

Heartburn was working its way up my innards. Relish and mustard, I thought, but I knew better. On a case like this I should try to stay strictly kosher. During the last couple of years I'd been finding that harder and harder to do. I guess that's why I enjoy going home on Friday nights for dinner with Ma and Pa. It gives me a new start for the week. In their own fashion, Ma and Pa keep a kosher house, without reading the fine print on the labels too closely. But it was better than I could do eating in restaurants all the time.

As I made my way up the unlighted stairs, a bubble was growing under my ribs. It loosened with movement and left a charred taste in my mouth. I found the right door and enough light from the window at the end of the hall to help me fit the key into the lock of Larry Geller's bolt-hole.

For the second time I stood in that small office. It didn't seem to have changed since my last visit. I hoped that it wouldn't end the same way. I turned on the light and for a second the brightness stung my eyes. I went at once to the telephone, lifted it and tried the redial button. I heard the usual telephone noises. They matched the ones now being made by my stomach. The phone rang and rang again. After the third and fourth ring, I started to lose confidence in the opening gambit I had in mind. It rang a fifth, sixth and seventh time without any additional

luck. I replaced the phone. I wasn't going to catch anyone out in a lie tonight, I thought.

The smell of burned paper was less clear in the air this
time. I could still see wisps of charred paper near the
discoloured waste-paper basket. I'd given the full Cooperman treatment to the room the first time around, so I
knew there weren't any secrets to be uncovered. But feeling a little caught up short by the telephone's failure to
cooperate, I shifted the desk, just to see if anything had
slipped through my fine-meshed net the first time around.

It was my foot that found it, not my eyes. I felt an
irregularity underfoot and looked down and saw nothing
but an uneven floor. A second glance proved more interesting. It was a scrap of cotton cloth. It was scorched
around the edges, and of double thickness. On the other
side there was writing; part of a printed label: "...*her-
stone, S.A.*" It didn't mean anything to me, but on the
probability that anyone with half an education might be
able to make something out of it, I put it carefully into
one of the plastic compartments of my wallets after re-
shuffling the gas company credit cards. Before I left the
office, I tried the redial button again, but with the same
unhelpful results.

As I parked at the curb in front of 40 Monck Street,
Martha's lights were on. Once again I felt like I was tread-
ing on her hospitality, even at fifty bucks a week. I was
hiding out at her place under false pretences. Glenn Bagot
was soon going to send his borrowed boys after me to
see why I hadn't accepted his five hundred dollars. I figured that he wasn't going to enjoy reading about Larry's
body being discovered on the building site a hell of a lot.
And I couldn't blame him. The name of the corpse was
sure to be Geller, and the name of the construction company was Bolduc. But at least if the provincial government noticed and picked another tender to the big

Niagara-on-the-Lake highway project, I couldn't see how
Bagot could find Mrs Cooperman's little boy at the bottom of it. Niagara Regional wasn't going to spread the
credit around, I hoped. And maybe, with Larry Geller's
whereabouts finally established as some fair distance
from Daytona Beach and his activities restricted to de-
composition, things would settle down around town.
Once more it had been demonstrated: greed begets serpents, and serpents sting.

"Well, you're home early! Couldn't keep away, could
you?"

"Hi, Martha."

"When are you going to help eat some of the grub you
bought? The fridge has never been so loaded with good
things, and I'm eating it myself."

"I was at a friend's barbecue. We had hamburgers,
salad, fruit salad and now heartburn."

"A little something to remember her by."

"How do you barbecue without doing yourself an
injury?"

"I'll show you sometime, if you're ever around here
that long."

Martha had been flipping through a magazine in front
of the TV set, which was turned off. It was a glamour
magazine. I'd never thought of Martha as a consumer of
glamour and all that stuff. You never know about people. I took out my wallet and retrieved the bit of cotton.
Palming it I held it out for Martha to see. "Can you
make anything of that?" I asked. She picked it up and
looked at the letters.

"S.A. means it's a European company most likely. It's
the same as our use of the word incorporated as part of
a company's name. So this is a big, non-North American
outfit. I suppose you could look it up in..." She broke
off without finishing the suggestion. Her face lit up like
a Coleman lantern in a dark cottage. She got up, left the
room and rummaged around in her room for a minute.

When she came back, she was waving a coloured page from a magazine. She turned over the coloured page showing the ads in small type on the other side. She tapped one of the ads and cocked a smiling face in my direction. "Benny, the missing letters are *At. Atherstone S.A.* is just about the biggest diamond exporter in the world, that's all." She handed me the piece of paper with the ad in it. As soon as I held it I knew that I'd seen it dozens of times. Martha handed back the scrap of cloth, and I was suddenly plunged into a brand new puzzle.

Chapter Twenty-Four

W hat I knew about diamonds could be written on the knee of a gnat. But I knew this much: a tidy way to make two point six million dollars disappear into a fairly compact space would be to convert them into cut, unmounted diamonds. I'd read somewhere about the diamond trade in New York, about how big deals were still settled with a handshake. If Larry Geller intended leaving town, diamonds would have made ideal travelling companions. Diamonds travel well because they are what they are and anyone with a jeweller's loupe can see whether they're real or not. No papers or signatures are required. You don't even need one of those Swiss bank accounts with the numbers. My diamond in the pocket of Mr X is Mr X's diamond if he says it's his. Larry Geller had prepared to leave town with a bag full of goodies. Somebody knew he had them. Goodbye Larry. Diamonds and secrets can be equally deadly.

I went back to my hotel for clean socks and an argument with my landlord about the weekly rent I was behind in paying. The fact that I hadn't been in the room for a few days, and that he had seven other unrented rooms was noted with some interest in an academic way, but it cut no ice. When I told him the cheque was in the mail he looked at me like I thought I was a comedian. I gave him twenty dollars on account. That left forty dollars between me and a heart-to-heart with the bank manager.

I managed to get both into the room and out without running into Glenn Bagot or three of his merry men. I felt silly coming down the stairs into the din of the Ladies and Escorts Beverage Room. If there was no threat, why was I holed up at Martha's? If I was in real danger of running into Bagot asking about his proposition, what was I doing looking for trouble around here? The country and western band didn't help my thinking. The lead singer was dressed in leather and silver from head to foot. I couldn't tell whether his outfit came from a couturier or a saddler. He was holding the microphone close to his mouth and distorting the sound at the beginning of every phrase.

"...and those shoes come walking back to me..."

Luc Bolduc was sitting in the living room watching TV when I knocked at the screen door of the house on Nelson Street. I'd driven up half an hour before, and watched until I saw Alex and his wife leave the house, take the car and drive off in some direction that held no interest for me. It was the old man I wanted to see.

"Oh, it's you," he said through the screen, seeing less than a sight for sore eyes. "Alex's not here. You want come back tomorrow."

"I want to talk to you, Mr Bolduc."

"Talk?" he said, "I got not'in' to say to you, mister. Better you come back, talk to Alex. Hokay?"

"Not hokay, Mr Bolduc, because we have to talk about things you don't want Alex to know about. Right?"

"I got not'in' to say," and he started to close the front door in my face. I opened the screen door and put my hand firmly on the handle of the door.

"He's worried about you drinking again, Mr Bolduc. And you're worried about Alex getting mixed up with Tony Pritchett. Right?"

"Tony Pritchett got not'in' to do with my Alex."

"That's your story and you're stuck with it. What I know is that you're right: Tony doesn't even know about Alex. Alex isn't doing any of Pritchett's dirty work."

"That's true. That's what I say."

"You say it, but you don't believe it. You told me last night. You think Pritchett called Alex on the phone. You heard him call him Tony."

"He not call Alex," he lied, looking me in the eye.

"You think he called last Saturday morning, and they had a hush-hush conversation. I'm telling you it wasn't Pritchett. It was Pia Morley. Sid Geller's girl. You remember she used to be Antonioni, used to be Alex's girl, right?"

"You say that Alex and Pia Morley...?"

"I'm not saying anything more than that they talked on the phone. You must remember when he played hockey, he used to call her Toni, from Antonioni?"

"Toni? Yes, that's right. He liked her when he was young. Called her Toni. That's right. So, it was not Tony Pritchett talk to my boy. That's good." He began to let a smile steal over his wrinkled features. Suddenly, he was holding the door open wider and motioning me into the living-room. The old man was plainly delighted by the news. Now I was hating myself for what I had in mind for him to do to pay for my good deed. I followed the hospitable gesture to the inside and snapped off the TV when I had my back to it and Luc was clearing newspapers off the sofa. I sat where I'd sat when I talked to Alex, the last time I was under the Bolduc roof. The old man sat in an overstuffed occasional chair. "You'll drink a glass of wine, mister? I made it last year." I agreed to the wine because I knew he would be more relaxed if I was holding a glass.

He was gone for less than a minute. I guessed that the wine came from the family stock and not from a covert supply of his own. He poured me a glass with a tired grin and waved away the suggestion that he should join me when I tried him out on his teetotal resolve. "Mr Bolduc, tell me about Larry Geller. We both know that you know his body is in that footing on the building site."

"Look, mister, I don' want to get involve'. I forget what I don' know."

"The cops are digging the body out of that footing tonight, Mr Bolduc. If you don't tell me, you'll soon have to talk to one of them."

"Better to wait. I sure don' have to talk to you." He shifted in his deep chair as I moved my drink from one hand to the other.

"Suit yourself. There's quite a bit I know already. And the rest I can guess. You knew Sid and his brothers, didn't you? Sid ran the yard and did the business, but his younger brothers were in the background. I'll bet Larry made a deal with you to let him get into the shed at the fire-hall site. He paid you to let him put some things there. Am I right?"

"You're doing the talkin'. I'll just listen, me."

"You made a deal with Larry, gave him a duplicate key. If you cut the key in Grantham, we'll have no trouble finding the guy who cut it for you. How many hardware stores are there? It won't take long to run a check." That rattled Luc. He stuck his thumbs in his belt like the cops were after him already.

"So what, eh? I cut lotsa keys, mister. Dat don' prove buttons."

"Look, Mr Bolduc, nobody's trying to hang Larry's death on you. But he didn't get into the cement by himself. That makes it murder. And murder is a word, Mr Bolduc, that the cops get excited over. They'll put in a lot of men and they'll pick up a lot of overtime."

"Why should I tell you dis t'ing?"

"It'll show that you've got a cooperative character, that you were willing to help without having three lawyers standing around collecting fat fees. Alex would see you had the best."

"Alex got nothin' to do wit' dis. I tol' you."

"And I believe you. I'm on your side. I want to know who killed Larry Geller. I don't think you did it, but when you throw up a smoke-screen, I don't know what to think."

"Hokay, hokay. I'll tell you what I know. It's not much. I t'ink I feel better after anyhow." He took a cigarette from the top pocket of his shirt and lit it after rolling it in his fingers like it was a fine old cigar. I tried not to lean forward in my seat. I sipped the wine and waited. "A couple weeks ago; no, more; beginning of the mont', Larry comes to me in Sid's yard and gives me twenty bucks. He says he wants to leave a suitcase under the boards in the shack, where I used to leave my beer. Larry, he knew about dat place. I guess everybody knew. Maybe dey laugh at me. You t'ink?" I shook my head and he went on. "Anyway, I get him a key. I don't know when he puts in dis suitcase, but I see it in dere. Den, a week later the suitcase is gone, and I forget all about it, excep' he leaves me another twenty in dere, the hidin' place I'm talkin' about." He took a new drag on the cigarette and continued slowly. "Den, one night I was checking dis place an' see dat ole feller Wally Moore hangin' around. He always been hangin' around, but dis night he's liquored up good and asks if I see not'in' funny about dis footing. I have a look, like I t'ink he fine some hairlines, cracks, bad t'ing like dat. But no. I look around, see not'in'. Den he show me. He show me the finger wit' da ring on it. He says dere's a man inside. He nods his head and shows me clear where da ring show t'rough. He tell me not to tell anybody, cause den we all have hell to pay, hokay? So, I don't say not'in'. Da next t'ing I hear in da yard is dat Sid's brother, Mr Larry's gone missing. Mr Sid looks bad, and I feel bad because I don' say not'in'. Maybe I should, but I keep still. I figure it's smarter to keep eyes open and mout' close. I get me some beer and keep quiet wit' da beer in da shed. Cover ring wit' new cement. Dat way nobody fin' hout not'in'."

"I told you that Wally Moore's dead, didn't I?"

"I t'ink 'bout dat las' night. I know I'm goin' to t'ink about it again tonight. That Wally was goin' to make a buck out of dat business, you bettcha. He say we keep quiet, but Wally, I bet he tell wrong person. Get killed."

"What could Wally know besides all this?"

"Wally, one smart feller in a dumb way. What he t'ink he is? Structural engineer? Make me laugh. He no see hairlines or ring or finger in footing wit'out seeing Mr Larry go into da cement. In t'ousand years you not see da ring. No, Wally see Mr Larry go into cement. And dat's for sure."

Chapter Twenty-Five

I drove by the site of the new fire hall where Niagara and Geneva come together at Queenston Road. If I counted one cop cruiser, I counted a half dozen. When I found a place to park, I could see the lights they'd wired up down below. I didn't want to get too close, because I figured that now that the cops were investigating a bona fide murder and not just a disappearance, they might want to have a further chat with me at Niagara Regional, just to fill in the time between digging Larry out of his cocoon and getting the official word from the forensic people.

The night was cool and a mist crowded low-lying areas. It seemed to overflow the valley of the canal and spill into the dark empty streets. I could see shadows moving down below with a fancy piece of machinery. Other figures were watching like sidewalk supervisors from the upper level near the shed. I recognized Chris Savas with his hands deep in his raincoat pockets. There were other cops running around the way they do when something like this happens. If it had been earlier, there would have been a crowd they could manage, but as it was I couldn't see anyone watching who wasn't directly involved. Sid was there, of course, and so was Glenn Bagot. They were standing on the upper level, Sid close enough to Savas to be within earshot. Glenn was farther off and not getting more involved than he had to by the look of him. Sid looked grim, like he'd already been up all night and had been drinking cold coffee from styrofoam cups for the past two days. Bagot looked like he'd been pulled out of a party. Under a light raincoat I could see what looked like evening clothes. Tonight he was getting mud on his patent leather shoes.

I watched Savas lean over to speak to one of the uniformed men, who nodded then came away from the site, crossed the street and approached a parked car a few yards up from mine on the other side of Geneva. A window was rolled down and through it I thought I saw one or other of the Kaufman sisters. I couldn't tell whether it was Ruth or Debbie in the rising mist. The officer made an attempt at a cross between a salute and a tip of his hat and returned to Savas. The window went up again and the car just sat there waiting. Even with the windows of my car closed, the smell of the paper-mills was in the air. There was sulphur in it and other stuff. Stuff I'd been smelling on nights like this since I was a kid.

I was certain that there was no news beyond what I already knew to be expected. But it was like a stage set that's just aching to be played on. This scene, for all of the dramatic equipment and the fancy cast, would never be played. The real drama would come on a slip of paper from the Forensic Centre in Toronto. If that was drama, I'll stick to Shakespeare in Montecello Park.

A cigarette was lit in the car across the street. I could see two heads. I had an idea that I wanted to say something to them. I don't exactly know what, but I had this urge that something had to be said. I opened the door of my car and began moving my bulk past the steering wheel, when I felt a hand on my arm assisting me, if that's the word. I came out looking into the smiling face of Gordon. Geoff and Len stood behind him.

"Well, Mr Cooperman! Small world, right?" I was standing now by the closed back door of the Olds.

Gordon slammed the front door, so I wouldn't attempt to re-enter the car unassisted.

"Hell, Mr Cooperman," said Geoff. "We been looking all over for you. Where you been?"

"Now, look, you guys. There are two dozen cops over there." I tried to make a snatch this close to trouble sound ridiculous. The boys laughed away the suggestion that this was a snatch.

"We just want conversation, that's all." I didn't want to encourage their kind of conversation. I hoped that I wasn't going to come down with a sudden case of broken kneecaps.

"We want to talk to you, Mr Cooperman. You come easy and there'll be no trouble." Len moved in behind me as Gordon pulled me away from the dubious redoubt offered by the Olds. By now I could see a large black Lincoln parked across the street. Even in the mist I could see it was one of the kind with the windows darkened. But I had the feeling it wasn't empty. There was someone in there watching what was going on and waiting.

Gordon had shifted his grip on my arm but he found a better one higher up. From the rear, Len offered encouragement. I was sure that as soon as we were across the street, I was going to feel another sap on the back of my head where I was still getting over the clout they'd given me at our last meeting. I moved as slowly as I could. The boys were going to have to earn their pay. I didn't want to wake up in the trunk of another car even if it was a Lincoln. Again I could smell the exhaust from the first car I'd tried out. I was glad I'd fixed their spare tire with my Swiss Army Knife. That, I thought, might be my very last unrecorded thought. I could see the light at the end of a cigar through the dark window of the car.

"Step lively," Geoff said. "Move along." He sounded like a London bobby in a movie directing traffic in front of Harrods.

"You wouldn't have a match, would you, Benny?" It was Pete Staziak. He was standing there on the sidewalk partly masked by the Lincoln. He'd been watching the building site from there.

"Good evening, Sergeant Staziak," I said, feeling Gordon's grip on my upper arm loosen. "A foggy night for honest people to be out." I thought I was sounding a little Irish in my relief at seeing Pete.

"Cool night for this time of year," Pete said.

"If these gentlemen can spare me, I'd like a word or two with you, Sergeant. You are finished with me, aren't you?" Gordon had stopped in his tracks and Geoff had bumped into him like boxcars in a shunting yard. Len managed to find his voice:

"We're all done, Mr Cooperman. Nice running inta yeh."

"Yeah," Geoff added. "We'll finish up some other time in the near future." The three men got into the Lincoln, two in the front, and Geoff in the back. I caught another glimpse of that cigar before the door closed and the car moved off silently down Geneva Street.

"Nice playmates," Pete said as we watched the car disappear. "You being taken up by a new crowd, Benny? If those guys are who I think they are, I don't think they play by the rules."

"Pete, if I didn't say I was never so glad to see a friend before, I'm saying it now. Where'd you come from?"

"Oh, I was sitting at home thinking of Savas and the rest digging out what you say is in that column, and then I got to getting restless until Shelley threw me out of the house. She said I'd been mooching around since you left. She exaggerates, Shelley does. But I guess I was doing a lot of getting up and sitting down. That sort of thing bring you out?"

"That and a little heartburn. I think I nearly got to meet the great Anthony Thorne Pritchett, head of the English mob."

"Well, that's a pleasure I'd rather postpone, if I got the chance." We had walked over towards the entrance to the building site, but had stopped where the fence would have cut us off it it had been closed. Everybody inside looked busy trying to look busy. Down below they had cut down the footing and column like it was a stump of a dead elm, and were hoisting it to the flatbed of a truck. You could see where the cement cutter had sliced through the footing to where the filling was. I wasn't sure how the procedure went from there. It would have been one post-mortem in a million to watch. Like trying to dissect the Cardiff Giant.

"Benny, we should have a little talk in the morning about all this. If we get a positive ID, we can call off the hounds of Interpol and get back to a nice local investigation. Right?"

"You just saved my hide, Pete. I'm not going to tell you to get a subpoena. What time you want to talk? I'll be there at eight o'clock."

"And I'll be there at nine."

"Cheap joke. I saw it in a Bogart movie. Good-night, Pete."

"Good-night, Benny. Sorry about the heartburn."

I woke up from a dream in which Gordon, Geoff and Len were trying to turn me into a lasting part of a bridge abutment. They were very polite about it, and I felt peculiar having self-centred feelings about it. Tony Pritchett supervised from his Lincoln with the smoky windows. When I opened my eyes it took more than a minute to find me in Martha Tracy's spare room. I rolled out of bed and headed for the bathroom.

Forty-five minutes later, I was waiting for Pete Staziak to check in at Niagara Regional Police. I never liked calling at Niagara Regional. Usually when I do it's after being up most of the night and feeling low in the self-esteem area. At least this Wednesday morning, I was fresh from the shower, with a cup of coffee and a bran muffin digesting in my stomach. The day shift at the counter looked starched and rested. The girl on the phones even had dimples. But I felt up to it. I just hoped that Pete had slept well.

Pete Staziak had slept well, as I found out when I got a chance to ask him. Unfortunately it wasn't Pete who tapped me on the shoulder with a sleep-hungry thumb, it was Staff Sergeant Chris Savas, who had been up all night with a lump of cement and its contents. He had driven to Toronto and back. He needed a shave and no backchat as I followed him down the linoleum-paved corridor to his private office. He breathed in as I passed his massive chest moving through the doorway to his office. I've been in Savas's office before, and I was getting used to the awards and photographs on the wall, the shooting trophies and other signs that made Savas feel at home when he was sitting on the other side of his banged-about metal desk.

"Okay, Cooperman, it's time. We always get there don't we?" He moved his chair closer to mine. "I been sitting up all night with a sick friend, so I'd just as soon we skipped the playing around, the games you and Pete play between the two of you. I got the murders of a brace of Geller brothers to figure out and I wanna hear what you got to say with all the crap edited out so I don't even know it's there. We talking the same language, Cooperman?" He looked up at me and I couldn't miss the bruise marks under his eyes nor the way the light from the venetian blind highlighted the stubble on his face.

"Okay. Where do you want to start?" I asked. "I don't think I know anything you don't know."

"So, right away you're into games. I told you I got no time for crapping around this morning."

"Listen, Chris, I want to get this thing cleared up as much as you do. Then I can get back to some honest work. The way they've been playing around will change the law on divorce even more and there won't be a buck left in it for a guy like me." Savas started sucking at his teeth the way he did whenever I began wandering from the subject at hand. He was looking at me the way I imagined I looked at Kogan under the same circumstances. I took a deep breath and tried to see a straight line in front of me. "I've been working this case since last Wednesday, Chris, when the Jewish community formally asked me to make some informal inquiries. I've been doing that for a week to the minute and I haven't seen any money. I came within an ace of taking a bribe to stop playing with this deck. I took it, but I sent it back."

"Petty larceny you'll be into next, Benny." I've noticed that I bring out strange word orders in the people I talk to. After a week in my company an outsider starts mixing up "lay" and "lie" and "like" and "as though" like the rest of us Granthamites. Savas continued, "Suppose we start with the bribe. How much was it and who did you take it from?"

"It was five hundred bucks that Glenn Bagot gave me to go fishing far away from home. He wanted to buy my time so I'd stop fooling with this case. But I told you, I sent the money back."

"You think Bagot iced the Geller boys? Is that how you figure it?"

"Chris, right now I don't figure it at all. Bagot has good business reasons for keeping the Geller name out of the papers, and since he can't buy off your gang, at least by trying to pay me off he's showing his partner that his heart's in the right place."

"You're not talking about the remaining Geller, to wit Sid, are you?"

"Geller's in there all right, but he's not the only partner. The other one was watching you and your excavation team last night on Geneva Street."

"Pritchett, eh? One of my men spotted his car. So he is in with Geller and Bagot. What's the scam?"

"As far as I know it's no scam at all, just business, but with the provincial government. Highway job that's pending. The consortium of Geller, Bagot and Pritchett are bidding on the Niagara-on-the-Lake highway job. Publicity about Geller's disappearance hasn't helped, and unless I miss my guess Sid doesn't know that Bagot has Pritchett as his partner. Some of their interest in keeping me off the case was aimed at keeping brother Sid in the dark. Besides, Pritchett's name isn't likely to help things in Toronto when they pull the winning tender out of the box."

"You got your medical insurance paid up? Broken kneecaps can be expensive. It gets you in the grey area of convalescence and rehabilitation. Crutches, you know, and wheelchairs, ramps and special buses."

"Cut it out, Chris. What else you want to know?" Savas looked at me sideways for a second, banged about in his top drawer for a minute, and then called to see if Pete Staziak had booked in yet. If he was trying to make me feel like a high school kid forced to cool his heels in front of the principal's desk, he was doing all right. I tried to squirm a little so we could get this over with. It must have worked because suddenly he was looking at me again, and I had that feeling TV newscasters must get when the little red light goes on.

"You ever hear of a Lewis Gosnold? Lewis Emmett Gosnold?" I shook my head and waited for more information. It came after Chris's natural sadism had its fill. "Name on the passport in Geller's pocket. The picture was him all right. And he was also carrying a first-class airline ticket in that name to Paris, France."

"Well you know a lot I don't know, Chris. But then, I don't have the can-opening equipment you borrowed to get into that inside breast pocket. Funny how people picking new names hold on to the initials of their old one."

"Yeah, I'm having convulsions over it. What else have you got for me?"

"Just questions. Is there any sign that our boy meant to leave town with anybody? Some woman, for instance?"

"No sign of that in his personal effects. Try me again."

"Let me see the ticket." Chris opened up a file in the middle of his desk and took from it a plastic envelope from which he removed a travel bureau's cover with the usual flimsy joined-together pages backed with red carbon. They looked very well preserved considering where they'd spent the last few weeks. The travel agent was located in Hamilton. The flight was one that left Toronto's Pearson International Airport at 9:10 P.M. on the evening of Larry Geller's disappearance. "The travel agent? Have you talked to him?"

"I've got a man on it. Give us in the public service a break, Benny. We got overnight developments we're working on. This whole case has been upgraded from a disappearance to homicide. What I want to know is what did the brother Nathan find out."

"Yeah, he seems to have come into deadly information late in the game. I told Pete that he called me the day before he was murdered."

"Yeah, with a song and dance about hearing from his brother down in Florida. He was playing games with you, Benny. You should know better."

"Thanks, Chris. Maybe I shouldn't have booked that flight. I could have saved a bundle if we'd had this talk last week."

"Go to hell. Sometimes, Cooperman, you're as touchy as—"

"As you are. It must be the company I keep."

"Okay, so who did all the icing in the Geller clan? I know for a fact that you're holding out on me. You always do. I've got pressure on me from every direction to bring about a speedy and tidy solution to this investigation. My ass is in the wringer. You've been doing a local snoop while we've been waiting by the phone. I gotta know what you got."

"Well, you got my theory that Geller was running away with somebody, right?"

"Check. Next?"

"Well, you know that this woman was a smoker."

"How do we know that?"

"The ticket cover requests a window seat in the smoking section."

"So what?"

"So Geller was a non-smoker. But being a perfect gentleman he arranged for a smoking seat for him and his girl-friend. What you gotta find out is who she was. Check car rental agencies in Hamilton for a car rented in the name of Gosnold. Check the travel people for the name of the other person travelling with Gosnold. When you've got her name you can get her picture from the passport division of External Affairs."

"You're not half-bad when I get you kicking over, Cooperman. As a matter of fact we are checking out some of that, but we missed some."

"You aren't going to tell me until I get down on my knees and ask, are you Chris?"

"Ask what?"

"You know damn well I want to know what killed Larry Geller."

"Oh, yeah. Right. I got the post-mortem results right here." He waved a sheet of foolscap at me, but didn't hand it over.

"Well?"

"Larry Geller was stabbed once through the heart. Very neat." Savas's hand went over his eyes like he was going to wipe away his scowl. When he brought his hand away, his expression was unchanged, except that now I felt one too many in Savas's office.

"Were they able to compare Larry's wound with the ones that killed Wally Moore and Geller's brother?"

"Cooperman, they can't get Larry Geller to lay down yet like a decent stiff should. How the hell are they going to probe a wound in a corpse that's stuck in the fetal position?" I tried to imagine the problem, then decided to take Savas's word for it. I got out of there as fast as I could.

Chapter Twenty-Six

I came out of the police station with a blank empty feeling. I'd just given the case away. The rabbi and Mr Tepperman had asked me to find Larry Geller. Tonight everybody in town would know where he was. I knew I owed the rabbi a phone call at least, so I walked up James Street without even the interest in life to see whether there were any bagels at Bagels Deli. The weather was spoiling to break the record for this day. The sun cut right through the back of my shirt. I tried to walk in the shade of the stores kind enough to have lowered their awnings. American tourists were walking down St Andrew Street in short sleeves and seersucker. At first I thought they were pushing the season, but this was the season. Maybe, I thought, I should take a bus tour to see the ruins of the neighbourhood. When was the last time I'd seen Brock's Monument? The only time I ever climbed to the top I came down to talk to an old custodian who'd been gassed at Ypres. At the time I didn't know what he was talking about. I somehow got World War I confused with the War of 1812, when General Brock led his famous last fatal charge. I could skip the rabbi and hear about it all over again. Or I could drive to the Falls and watch the not overrated splendour of the great cataracts. Nuts, I thought. You've seen the falls.

I crossed St Andrew Street. My haunches reacted stiffly to climbing the twenty-eight steps to the office door with its peeling gold-lettering.

I lit a cigarette and called the rabbi. I told him the news and he thanked me for being a big help. He said that in spite of the fact that Larry Geller was now in no shape to undertake the restitution of his ill-gotten gains, I was to be commended for the work I'd put in. He said that I could expect payment of my bill as soon as they had my invoice.

After I hung up, I felt worse. I'd found what they wanted, the cops were sorting out the last parts of the puzzle, and now I had to bill the Jewish community in order to get some money. I knew that I was incapable of writing up the invoice, and so I would never see a dime. I felt sunburned top and bottom; there was no comfortable way to sit. I lit a second smoke from the first. I could tell this was going to be a great day.

And suddenly there was Kogan standing in the doorway. Just when you think your life is brimful of headaches, it overflows. "Kogan," I yelled across the room, "I've got no time for you today. I'm a busy man. Go haunt some other citizen. Go see Dr Bushmill." Kogan was very good at looking hurt. He did that best. I caught him with only one foot on the stairs and watched him consider my apology. "I didn't sleep well, Kogan. I'm in a lousy mood. I would have yelled at anybody. My own mother even." Slowly Kogan shifted his weight back to the leg that was on the top step, and he followed me back through the open door.

"That's no way to do business, Mr Cooperman."

"I know that, Kogan. I'm sorry." I sat down behind the desk and watched while Kogan rounded one of the chairs, like a dog trampling the vanished grass in his dreams, and finally settled and pulled the chair closer to the desk.

"What's the report, Mr Cooperman?"

"Report on what?"

"Do you know who killed Wally yet?" He looked at me as though I had forgotten the date of the discovery of America.

"Oh, Wally," I bluffed. "No, I haven't forgotten him."
"You say that, but what news have you got?" I stirred uneasily in my chair. Kogan must have taken lessons from Savas, or I was more than normally vulnerable that morning.

"I know a few things, Kogan. But they don't add up to who killed your friend. I know that he used to hang around that building site where you found the discharge pin."

"Holy Christ, I told you that when I talked to you!"

"You want to talk or listen, Kogan?"

"Okay, I'm listening."

"He had a private kip arranged down below between piles of lumber. The watchman knew him and didn't make a fuss. One night your pal witnessed a murder. He didn't show himself, but when he saw the victim's picture and name in the paper, saying that he was missing, that's when he blew his cover. He told the wrong person about it, and that's how he was murdered."

"Are you telling me he told the wife that he saw the murder? He didn't even tell *me* what he saw."

"That's what it looks like, Kogan."

"She must of done it, right?"

"She denies any knowledge of Wally."

"You can't trust a bloody murderer! Why would she tell you the truth?" This was going to be one of those days when everybody knew more about my business than I did.

"Take it easy, Kogan. I didn't say I believed her. But with Wally unavailable to make an accusation, what he told you is hearsay and about as useful in court as a movie ticket stub. To build a case you need evidence. And evidence is what we have least of."

"So nothing Wally told me is any good?"

"Come on, Kogan. What did he tell you? He told you he was going to see Mrs Geller, that they had business, and that you were eating your last can of cat food. You see, I remember."

"Yeah, but Wally had that bottle of gin. The guy in the liquor store said he broke a fifty-dollar bill for him. Where'd that come from? You're supposed to be the investigator!" Kogan screwed up his lined face so that it looked like an ordinance survey map. He was practically rubbing his hands together.

"Right," I said. "He must have met her, got the fifty and made an appointment to meet her in the park later on, before going for the gin and finishing up the cat food. Why didn't he spend some of that fifty on people-type tuna?"

"Wally was never one for sudden change."

"Let me think. Wally figured he could turn what he saw down in the cellar of the building site into cash. He tried it out and it worked. Not only that, but there was promise of more to come. He must have recognized that the victim was Larry when the paper first did a story on his disappearance." I chewed on that for a minute, but I couldn't see how the cops would make more than mashed potatoes out of it. "Kogan, what we've got here is a lot of conjecture. It could have happened this way, but it could have happened other ways too. We can't prove it happened one way over another."

"So, what do we do? Here we are sittin' twiddlin' our toes and there she is smokin' Mexican grass and laughin' at us. There's gotta be some way we can stop..."

"What's this about grass? She was smoking marijuana? How do you know that?" I was getting a little excited, so I tried to calm down. I took a breath, then started in again. "Wally told you, right?" Kogan nodded proudly. "But you didn't bother to pass it on. You didn't tell me anything about his meeting with Mrs Geller. What else are you saving? You going to gift wrap it and wait till Christmas?" Kogan's smile went indoors. "What else are you saving for later bulletins? I have to know everything, Kogan. I can't help you if I'm playing with only thirty-eight cards. I need the whole fifty-two."

"I already told you everything. I forgot about the grass. He said she lit up right in front of him. He could tell it wasn't a regular smoke by the smell."

"What else did he say? Did he describe her? Was she short, fat, tall, cross-eyed, what?"

"He didn't say nothin' about that, except that she wasn't hard to look at."

"Kogan, we may be getting somewhere." Kogan grinned. "We've just eliminated 'fat' and 'cross-eyed' from the description."

"Well, I dunno. Wally didn't hold much with women at all, so there's no tellin' what wasn't hard to look at from his standpoint."

"Welcome home 'fat' and 'cross-eyed.' " I tried to picture Ruth Geller lighting up a joint and it didn't work. That was not the Ruth Geller I knew. Instead, I saw another face and it wasn't the face I wanted to see.

Ten minutes later, I had given Kogan a couple of dollars for a cup of coffee and he gave me a dirty look by way of change. I left him at his usual stand, the corner of Queen and St Andrew, with his hand out. I headed for the marble mausoleum that Tom MacIntyre used as an office. Ever since I'd borrowed the keys to the Woodland Avenue building from MacIntyre, I'd been meaning either to have them copied or to return them. I wasn't sure what I wanted to do, but I was sure that I wanted to have a heart-to-heart with Larry Geller's former landlord.

The redhead was at her desk surrounded by the cold marble of business trying to ape classic architecture. As long as the receptionist took the occasional breath or reached for the remaining half of her morning blueberry muffin, the room would never work. Replace the girl with a stone column and you might achieve an effect but whether or not you'd do any business was another question. I began by telling her that once again I didn't have an appointment. With some badly concealed pleasure she told me that Mr MacIntyre was not in the office and wasn't expected until later in the day if at all. I figured she was telling the truth. If she was expecting her boss, the blueberry muffin on her desk blotter would have been out of sight. I told her that MacIntyre wanted to see me. She looked suspicious but smiled with guile: "Then why did he tell you to come here instead of having you meet him at the boat? I don't think you are telling the truth." I looked hurt, and offered her my pack of Player's. She fooled me and took one.

"Is that the one in the marina at Niagara-on-the-Lake?" I asked her as she held my hand steady for the match.

"I only know about the Port Richmond boat. If he has another, he hasn't told me about it."

"Well, if I miss him, you can tell him I dropped by."

"Yes, Mr Cooperman."

The road to Port Richmond led to the north end, past my parents' town house. The marina was bunched up into the funnel-like opening of the entrance to a lock in the old canal. It was a forest of aluminum masts each emitting a ping as loose cables hit the metal uprights. I parked the car across from the main street, which looked like the set for a western movie in the back lot of one of the old Hollywood studios. The view from the shaded balconies looked across to what locals still called the "Michigan" side, even though the Michigan Central tracks had been pulled up before most of them were born. From the wharf, where as a kid I remember the two lake steamers from Toronto used to tie up, I could see the two wooden lighthouses on the twin piers jutting out into the lake towards Toronto. A couple of huge trees, left over from the heyday of Lakeside Park, now sheltered only a few sunbathers. The beach had, of course, been condemned for swimming at the beginning of the month, but a few kids in bathing suits were beachcombing with an active fox terrier. I couldn't see the skyline of the provincial capital in the summer haze, but remembered the CN Tower and a few other tall buildings standing out on frostier days than this one. I wanted to take my shirt off, or wander down the now vanished corridor of ride and refreshment stands. Only the old merry-go-round survived, and that in a new location.

I could see no activity on any of the boats from the wooden catwalks that separated the marina into berths for some hundreds of boats. The hatches were covered with canvas, the booms wrapped in coloured plastic. I watched and listened to the ping-ping-ping of the masts for a couple of minutes, but heard no other sound.

The antique store I went into for information looked pitch dark when I came in out of the sun. A woman on a ladder ignored me and spoke to the gnarled old man who'd just come in from the back of the store. "Mr Helwig, I moved 'God is Love' down there. Hope you don't mind." I asked where the sailors went to eat. "You'll find most of them drinking in the pub at the end of the road, but a few eat at Marie's or Murphy's."

"Who are you looking for?" the old man asked.

"Tom MacIntyre. White-haired man, owns a boat in the marina."

"He'll be at Murphy's feeding the piranha."

"I never been in there," the woman on the ladder volunteered.

"I should think not," said Mr Helwig as I found my way out towards the light.

I found him as advertised, with a paper carton of goldfish in one hand and a lobster claw in the other. Except for the piranha and the goldfish, he was alone at a wooden table laminated in transparent plastic.

"Well, well, Mr Cooperman! Are you still hot on the trail of Larry Geller?"

"Mr Geller's dead, Mr MacIntyre. The police are holding his body."

"Well, well, how does it go? 'The weed of crime bears bitter fruit...' You'd better sit down and join us." I did that, and as I collected a chair I took in the heavily nautical trappings of the room: everything from anchor chains and fish-nets to model ships in bottles and polished brass-work. The bar was a lifeboat levelled off for landlubber duties.

A white suit in July is dramatic enough, but when it's filled by a large pink-knuckled albino, you've moved from dramatic to sensational or whatever the next step is. He could see me checking him out as he sipped an amber drink without ice. "Will you join me in a drink, Mr Cooperman?"

"I'll have a beer, I think. It's warm enough." I noticed that I was sweating. MacIntyre grinned, then called out for a round of drinks. I could see his bluey-pink eyes were vibrating. The piranha nipped at the tail of one of half a dozen goldfish in the tank. The others were sheltering under a curve in the ornamental driftwood inside. But not for long.

"Have you sought me out to return the keys you borrowed, Mr Cooperman? I had to send Vicki out to have another set cut. I should charge you."

"I borrowed the keys because you wanted me to. Let's not run around in circles, Mr MacIntyre. You tipped Glenn Bagot off about my visit last Friday, didn't you? He borrowed some help from a friend and they met me coming out of Larry's little hideaway on Woodland."

"You have the Levantine imagination, Mr Cooperman."

"Nobody else knew I was headed over there. Only you."

"Why would I want to set you up? You're nothing to me but a break in the routine. You remind me that I was a one-man band not so many years ago. You reminded me of my youth." He tried to end things there with a winning grin, but I wasn't in the market for winning grins. I wanted to nail MacIntyre for all he knew.

"You knew that Geller rented that place from you. You don't forget just because he took French leave. You had guilty knowledge, which wasn't so bad until I came snooping. But after me would come Grantham's finest with more questions of an embarrassing kind. So you phoned Bagot in a panic: Cooperman's on his way over to 44 Woodland. What are we going to do? Bagot told you to leave it to him. He'd throw a little scare into me. He knew how to handle my type. Something like that? Am I close?"

"I'll deny it all. I honestly forgot that Geller had that place. You'll have to believe that."

"I don't take a lot of convincing, Mr MacIntyre. But juries do. And for what it's worth I'm not trying to see how muddy I can make the water. I just once in a while want to meet a half-way honest man."

"You and Diogenes the cynic."

"I haven't come to him yet. How long have I got before you'll be renting that place?"

"Geller's? Since it's paid up until the end of the year, I think I can afford to let it rest fallow until the end of the month. Are you thinking of moving in?"

"It might help me to think through this business."

"Then, help yourself."

"If I do, Mr MacIntyre, I'd prefer to think that just the two of us know about it. In fact I might leave a memorandum to that effect somewhere. I wouldn't like to run into that trio of goons again without knowing that your part in it wouldn't go unrewarded." The goldfish in the tank now numbered four. MacIntyre wasn't even watching. "And since you forgot to call the cops on Friday, let me tell them about the hideaway when I'm ready for them."

I tried to look him in his shaky eyes, but he was looking to the window where a starfish caught in a fish-net was silhouetted against the light. My last view of him, before I went out the door, was of a totally white figure pouring a stiff drink from a flask of Irish whiskey.

Chapter Twenty-Seven

S teve Tulk worked for the telephone company. He was a big guy even in high school where he made a better captain of the football team than he did a Duke in *Twelfth Night*. I played Curio, and we had a scene together near the beginning. The scene goes like this:

Curio: Will you go hunt, my lord?

Duke: What, Curio?

Curio: The hart.

After that I was ready for the showers, while Steve had the rest of the play and a curtain call. A few years later I was able to do him a favour professionally when his ex-wife disappeared with his two kids. He wanted me to snatch them for him, but I simply gave him the address in Barrie and let him do what he wanted himself. When I talked to him on the phone, I didn't have to remind him of all this. In fact he sounded glad to hear from me. I was able to let him know that the time had come to return the favour without putting that short temper of his out of joint. We met for a beer and there, in the Men's Beverage Room of the Harding House, I explained what I wanted him to do in Larry's hideaway at 44 Woodland Avenue. Steve shrugged when I asked him if he could handle it, so I took it that the job was as good as done. Just the same, I arranged for him to call me at my office when the dirty deed was done. The call came a little after six.

An hour later, I presented myself at the front door of Debbie Geller's house on Francis Street off Welland Avenue. It was a hot night, but I'd put on a jacket and tie just to show that I knew about the little things that divide society up the middle into those who know better and those who are comfortable. I heard the chime sound on the inside and saw a shadow approaching through the cranberry stained-glass windows that ran up either side of the door.

"Mr Cooperman! This is a surprise. I was expecting Sid. You're early for the minyan. Won't you come in?" Debbie looked mildly shocked to see me, but spoke with a voice that was too tired to put much expression into her reading of the line. "It's not Sid," Debbie called ahead of us. "It's Mr Cooperman from the...It's Mr Cooperman."

"Like a bad penny," I said. She led the way through the vestibule and through an arch into the living-room. Instinctively, I found my eyes drawn to the spot where I'd last seen the tray of cold cuts. They had vanished, of course. Debbie's sister, Ruth, was sitting in the centre of a large chintz-covered couch. The room looked bigger without a hundred people shoving their way towards the smoked carp and carved turkey. That was a funeral to remember. Now they would have to have one for Nathan's brother Larry. Would anybody come? Two brothers within a week. I could see from the faces of the two women, as Debbie slipped into a Queen Anne chair nearest the archway, that they had been thinking along similar lines. Ruth hardly looked up. She was examining the pattern cut into the wall-to-wall broadloom. "I'm sorry for your trouble, Mrs Geller," I said, echoing both myself a few short days ago and Frank Bushmill, the neighbour who taught me this useful Irish expression of sympathy. I thought of adding about it being all for the best and another observation about how certainty beats uncertainty every time, but I couldn't find the right words. I gave them a break and sat down and kept my mouth shut.

"As you can see, Mr Cooperman," Debbie said, "we are still stunned by the news. Even though he's been away all these weeks, it's still a shock." Ruth raised her eyes from the floor and looked at her sister as though she was trying to see how close what Debbie said came to what she was feeling. Debbie went on: "I invited Ruth over here. I didn't want her to be alone in that big house to-night. She's going to be staying with me, aren't you Ruthie?" Ruth made an inaudible response. "May I get you some coffee, Mr Cooperman, or would you prefer a drink? Sid will be here in a few minutes. Maybe then we'll all have a drink? In the meantime, coffee?" I nod-ded, and Debbie left the room. Ruth had returned to the pattern of the smokey-blue carpet. Sharing a silence with her was next door to sitting by myself. I couldn't think of anything to say anyway, so I thought I could be build-ing up points on tact by just keeping still.

About the same time I could hear crockery on a tray coming from the direction of the kitchen, a big car pulled up and parked in front of the house. Sid and Pia came in and Debbie greeted them, managing the coffee tray at the same time. Ruth got to her feet and Sid held her close with his arms around her for a long time. When they broke the clinch, both of them had tears in their eyes. Pia was the first to light a cigarette. It gave her some-thing to do. This couldn't be easy for her. After the funeral all those people made for substantial insulation between herself and Debbie. As for me, I'd tried to make myself into a fly on the wall.

For the first few minutes, I don't think anyone but Pia noticed me. Everybody but me got a hug from some-body. Pia was short-changed by Debbie, but she was still holding the tray. It was Sid who first took official notice of me. He didn't sound unfriendly but his greet-ing needed more work before it could convince a drama critic. "So, Mr Cooperman, bad news travels fast. No sooner is my brother found than you turn up. Have you started chasing ambulances in your old age?"

"Mr Geller," I tried to say in an even voice, "I'm sorry about your brother."

"Which one?" He shrugged, which is hard to do with as short a neck as Sid had. "Did you come over here to ask more questions, Mr Cooperman? Why don't you let the cops handle this?"

"Sid has a point," Pia put in. Even Ruth was nodding agreement. I sipped my coffee then replaced the cup on the saucer with a racket that sounded like a gunshot.

"Look, this might be as good a time as any to tell you that my involvement with this case is over," I said. Debbie exchanged a look with her former husband. "I was brought into this by Rabbi Meltzer and Saul Tepperman. They had some idea that I could do something on behalf of the Jewish community. While there was a chance that Larry was alive somewhere, there was a chance that he might be persuaded to return the money he took and make good on his obligations. Now that we know that he can't do that, there's no way I can help Mr Tepperman, the rabbi or the community. So, I'm bowing out. Since I guess I've bothered all of you most, I thought I should let you know in person. That's all. End of speech. And if you need a tenth man for the minyan, I'm here." I picked up my coffee and nearly choked taking a badly gauged swig. Sid pounded my back and I came back to life.

"I don't get you, Cooperman," Sid Geller said, as he took a seat beside his sister-in-law on the couch. "Just when the case has taken a big turn, you drop it. Why?"

"Well, in the first place, this is a case for the cops. I keep telling everybody that most cases are, but luckily some of them don't believe me. As far as this one goes, the cops are now putting all available men on it. It's no longer a matter of waiting for Larry to make a move down in Florida or try using a credit card in Paris. The cops have his passport and the name he planned to use in his new life. From that they can move on quickly. They'll have the murderer before you know it."

"That's reassuring," said Debbie, lighting up one of her menthol cigarettes and accepting a light from Pia's familiar lighter. "But how long will all this take? You have no idea what this has done to all our lives. To think of it dragging on much longer, well..."

"I shouldn't think it will take them a lot longer. I was talking with Staff Sergeant Savas earlier today, and he said that they are trying to locate an office somewhere here in town where Larry did the paperwork for his..." I didn't know how to end the sentence with so many of his relations looking on, so I went back and ended it with "paperwork" and left it at that. "When they get there they'll go over it with a microscope. If there's a shred of evidence, they'll find it. I was on a case a year ago where the husband I was trying to locate was found just by discovering information on the redial memory of his girl-friend's telephone. You know, one of those cheap, made-in-Taiwan jobs. It shouldn't take more than a day or so for them to find the hideaway, and then it will be very fast work to close the noose on the guilty party." I'd ended with more of a dramatic flourish than I'd meant to, but I could see that all of the Geller relatives and friends were paying attention.

"What else have the police found out, Mr C? You seem to be the first to hear what's going on." Pia Morley was smiling at me, but it wasn't quite as friendly as I remembered her smile the last time we'd met.

"Well, it's true," I said. "They have told me a few things that the reporters at the *Beacon* don't know about yet."

"Sid, why don't you get us all a drink. You know where the liquor is. There's ice in the fridge under the bar." Sid got up and moved past his former wife and current mistress to the dining-room, where the tinkling of crystal and the ping of ice-cubes could soon be heard. In the meantime, we waited. After what seemed long enough for a jury to make up its mind, Sid returned with drinks on a tray.

"I brought rye. Debbie's out of Scotch," Sid said.

"Idiot. You don't know where to look for it, that's all." She got up and went into the kitchen.

"Rye's fine with me," Ruth said, trying out a smile.

"Sure," said Pia, "just as long as it stings." She collected a glass for Sid and herself. I took one of the remaining two glasses.

With the exception of Debbie, we were all sitting down again, watching the ice-cubes melt in our drinks. In a few minutes, conversation started up again. It was about Ruth's kids in Toronto. She'd had a call from them, but hadn't told them about the death of their father yet. Sid suggested that there was no need to rush to be first with the bad news. Soon Debbie could be heard in the dining-room. "Anyone for Scotch?" she called. "I had to go down to the rec room to find it." There were no takers apart from herself. She appeared carrying her drink in a glass that matched the crystal of the orphan on the tray. "Now tell us," she said, "if you haven't told everybody already." She settled herself back in her chair, leaning towards the rest of us in the group. She seemed like a fellow-conspirator waiting to hear the rest of the plot. The others, except for Ruth, were just as bad.

"Are you sure you want to hear this?" I asked. "It may not come out the way you expect. It may only raise more issues than it settles."

"We want to know what's been going on," Sid said. "If you think you know so much, we want to hear it."

"Well, I don't quite know where to begin. I guess I'll begin with Larry. His was the first of the murders. From the papers you know that he had been defrauding many of his clients over a long period of time. He had been illegally converting assets over to himself and...well, I won't go into it. He further converted over two million dollars worth of these assets into commercial diamonds. What this tells us is at least two things: he wasn't, as some lawyers are, temporarily embarrassed for funds and dipping into the trust accounts as a short-term stopgap. It was part of a carefully worked out plan. That leads up to the other item: he was intending to leave town, using the diamonds to finance his departure and subsequent settling down somewhere in a brand new life under a brand new name.

"We don't know where he planned to end up, but his route went through Paris. We have a ticket confirmed on a flight from Toronto on the night he disappeared. The name on the ticket matches the name on the new passport he was carrying at the time of his death."

I could feel that I had the audience, and I wished that I had lines as good as Steve Tulk had in *Twelfth Night*, but all I had were a handful of facts and a lot of conjecture. I took a sip of rye and put the glass down on the coffee-table harder than I intended. "From the plane ticket and a few other things we know that Larry was planning to leave town with somebody. Plane tickets were bought in the name of Mr and Mrs Lewis Gosnold. We know that the woman appeared to be ready to run away with Larry. She may have encouraged, even masterminded, the whole scam. Larry's legal friends all agree that when they first knew him, Larry was very serious about the law. It was only fairly recently that his attitude changed. Blame that on the lady. From what we know about her, she could be capable of anything. We don't have a picture of her yet, but I've learned a few things about her. She double-crossed Larry. They arranged to meet at the Bolduc site where they're building the new fire hall. Larry had used the construction shack there to hide his suitcase with the diamonds in it. It was on the way out of town. The perfect rendezvous.

"Only Larry didn't expect that his partner had figured out that half of the diamonds was too big a fraction to lose. She pretended that everything was going as arranged until she slipped a knife between his ribs and dumped his body into a frame where footings for the fire hall were about to be poured the next day.

"What she didn't figure on was the fact that the murder was seen by a down-and-outer by the name of Wally Moore. He was hiding in a nest he'd built safe from the wind and weather. Wally Moore was her next victim. Simply because he'd been foolish enough to try to get in touch with the wife of the victim. He was only trying to help out: the paper said that Larry was missing; he knew that he'd been murdered. Further, he knew where the body was. He went to see Mrs Geller. Mrs Geller gave him fifty dollars to keep quiet about it until she had a chance to hear the whole story. They arranged to meet in Montecello Park, where she knifed him too."

"That's a goddamned lie!" It was Ruth Geller. She was on her feet, her eyes wide with anger. "I told you it wasn't me. I told you, but you won't believe the truth!" She had walked to the centre of the room, with her eyes fixed on me. "You hateful, spiteful man, I despise you!" Sid got up and tried to put an arm on Ruth's shoulder, but she brushed it off. "Why do you allow this man in your house, Debbie?" Ruth asked. "I really thought you had more sense."

"In the circumstances, Mr Cooperman..." Debbie never got to finish what she started to say. Ruth was now walking towards Pia.

"You were the one he meant, weren't you? You were the double-dealer he was talking about."

"Ruth! Sit down!" Sid pulled at her, but she wouldn't budge.

"You killed all of them, didn't you? You took my sister's husband and killed his brothers. It was you. I don't care what they do to you, I just don't want to have to

look at you. Will you please get out of here?" She slapped
Pia in the face. It wasn't a very good slap, but Pia's face
went quite red except at the place where the blow had
landed. Sid had a grip on Ruth now, and led her sobbing
back to her place on the couch. Near perfect silence. If I
was bluffing my way forward, trying to provoke some
accusations or confessions, I wasn't doing bad. I only
hoped that nobody called my bluff before I'd guessed
the cards everybody else was holding.

Chapter Twenty-Eight

Shock waves from the slap that Ruth landed on Pia lingered in the living-room like a bad smell. Pia quietly excused herself and went upstairs, where in a moment I could hear water running. In a moment she returned, having splashed water on her face and rubbed it a little too hard with one of Debbie's luxurious towels. To her I guess we looked like a tableau vivant from some old play, or a grouping by Nathan Geller, for there we stood very much the way she'd left us: Debbie looking daggers at me for hurting Ruth, who was sobbing on Sid's shoulder. I didn't know whether I was still under sentence to leave the house or whether Ruth's more recent accusation meant that the action had stepped over my body to more important things. I decided that I wasn't going to leave the house unless my unwanted presence came up again. I had a seat front and centre, the curtains were opening on the last act, and I'd be damned if I'd willingly leave my seat for a smoke in the lobby.

Pia went directly to Sid. She touched him lightly on the back and said in a low, artificial voice: "I think we should go, Sid." Sid nodded, and patted his sister-in-law on the shoulders. He slowly pulled her body away from his, pausing when he had her at arm's length to see if Ruth was going to be able to stand on her own.

"There, there," he said. "There, there."

"For what it's worth," Pia Morley said in a steady voice, "I want you all to know that in spite of being the crazy broad you have known all these years, I am not, on top of it all, a murderer. I don't run away with other people's husbands, even though I plead guilty to being a bitch in countless other ways. Debbie knows I didn't take Sid away from her, and Ruth, you should try to remember that I'm very happy with Sid. Why would I want to run away with Larry? And if I ran away with him, why didn't I leave town?" Ruth looked at her sister, who tried to catch my eye. I was watching Sid, who was twitching inside his suit. "Sid isn't some kind of human pinball," Pia said. "He does what he wants to do, like the rest of us when we can. God knows I've got a checkered past, Ruth, but why would I want to...I'm sorry, why would I run away with Larry?" She was speaking in a measured voice that only slightly resembled her normally exaggerated style of speaking. She rationed her breath to make sure she had enough to say all of the things she'd put together since leaving the room.

"What about *this*?" Ruth asked, holding up the photograph of Larry with his hands over Pia's eyes. Pia took the snapshot from her and looked at it, then smiled. She handed it back again.

"That was at that party here last fall. Remember, Debbie, I got tanked on white wine and about six men walked me around the block. Damn it, I can't help it when somebody puts their hands on me. It's been happening all my life. Nathan used to say I was a very tactile broad." Right then Pia was looking more than just tactilely interesting.

"Then where were you on the day that Larry disappeared?"

"How should I know? I haven't been out of town since my trip to my gynaecologist in Toronto. If you want to check, his name is Walter Shankman in the Medical Arts Building, damn it. Sid, why am I defending myself, when I haven't done anything?" Sid didn't answer, he simply pressed the rounded shoulder of his sister-in-law, to which he was still attached. Pia saw that Ruth was still holding the photograph in an accusatory way. "Look," Pia said, "a half-wit could see he was clowning. Ruth? Ruth, can't you understand? I wasn't in love with your husband. His brother absorbs all my attention. Benny, can't you see that?"

I was glad to get some status back, and nodded earnestly. "I believe you, Pia," I said, "and maybe Ruth is beginning to. Tell us, Ruth, where did you get the idea that Pia was fooling around with Larry?" Ruth raised her eyes, looking a little wilted and damp.

"It just looked that way. I don't know. I know he wasn't spending his idle hours at our house. So I thought...And then when Debbie showed me the picture...Well, I guess I just jumped at the idea. It was something, after all. And I'd been living with nothing." She looked up at Pia. "I'm sorry, Pia, but you don't know what I've been going through."

At that moment the door-chime sounded like a summons in a minor key. Ruth looked up, and Debbie went to the door. When she returned she had Pete Staziak with her. He was looking awkward and large the way he always did in public. He reintroduced himself to the group and apologized for coming without calling first. "There has been a development which we feel you should know about." Pete used the word "feel" a lot when he must have meant "think" or something with sharper edges. "We have located Larry Geller's satellite office. And I'd like permission to bring over a witness to meet you. As a matter of fact, I'm expecting a call from him here." He glanced over at Debbie and added, "If you don't mind." Debbie shrugged her indifference.

"Since you're on duty, Sergeant, I suppose I can't offer you a drink?" Debbie said, almost coquettishly.

"You can offer, and I appreciate your offer, but you're right, I'm on the job. Unlike my colleague from the private sector here, we have our standing orders about drinking on duty. But thank-you just the same. Frankly, on a hot night like this, I could use a cold beer the same as anybody."

The phone rang at that moment, and it came so quickly on Pete's heels that the two events seemed to have happened together. Debbie caught the phone in the kitchen and came back to announce that it was for Staff Sergeant Staziak. Sid muttered something about Pete being well organized as Staziak bowed out of the living-room and out of sight. While he was gone, the doorbell rang its version of the Westminster chimes again, and Rabbi Meltzer and Saul Tepperman came into the vestibule without waiting for the door to be answered. "Rabbi Meltzer! Oh, it's good of you to come. How are you, Saul?" said Debbie, the perfect surprised hostess.

"We thought," Saul Tepperman said, clearing his throat, "that we'd just drop around for a minute to pay our respects. I had an idea you'd all be over here for the minyan anyway." He went over to Ruth and shook her by the hand and brushed a kiss on her passing cheek. Debbie made a round of introductions, and repeated them again when Pete rejoined us from the kitchen. Saul hadn't met him before and clasped his hand warmly in a manner that seemed to say I hope we never have to do this again. Both Saul and the rabbi seemed curious about Sid's live-in friend. They looked at her as though they thought they might catch a glimpse of walking, breathing, palpitating evil on the hoof just by being in the same room with Pia Morley. They were both of them smiling with a brightness that made their teeth look like dentures.

"Benny here," Debbie said, with a sweep of her arm to let the uninitiated know whom she was talking about, "was just giving us a review of his findings over the past two weeks."

"It only seems that long. I came into this exactly a week ago."

"Benny has been a great help to us on the case," Pete said. It was Pete the friend talking, putting in a good word for me with my people. I felt like the owner of a restaurant who has been mistaken for a waiter and given a tip. But he was right, I had been a big help to Niagara Regional, and now that Pete had said it that way, nobody would ever believe it. Pete was a clever son of a bitch.

Debbie tried to make people comfortable. Sid brought in chairs from the dining-room, like we were about to hear a lieder recital. Pia tried to catch up with the drinks. Debbie shouted that there was lots of ice in the fridge under the bar. I held on to my coffee. It was cold by now but I was sure there wouldn't be fresh for some time to come.

Just when we were all settled, the door-chime sounded again. Sid went, and returned looking annoyed and at me. "There's a guy at the door asking for you, Cooperman. He looks like a rummy of some kind. Should I get rid of him?"

"That will be Victor Kogan. He's the witness that Pete Staziak was talking about. He's the man who just phoned." I got up and brought a reluctant Kogan into the room and made a stab at the introductions all over again. As a matter of fact, I was getting good at it. Kogan acted like he was at his favourite intersection. He greeted Sid like they were regular acquaintances. Pete smiled, so there was nothing the women could do. Why is it that a guy like Kogan seems to undermine the structure of our society? He doesn't say you can never sell another raffle ticket on a car again, he doesn't preach that our values are up the chimney. But Ruth, Pia and Debbie behaved as though he had just climbed off the soap box.

"I done like you told me, Mr Cooperman," Kogan said, sitting down on an expanse of light-coloured chintz between two of the women. "I phoned as soon as I could afterwards."

"I should explain," I said. We have been running a little test on all of you, or at least some of you. Rabbi and Mr Tepperman, you arrived after I had thrown out the bait."

"Mr Cooperman, this happens to be a house of mourning. Let me remind you we are sitting *shiva*. I'm shocked and disgusted by your boorish insensitivity. There have been two deaths in this family!" Debbie looked her best when she was playing the watch-dog for her sister. I remembered the skirmishes of our first meetings.

"We all appreciate the situation, Mrs Geller, and nobody's trying to make it into a three-ring circus. But, I admit, we did engage in a simple stratagem." Ruth looked stunned and glanced at her sister, Debbie moved closer to Ruth, Pia held on to Sid's arm. Sid looked like he wasn't sure whether to sock me or shut up and listen. "A couple of days ago, I blundered into the office that Larry used to keep the papers he required for the complicated scam he was operating within the Jewish community. That was where he kept his books, and where he organized the escape route for himself and his girlfriend.

"One of the things I found, was the burned fragment of a bag that had contained diamonds. So I knew the form the loot Larry had acquired had taken. He could have gone for negotiable bonds, gold certificates, that sort of thing. But his way was diamonds, and it's as good a way as any. Any jeweller around the world will give you a fair price for a good diamond with a clear pedigree. The other thing I found was that Larry's phone had a built-in memory. When I phoned out using the redial button, I got his wife. Now, what could be more natural than that? Husband phones home to say that he'll be held up, or that he'll be right there. The trouble is we know that for the last couple of months, Larry never phoned home. All messages to Ruth were relayed through Rose Craig, Larry's legal secretary. Still, when I used the phone, I got Ruth. I didn't tell her where I was calling from of course, but I'm sure that she'll remember our conversation." Eyes went to Ruth, who was sitting on the edge of the couch, her back very straight and her thin fingers entwined around one another.

"Yes, I think I remember the call you mean. We talked about Nathan, who'd called you in the middle of the night."

"That's right," I said. "Ruth, how do you account for the fact that the memory on that phone got you?"

"Well, I think I can..."

"Just one little minute, Mr Cooperman," Pia said, "are you saying that the centre of this case is in the memory of the telephone in Larry's secret office?"

"I guess I'm saying that. Or at least that's part of what I'm saying."

"Well, I for one would like to see this telephone for myself." I glanced at Pete, who shrugged his shoulders.

"We can go there, sure," he said. "Even if we walk, it won't take us more than a few minutes." I looked at Debbie, who looked at her sister, who began to get to her feet. Rabbi Meltzer looked to Saul Tepperman for guidance. They were the last to get up.

"This is very exciting," the rabbi said perhaps a little more loudly than he'd intended.

It only took about eight minutes to walk up Francis to Welland Avenue, along Welland Avenue for a block, then down Woodland to the office building at number 44. Kogan had my keys, so he opened the front door and led the way up the front stairs and along the corridor to the rear of the building, where he unlocked the door. The nine of us moved into the small room, which didn't get any larger when the lights were turned on. All eyes went around the office, each pair finding the headland it needed to make sense of the scene. When they had finished with the filing cabinet, the chairs, the desk and the wastepaper basket with the scorch marks, they settled on the telephone in the middle of the desk. "It's one of those cheap Formosa jobs," Sid said, as though he expected more from an important clue in a human drama like this. "Well," he went on, "let's see where it takes us." He looked around for volunteers. "Who wants to see where this thing takes us? Pia?"

"No thanks. I'm content to watch." She held on to Sid's arm tightly.

"Well, who's going to push the redial button? What about you, Mrs Geller?" Pete was making room for Ruth, but her sister pushed her way in.

"Sergeant, my sister has gone through a lot today. If you want to experiment, let me be the guinea pig."

"Thank-you, Mrs Geller. Your finger will do just as well." Debbie stepped up and lifted the one-piece instrument from the desk. "Is this the button you want?" she asked, looking up at Staziak, and pointing to the "redial" button.

"That's the one, on the lower right-hand side." Debbie pushed the button and held the phone to her ear. When it began to ring, she held the instrument so that we all could hear. It was on the dying end of the third ring when the ring stopped abruptly and someone answered on the other end.

"Hello? This is Mrs Geller, who is this please?" We all could hear the sound of the response without being able to make out the words. Debbie said. "Hold the line, please." She rested the phone on her shoulder and said to no one in particular "It's Rona Bagot, Glenn's wife!"

"Rona!" said Pia, with disbelief. "But she's visiting Sid and me at my place. She's in my apartment!"

"Can you confirm that?" Staziak was speaking to Debbie.

"Rona, this is Debbie Geller again. Could you give me the number on the telephone you're using?" There was a brief pause. "Yes, it is a kind of experiment we're conducting." She repeated the number.

"What's going on here?" said Sid, taking the phone from his sister-in-law. "Rona, is that you? No, we haven't all gone crazy. I'll explain when we get back. No, it shouldn't be much longer. Goodbye. Just a minute!" He waved the instrument at Pete. "You wanna take a crack?" Pete shook his head, and Sid told the unseen Mrs Bagot to hang up. He did the same and then faced the rest of us. "Well?" he said, "I think we just proved something, but what is it?"

"You're not going to say that Pia had anything to do with any of these crimes," Debbie Geller said, looking a little like a mamma fox protecting her brood. "She couldn't have had anything to do with any of this."

"Well, I don't know," Pete said. "The person who last made a call on that phone was Larry Geller. We figure that it must have been made close to the time that Larry made his flit. We know that it had to be around then because he had no later opportunity. He was dead within an hour of placing that call."

"But why to my place?" Pia cried. "I don't understand."

"Are you accusing Pia of these murders, Sergeant?" asked Mr Tepperman. Sid was glowering at Pete, but unable to make a sound.

"We'll stand by you, Pia," Debbie said. "We won't let the police railroad you on evidence as flimsy as that." She looked at Pete and then at me. "You can't make a charge stick that's only based on a telephone call." She said this like it was the cornerstone of Canadian jurisprudence. "The telephone just proves that someone, possibly Larry, called Pia at some time prior to his death. You can't tie a noose with telephone cord, Sergeant Staziak." Pete nodded, and let his eyes look in my direction.

"There is the question of the lighter," I offered.

"What lighter?" Ruth Geller asked, suddenly taking more interest in the proceedings since Pia had become the central figure. Pete glanced my way but didn't say anything.

"Pia's Dunhill," I said. "It was found at the scene." Pia glared hatred at me. I felt Sid's substantial bulk moving towards me.

"Benny, I told you how that happened," Pia said, with her eyes half-closed. "I told you the truth about the lighter."

"Mr Cooperman, Pia could have left the lighter in Nathan's studio hundreds of times. As a clue the lighter is as pathetic a piece of evidence as the telephone." Debbie's eyes were bright with defiance. "They're both clutching at straws, aren't they Sid?"

"If there wasn't a cop here, Cooperman, your brains would be on the sidewalk outside."

"Just don't hit me for a minute, Mr Geller. We still have a way to go." Geller wasn't mollified much, but there wasn't a lot of swinging room uncluttered with relatives, rabbis and the president of the shul. For the moment, Sid had to take out his feelings on his molars. I turned to Debbie: "How did you know that the lighter we were talking about was found at Nathan's studio?" Debbie's eyes smiled as she collected her thoughts.

"Why, you yourself said it was found there. You heard him, Ruth?"

"What everybody heard me say was that the lighter was found at the scene. I didn't say whether it was the fire-hall site where Larry was murdered, or whether it was the park where another related crime took place. But you knew which scene I meant, and I wonder how."

"Well, if I didn't hear it from you, I must have learned it from one of the dozen policemen that have been in and out of my house since the murder of poor Nathan."

"That would be fair enough if the cops knew about the lighter, but they didn't." Pete was glaring at me. I could tell, even though I could only see him out of the corner of my eye. I turned to face him. "Sorry, Pete, it was one of those things I forgot to tell you and Chris about. The lighter was left at the scene in Nathan's studio, but it was removed from there before you were called in. Before I got there too." I thought that I'd better add that last part or I'd find that Pete and Sid were going to join forces to find a way to push me out the window. I turned back to Debbie. "Debbie, how did you know about the lighter when no one else did?"

"You're out of your depth, Benny. You've got things twisted again," she said, trying to smile, as though the proper expression could make this ugly scene disappear.

"There's only one way I can figure it," I said. "You're the one, Debbie. You did it. You did it to Larry, to Kogan's pal Wally, when he got too close, and you did it to Nathan too. Bringing in Pia as a prime suspect was part of the scheme, but just a minor part, not on a par with the rest of your very clever scam."

"There are laws in this country, Mr Cooperman," Debbie said steadily, "to protect people like me from people like you who say damaging things in front of witnesses. I think I've heard enough. This is a very stuffy room, I think I'll go home." Debbie turned, and said her sister's name, and they both made a move towards the door. At this moment a uniformed man from Niagara Regional made himself visible by filling the doorway with his two hundred pounds. Debbie and Ruth looked at the rest of us. Ruth was confused and disbelieving. She looked around the room at each of us and then at Debbie. Debbie stood very still, like she was gathering in her strength for a move she had not the resolution to make. There is only one word to describe her as she turned to face the rest of us and that word is "caught."

Chapter Twenty-Nine

I t was some time before anyone spoke. What at first appeared as a gross slander was now being considered, not believed or taken for gospel, but it had been born, had a life and weight of its own. The silence brought with it the distant sounds of traffic moving along Welland Avenue. It was Sid who finally spoke. "First you make damaging statements about Pia, and now you're giving Debbie a working over. What kind of guy are you, Cooperman?"

"Well, Sid, I had to pretend that I suspected Pia in order to catch Debbie off balance. Debbie intended us to suspect Pia and built a trail of phony evidence leading to her door. You saw what happened on the phone. Debbie did that, a bit of inspired malice Debbie dreamed up when I told all of you about how we'd nailed somebody through the redial memory on the phone. You remember that Debbie then went to look for the Scotch. What she really did was go out across to this building to remove the redial memory that pointed at her, and replace it with the one you heard."

"But she wasn't gone for more than a few minutes."

"The back door of this building is practically at the foot of Debbie's backyard. How long does it take to cross the garden, run up three flights and dial a telephone number?"

"Francis Street and Woodland. He's right. They're next to one another and both about the same distance down the block."

"Debbie had used the short cut many times before when she went to visit Larry. And, I'm sorry to say, Ruth, that Larry used it when he visited your sister."

"You'll never make me believe you," Ruth said, holding on to her sister to show the strength of her belief. "You have no proof, no rationale, nothing but malice. Why do you hate us, Mr Cooperman?" Ruth said this so simply that Staziak looked at me with the same question.

"I don't hate anybody, Mrs Geller. I don't like the things I've come across, but after being in the divorce business for so long, I'm used to unpleasant surprises. I'm sorry for the hurt in all this. I wanted to hurt you least of all, because they took advantage of you from the start. Nathan was aware that something was going on. That's why he was killed. That's what he wanted to talk to Pia about the night he was murdered. She got there just after Debbie had stabbed him, before she had even left the studio. That gave her an idea. So she left the lighter, which she had found earlier in the day. She didn't know, and couldn't have known, that Pia noticed the loss and arranged to have it picked up.

"In one way you're right, Ruth, I don't have a lot of proof. But I do have this." Here I pulled the desk away from the wall and showed where Steve Tulk had installed a second telephone, and where I'd hidden the phone that Larry had been using.

"Two telephones? In an office this size? I don't get it."

"Well, Mr Tepperman, I wanted to trap the murderer. I told that story back at Debbie's house, knowing that the phone up here in the office was a newly installed one. It was put in today as a matter of fact. There was nothing on the redial memory, nothing important anyway. But this other phone, hidden back of the desk, is the one Larry used. It's the one I used too that day I

talked to you, Ruth. When I questioned you about getting a call from Nathan, you threw me for a loop. You
answered the phone, therefore it followed that Larry had
called you. You said that maybe I had the facts but wasn't
reading them right. You were dead on. It took me a long
time to get the idea that you were visiting Debbie when I
called not your house but Debbie's. Larry placed that
call to your sister to say that he had finished burning all
his papers and was ready to make a dash to Toronto
International with her, after making a short stop to pick
up his suitcase with the diamonds at the Bolduc building
site on Geneva."

Tepperman was whispering to the rabbi, but the rest
of the people in the room, including Kogan, were waiting, looking like they had just felt the floor tremble. "I
know we don't have a lot of proof. Much of what we've
got is circumstantial. But we do know for a fact that
someone from Debbie's house crossed the garden and
came into this office alone less than an hour ago. She
may have thought she was unobserved, but there was a
witness. Kogan, do you see the person who came to this
office before we came as a group?"

"I do," said Kogan like he was under oath. "That's her
with her arm on Mrs Geller."

"You're pointing at Mrs Debbie Geller, right?"

"Yes, sir."

"Since I had Mr MacIntyre's keys to this building, I
made use of them. Kogan was in the office across the
way which has a glass panel in the door."

"I thought she saw me once," said Kogan. "She looked
right at me. You forgot to mention," Kogan said, "that
when I called a few minutes ago and asked for Sergeant
Staziak, I used the other phone and the redial button."
Kogan looked like he had more of his adventure to share
with us, when he was interrupted by Debbie Geller making a sudden move. I missed the first part, I was looking
at Kogan. So were the rest of us, including the hefty cop

that Staziak had assigned to the possibilities of the night, as he called them.

"Look out!" Rabbi Meltzer was shoved out of the way, and Debbie darted past the uniformed man to the corridor. She was on the stairs before the rest of us, except the rabbi, knew what was going on.

"Carswell, catch her! Don't let her get away!" Carswell was in a better position to get her than the rest of us. We all had to take turns going through the narrow office door. By the time I got to the stair landing, she had reached the first floor. I stumbled on the first half of the second flight and almost crashed down the rest of the steps. I grabbed the rail and nearly pulled my arm out of its socket breaking my fall. When I got up, I looked behind me. I was the only one in hot pursuit. Cool at the top of the stairs, Staziak was looking down at me.

"Pete, for Christ's sake, she's getting away!" Pete walked down towards me and helped me test the foot that had let me down. "Pete, are you crazy? She's got a car in the driveway!" Staziak beamed at me. "It's all taken care of; I've got a man on each of the doors. She's going nowhere."

"But what the hell were you yelling at Carswell for?"

"I lost my cool, Benny. Have you ever lost your cool?"

Half an hour later, with the exception of Debbie Geller, who had been taken back to Niagara Regional, warned and booked, and her sister Ruth, who was upstairs sedated, we were all back in her living-room drinking Debbie's rye when Staziak returned from Niagara Regional. He reported that she was in good hands, and a doctor had given her something to help her get through the night. He further announced that he was no longer officially on duty. So Sid fixed him a rye with water. I was working on a weak rye with ginger ale while my right ankle was using up all of the remaining ice-cubes in the house. Pia had made an attempt at first aid with the ice wrapped in a dishtowel. To protect the rug, my foot was sitting in a shallow basin with the melt-waters. Pia was sitting near by just to check on the patient.

When we left 44 Woodland Avenue, Ruth went downtown with Pete. She returned after a few minutes, when she found that there was little she could do after getting in touch with a lawyer. Irving Bernstein, Larry's old friend from Osgoode Hall days, had agreed to defend Debbie, at least until Debbie's own wishes were known. I thought of Irving, and wondered if he was still wearing his ring from law school the way Larry was.

"I hope you haven't been shooting your mouth off while I was gone, Benny. I want to hear your version of what you think was going on in this town."

"For you, Pete, I've got a cleaned-up version all prepared."

"Good, that way we'll know it's a load of sheep-dip from the beginning and not have to wait till the end."

"You don't have to wait at all." I said, calling his bluff. "I'd as soon listen as talk any day." There was a protest from Saul Tepperman, who had been trying to explain things to Rabbi Meltzer, without much success.

"You're not going to get out of it that way," said Pete settling down in a chair near Sid Geller. "We want a full confession, don't we, people?" For a minute, Pete reminded me of an old music teacher who plied his trade in the public-school system. He called the pupils "people" as though it was his private joke and we weren't people at all, just little horrors with bad pitch. I don't know why I thought of Mr C. Lawson Raven and his "Now, people, pay attention."

"You don't have to do anything if you don't want to, Benny. You should have a doctor look at your foot in the morning if the swelling hasn't gone down." Pia was being very helpful, but I suspected that this was a bad time for everybody. Here we were in Debbie's house, drinking her booze and about to talk about why she'd killed three men. I was glad about my foot. I could have been like the rabbi or Kogan, just sitting and waiting.

"Well, Benny," the rabbi prompted, "when you're ready, we're ready."

"Okay," I said, lighting one of the last of my Player's. I knew there were only other brands in the room so I resolved to make fast work of my explanation. "When Debbie left Sid, she was happy enough for a while. She had a good settlement, which meant that she would never have to go out to work. Not a bad spot for a divorced woman without any kids. So, she devoted herself to the arts, helped her former brother-in-law Nathan get established, but that wasn't enough. There was an unfinished part to Debbie, she was on the lookout for a main chance, an entry into the big time. Fixing up this place didn't begin to consume her energies. Then she recognized in Larry, her sister's husband, the way to satisfy that craving. First there was the adventure of a secret affair in a small town. A world first for Grantham, probably. Then she encouraged him to dip into his trust funds and stockpile securities against the day when they would be able to make a flit that would shake the dust of Grantham off their feet forever. Larry arranged to have an office for his dark deeds near Debbie's place. Underneath almost everything Debbie planned and did was a sense of the practical. She has a very tidy, uncluttered, unsentimental mind. When the time for the great escape grew closer, she began to try to imagine herself in foreign places— this is conjecture of course—travelling with Larry. Larry would have a price on his head, naturally. They would forever be on the lookout for the police wherever they went. And she knew that Larry had the power to implicate her if he were ever cornered. She had to think about the part she'd played in taking advantage of those fifty families back home. Not easy to sleep on, I guess, especially when you know that your bed-partner has his picture in every police station where Interpol circulars are sent. About that time, Larry hit upon the idea of converting the bonds and securities to diamonds. He went to Toronto and New York often enough to convert his fortune to a tidy, easily hidden bag of diamonds.

"I don't think it was greed. It was that practical side of her nature coming front and centre again. It was more practical for Debbie to have all of the diamonds. It was more practical not to leave town with Larry. And above all, it was very practical to have Larry out of the way, where he could never double-cross her. She'd never wake up in some casino town in the south of France and find him gone off with a cute croupier. So that short stopover at the construction shack became the last stop for Larry. I gather, Sid, that Debbie wasn't completely at sea on a construction site?"

"Hell, no. She used to follow me around when we were first married. She even had her own hard hat for when she was visiting me on a job. I don't know whether she could do all the jobs, but she sure saw most of them being done. She could even trade a few choice Italian expressions with the boys. No, she wasn't strange around a building site of any kind."

"Well, there you go. She knew what she was doing. What she missed didn't have anything to do with her knowledge of construction. She didn't see that an old rubby, a friend of my pal Kogan..."

"Wally was no rubby. Call him a wino, if you want, but he was no rubby." Kogan had looked like he was dozing off, but he hadn't missed a word. "Sorry, Kogan, didn't mean to give offence. Anyway, Wally Moore saw what happened. He was smart enough not to show himself. When he saw that the paper was asking for information about the missing Larry Geller, and printed his picture, Wally knew that first of all he had to tell the poor man's wife. He also thought that it might be good for some sort of reward. He called Mrs Geller over on Burgoyne Boulevard, and Mrs Geller met him briefly and gave him fifty dollars down on a reward."

"She told you she never met him," Pia said, showing the strain of these last few days in her voice pulled tight as a piano string.

"I thought she was lying when I first asked her, thought she was covering up for somebody, but now I can see what happened. Debbie had come over to visit her, to deal with the phone and the door. It was only natural that she was the Mrs Geller that Wally met."

"I'm not sure I understand. You mean Debbie pretended to be Ruth?" Pia was entwining her fingers, making steeples. The nervous gesture didn't suit her.

"She met Wally at the front door. If he asked her if she was Mrs Geller, she wasn't being inaccurate, just a little misleading."

"What about the grass she was smokin'? Remember Wally said she was smokin' up some pot?" Kogan asked, hoping that I'd forgotten all about it.

"I'll get to that, Kogan. Give me breathing room. Debbie arranged to meet Wally someplace quiet where they wouldn't be interrupted. I don't think Wally would be too suspicious of her picking the pavilion in Montecello Park. It was out of the way, but not sinister in any degree. And after all, Wally thought he was dealing with the widow, not the killer. So, she stabbed him too and left him lying in a corner, where some other down-and-out citizens encountered him and thought that he was asleep.

"Now we come to Nathan. Nathan was the youngest of the Geller brothers and very fond of his two sisters-in-law. He pretended that he didn't notice much of what was going on around him. He isn't the first artist to adopt that kind of protective colouring. But in fact he noticed a lot more than he pretended to. As I once told someone, nobody could make the kind of sculptures he made without an excellent eye for the behaviour of his fellow man.

For a long time Nathan had been suspecting that something was going on between his brother Larry and Debbie. I don't know how he knew, but he knew. He saw them in every sort of family gathering, and maybe he got lucky; saw them when they didn't know they were being observed. Or maybe it was his artist's radar. Who knows? When Debbie asked him to try to put me off the scent by saying that he had heard from Larry, Nathan got worried. Perhaps for the first time he wondered where his brother had got to. If he ran away with Debbie, why was Debbie still at home? I think that's why he told me such a dumb story. He didn't want me to go down to Daytona Beach; he wanted me here. He got in touch with his old friend Pia Morley and asked her to come around for a talk. He was worried, but he didn't know what to do about it. After all, everybody in this case is family. Where should he turn? Pia was at least only a member of the family by association. He could talk to her without the alarm bells going off.

"If Debbie's scheme had a weak point, it was Nathan. He was bright and intuitive. Once he began to wonder about things, to speculate out loud, Debbie feared her days were numbered. So, she developed a secondary plan, one which she'd fall back on if Nathan began wondering aloud about Larry's whereabouts. She knew about Nathan's friendship with Pia, so Pia had to become part of the plan. When she talked to Wally, she was smoking a joint of pot, just in case Wally did any talking before she could silence him for good. When the chance came to take Pia's lighter, she snapped it up and left it at the scene of the crime. Everything seemed perfect when Pia herself arrived just after Debbie'd iced Nathan. She hid until Pia left and placed the lighter where the police were sure to find it. The fact that they didn't wasn't her fault. Pia noticing the loss sent a friend to collect it.

"Does that cover all the loose ends, Pete? Does anybody have any questions?"

"How could she do it, Benny?" Pia asked. "She knew all of us. She was our friend. We all loved and trusted her."

"Well, I'm no psychiatrist. Blame it on the rivalry between the sisters when they were being brought up by their father on his own. Blame it on jealousy. Ruth had a husband and kids, Debbie had thrown away her chance at both. Blame it on the fact that she was bored by the ordinary lives most people around her were living. She always had a short attention span. She left school early, married and divorced early, never settled to anything but being big sister. Maybe you can get your fill of being big sister. I don't know. And don't forget the fun she had in using Larry to pull the rug out from under all of you. Yes, the whole Jewish community was up in arms over the defrauding of innocent people. A mind like hers might glory in that."

"But she was at Ruth's side right through the worst of it," Pia said.

"That's right," echoed Saul Tepperman. "I never saw the like. They were the picture of dedication."

"I don't think that was an act," I said. "I think that Debbie was honestly devoted to Ruth. She wasn't playing a part. But that wasn't all there was to Debbie. There was this whole buried part, hidden in shadow and full of envy and guilt and blame. There were more than half the original deadly sins walking arm in arm with the loyal, leave-it-to-Debbie side of her. She makes me wish I knew more about this kind of thing."

"What about all that money?" Pete asked. "You say Larry converted it into diamonds, two point six million dollars' worth. What happened to the diamonds, Benny?"

"Like the fellow in the hot seat says, I'm glad you asked me that. I figured that they were hidden someplace here in the house. I knew that the original bag had been burned in Larry's hideaway. Diamonds are fairly easy to hide. She could have planted them in the hems of some of the curtains in this room or upstairs. She could have put them in holes behind pictures. She could have done two point six million different things with them. I thought that maybe, Pete, you'd have to get a team of demolition experts over here and take the place apart stone by stone, board by board."

"But you don't think that any more?" Pete was great at noticing tenses. And he could tell from mine that I had found out something very recently.

"While I was talking, my ankle began bothering me. Now Pia went to a lot of trouble to put together an ice pack for my poor sprained foot, so I was reluctant to complain. A few minutes ago I opened up the dishtowel to see why the ice was not cooling my foot any better than it was. What I found was ice of a different kind. She must have got the idea from a movie. Diamonds in an ice-tray are invisible. Dissolved in a foot basin, they have limited cold-producing qualities. But a fortune in diamonds is nothing to trouble a sprained ankle about."

Everybody got up and came over to see the hard particles in the melt-waters and in the dishtowel. "Remember how Debbie insisted that we get ice from the fridge under the bar. She didn't want to give away a fortune with a couple of free drinks. I've heard of crooks hiding single diamonds in ice, but this takes the Nobel prize for hiding places." I turned to Pia: "Pia, I think you'll find some real ice-cubes left under the bar. This stuff might look lovely on you, but on my foot it leaves a lot to be desired." She looked at me as though she had completely forgotten the fact that my ankle had swollen to twice its normal size. Some people just can't keep their perspectives straight.